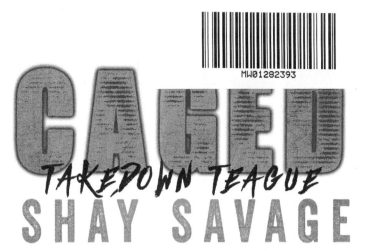

CAGED

TAKEDOWN TEAGUE

SHAY SAVAGE

# DEDICATION

For Jadalulu, who sent a Tweet in July of 2012 wanting to read a story about a cage fighter. Thanks for always inspiring me, encouraging me, and keeping me entertained!

# TABLE OF CONTENTS

CHAPTER ONE | WIN THE FIGHT     1

CHAPTER TWO | SAVE THE GIRL     17

CHAPTER THREE | MAKE THE MOVE     33

CHAPTER FOUR | FIND THE STEP     49

CHAPTER FIVE | QUESTION THE MOTIVE     57

CHAPTER SIX | MEET THE EX     71

CHAPTER SEVEN | STAKE THE CLAIM     91

CHAPTER EIGHT | REALIZE THE TRUTH     101

CHAPTER NINE | CLEAN THE MESS     113

CHAPTER TEN | ACCEPT THE ARRANGEMENTS     127

CHAPTER ELEVEN | KEEP THE DISTANCE     137

CHAPTER TWELVE | ADMIT THE REALITY     151

CHAPTER THIRTEEN | SET THE RHYTHM     159

CHAPTER FOURTEEN | SEIZE THE OPPORTUNITY     173

CHAPTER FIFTEEN | TOE THE LINE     183

CHAPTER SIXTEEN | FEAR THE WORST     201

CHAPTER SEVENTEEN | KISS THE GIRL     209

CHAPTER EIGHTEEN | TAKE THE TRIP     227

CHAPTER NINETEEN | TELL THE TALE                    239

CHAPTER TWENTY | REACH THE DESTINATION              253

CHAPTER TWENTY-ONE | CHALLENGE THE BELIEFS          265

CHAPTER TWENTY-TWO | REVEAL THE PAST                275

CHAPTER TWENTY-THREE | TAKE THE PLUNGE              287

AUTHOR'S NOTES                                      297

EXCERPT FROM CAGED: BOOK TWO - TRAPPED              299

MORE BOOKS BY SHAY SAVAGE                           303

ABOUT THE AUTHOR                                    305

# CHAPTER ONE
## Win the Fight

I paced.

The cold cement of the hallway floor made my feet tingle a little even through the tape wrapped around my insteps. My hands clenched into fists, unclenched, and then clenched again. I didn't know why I was feeling particularly fidgety—this night was like every other night when I worked. Something just seemed to have me on edge, and I didn't know what. I danced back and forth on the balls of my feet a few times, tilted my head to the ceiling with my eyes closed, and blew out a long, slow breath.

Maybe I just needed to get laid.

The deep base of "Sonne" by Rammstein started thumping through the sound system, and the door in front of me opened. My muscles flexed from shoulders to ass, and I prowled out of the empty, slanted hallway and into the crowd.

*"Eins…Hier kommt die Sonne…"*

The noise was insane for such a small place. It always was. Feet First was a hole-in-the-wall drinking establishment in the crappier part of the city and probably couldn't fit more than three hundred people inside of it and keep a fire marshal happy, not that anyone in a uniform came around that area. That was just asking for trouble, and the cops and other officials would just as soon go give someone a parking ticket. They were less likely to get a bottle over the head or a knife in the back that way.

"*Zwei…Hier kommt die Sonne…*"

Hands reached through the holes in the chain-link fence to try to grab at me as I raised my arms up over my head and roared at the crowd like some kind of half-domesticated circus animal. I spun in a small circle and absorbed the screams of the crowd into my skin as I made my way to the cage.

"Takedown! Takedown!"

I glared menacingly toward the onlookers, baring my teeth and growling. Near the end of the ramp and the door of the cage, I flung myself at the chain link between me and the patrons of the bar, snarling through clenched teeth and causing a group of them to scurry backwards. Their eyes were wide and bright as they laughed nervously before moving back toward the fence. Again, they tried to reach through with their hands.

"*Drei…Sie ist der hellste Stern von allen…*"

Executing another slow spin with my arms raised, I ducked slightly to enter the fighting cage. From across the other side, Yolanda sauntered over in shorts that looked about the size Barbie would wear, and a bikini top that left nothing to the imagination except for the bottom half of her nipples. She also took a little spin as she moved closer to me and tossed her sleek, black hair over her shoulder. More screams came from the audience—this time mostly from the guys.

The patrons of Feet First were mostly men though there were always more women watching the bloodshed than you might think. Probably at least two women to every five men would enter the bar

2

nightly, and those that made it through the first two minutes of a fight usually came back for more. Yolanda thought they came back to watch me, but I thought they were just as bloodthirsty as the guys —they just didn't admit it as readily.

Hoots and hollers came from all sides as Yolanda sauntered over to me and looked me up and down. I gazed right back at her, turning my head slightly as she began to circle. She was more familiar with the scene than I was, having been a fighter years before I ever even thought of it. In her mid-thirties, she could still pass for twenty-five with ease.

She walked around me like a cat, a single finger stroking over my shoulders and neck. She ran her fingernails lightly over the tribal tattoos covering my back and then dipped the tips of her fingers into my emerald green trunks. With still slow movements, she checked all around the hem of my shorts.

The maneuver was to verify the fighters didn't have anything hard, sharp, or hidden inside, but in reality it was nothing more than foreplay for the audience. Classical conditioning. They were drooling now, and they'd all orgasm by the time the fight was over. I eyed her with a cocky half grin as she finished it off by running her hand over my dick, much to the pleasure of the crowd.

*"Lässt dich hart zu Boden gehen*
*Und die Welt zählt laut bis zehn..."*

My song faded, and some rap song started up instead. A big bald-headed guy emerged from the opposite side and yelled obscenities at the booing members of the audience. He had a cheering section as well, but this was my venue, and I was the favored fighter. He was shorter than me by quite a bit but stocky with long, hairy arms.

Yolanda handed me a mouth guard. I slipped it into my mouth and bit down. I stretched my arms up above my head once more and danced around on the balls of my feet. My opponent entered the cage, was given the same treatment from the sleek bronze woman, and the door was shut with a clang.

There was no referee.

There were no rounds.

There was really only one rule—whoever taps out or goes unconscious loses.

We circled each other, moving slowly without getting any closer. The noise of the audience lessened, and my eyes focused on the man in the cage with me. He crouched slightly, and his nostrils flared as he breathed heavily through them. His fists tightened as he raised them up in front of his body.

Awareness covered me. I knew the position of every muscle in my body, and I positioned each one in preparation for what was to come.

This was my element.

My show.

My life.

My one and only love.

I let him come at me first, gauging his tempo, favored hand, and which foot he liked to put forward. Leaning back quickly, I dodged his first blow and smacked him with an open palm across his left temple. He shook it off easily—it wasn't a very hard blow—and backed off as I jumped toward him, which left me open for his foot into my lower back. I gasped through the mouthpiece at the clean hit and backed off a bit to recover.

He didn't give me much time.

I kept my left hand up to block whatever blows he sent in my direction, while I jabbed with my right to punch him in the stomach. As he brought up his knee to connect with my kidney again, I wrapped my arm around his leg and held tight but didn't let him fall. I turned to the side and followed the blow with my foot into his ribs. He fell backwards, recovered, crouched and jumped at me, landing a good blow across my temple.

I was stunned for a moment as lights flashed in the back of my head. I felt his arms wrapping around my chest and shoulders as he shoved me backwards and into the cage, his fist coming up and smacking me in the head again as my shoulder scraped against the chain links. I leaned back into the cage wall and lifted my feet to wrap my legs around his waist.

A fist landed forcefully against my thigh, causing the muscle there to clench, but I didn't let go. I twisted to the right and then the left and smashed my forehead into his nose. He lost his footing, and we both toppled to the floor as the crowd screamed at us.

I landed on my back, but I kept my legs gripped around his middle. My vision blurred slightly as I twisted again and flipped us over. His feet were up in the air behind me, and as my thigh muscles gripped him tighter, I started raining open handed blows to his head and face.

Without gloves, closed fists hurt my hands almost as much as they hurt his face, but that didn't stop me from switching to them. I could feel blood on my fingers, but I wasn't sure if it was from my knuckles or his battered nose. His arms came up to shield him from the pounding, so I leaned back to punch his ribs.

Sweat ran down my back, and I had to work hard to keep breathing steadily through my nose. My ear was ringing a bit from the earlier punch to my temple, but my vision was clear again. My opponent tried to bring his leg up to kick at my back, but my hold was too strong. I kept up the punches with my right hand as my left arm sought his neck.

Once I had my forearm across his throat, the fight was all but over. I felt him struggling under me, but the intensity became muted and shallow. I hit him on the side of the head a couple more times before I felt the tap of his fingers on my bicep.

I released my hold on him, jumped backwards, and spit the

mouthpiece out on the floor. I watched as he went nearly limp below me, a trickle of blood staining his cheek and forehead. I stumbled a little as I backed away, and the sting near my temple finally registered with my brain. My head throbbed, but I could still focus okay. I heard the door of the cage open behind me and felt Yolanda's hand around my wrist, but I shook her off, still dazed.

The screams from those outside the cage filled my ears, and the sound rippled through my skin as I collected my thoughts, realized it was over, and reached up toward the ceiling. I screamed in victory as the fans chanted in unison.

"Takedown! Takedown!"

Yolanda's hand reached up and grabbed my elbow, since at her height she couldn't reach my wrist, and she shook at my arm as she cried out to the crowd.

"Takedown Teague—victor again for his twenty-seventh consecutive fight!"

The guy I was fighting rolled over and propped himself up on his hands and knees. Yolanda went to help him to his feet, and he moved over to toss his arm around my neck for what I guess was supposed to be a manly hug.

"One of these days, I'm gonna beat you, Teague. I swear it!" he laughed.

"Have we fought before?" I asked. The guy didn't even look familiar, but then again, the fights all run together in my head.

He just laughed and shook his head.

"This is the third time you've kicked my ass."

"I must owe you a beer," I said, and we both grinned at each other.

Turning back toward the crowd, I was bombarded with faces and hands poking through the fence as well as cries of congratulations as I stepped through the cage door. I high-fived a couple dozen people on my way back down the ramp to the make-shift locker room on the lower floor for a moment of peace before I had to go out and meet the public again.

As the door closed behind me, the noise was at least partially cut off, and my head throbbed less as I made my way to the sink. Wincing a bit, I splashed cold water on the cut above my eye. It wasn't bad and only barely bleeding. There was a place on my back where I hit the cage that was likely worse, but I couldn't see how bad the cut was. Vanity was my main concern; I hoped it hadn't fucked up my tattoo. That shit cost me a lot of money.

I stripped and headed to the single stand-up shower in the locker room. The water wasn't hot enough to feel very good or relax my muscles, but it was certainly better than nothing. I washed quickly and grabbed one of the little towels folded up on a table next to the wall. They weren't big enough to be considered actual bath towels, so I just ran one of them over my chest, ass, and crotch before tossing it in the corner. It wouldn't fit around my waist, so there was no point in even trying to cover myself. Crouching down in front of a group of metal lockers, I started rummaging through my gym bag for clothes.

"Nice..."

Yolanda waltzed in without knocking, as usual, and emitted a low whistle. I glanced at her over my shoulder before going back to the items in my bag. She just kept eyeing me, clearly checking out my junk as I squatted down in front of my locker.

Whatever. I didn't have anything to hide.

Grabbing a pair of boxers, I stood and slipped them on before turning around and sitting on the little bench against the concrete wall. Yolanda knelt down in front of me and deftly removed the tape from my feet and ankles while I unwound it from my wrists. Once that was done, I grabbed a pair of ripped up jeans and pulled them on.

"Turn around," Yolanda ordered, and I did as she said. "Sit. I can't reach you from there."

I sighed but couldn't really argue. She was maybe all of five-two, and I was nearly a foot taller. She wouldn't be able to check me out if I remained standing. I sat on the bench and she looked at my shoulder.

"What's the damage?" I asked. "Tats okay?"

"Just a scratch," she confirmed. "Tats survived."

Yolanda pulled a bottle of rubbing alcohol out of her bag. Aside from being a cage fighter before she tore her ACL, she claimed to be a registered nurse. She certainly seemed to know what she was doing and even stitched up my side once when someone pulled a knife on me after losing a fight. The stitches weren't pretty, but they kept me from losing a lot of blood on the way to the hospital. Yolanda tipped the bottle upside down with a piece of gauze over the opened lid and rubbed some of the alcohol on my shoulder, which made me hiss.

"Don't be such a baby." She clicked her tongue at me.

"That fucking hurts."

"You'll go nine minutes getting punched in the face, but a little alcohol always makes you whine."

"I'm not whining," I insisted, shrugging her off. It didn't work, because she went after the cut over my eye next. Once she was done with her mothering, I opened my locker, located the small felt bag on the top shelf, and dumped the contents into my hand—two round silver earrings. I slipped them both through the matching holes in my left ear. "Don't you have anything in there that doesn't fucking sting like a bitch?"

"Pussy."

I snorted, rolled my shoulder a couple of times, and then reached into my gym bag for a T-shirt.

"Don't put that on," Yolanda said with another exaggerated sigh.

"Why not?"

"Well, for one, you've got a lot of female fans out there tonight," she explained. "You know they want you half naked, and you also know you love to show off the ink. Besides, you just pulled that nasty, wrinkled thing out of your gym bag."

"So?"

"So, it smells like a dead dog."

"Nice." I tossed the shirt back in the bag and zipped it up. "Let's do this."

Back inside the bar, it was a madhouse. I shoved my way through, using my bulk and notoriety to get myself through the crowd and up to the bar. I maneuvered up to the very end to keep from being completely surrounded and stood next to a big poster on the wall. It depicted an old guy with a long, white beard holding up a rat. At the bottom it read:

*"Feet first, Arthur. It's the only way out of here!"*

I had no fucking clue what it was supposed to mean, but Dordy, the owner of the bar, thought it was hysterical. He was a short, lanky guy with black hair and eyes. He was from the Philippines or maybe Malaysia; I could never remember exactly. He was behind the bar nearly every night and apparently bought the place because he liked talking to drunk people though he never had a drink himself. He used to work on a cruise ship and made killer frozen drinks.

About fifteen people tried to buy me drinks, holding out long neck domestic beers and other shit I wouldn't touch. I did hand two of them to my now bandaged opponent, who seemed to need them more than I did anyway. I politely declined the rest of the drinks until Dordy placed a rocks glass with a single malt scotch in front of me—neat. When I looked up at him, Dordy motioned to a guy at the end of the bar, sitting there with a similar drink. His neatly styled dark hair was slicked back over his temples, and as our eyes met, he raised his glass.

I copied his motion and sipped at the whiskey. It was top shelf —well, for this place, anyway—and went down pretty smooth. I raised an eyebrow at him before turning away and smiling seductively at a young woman in leather shorts and a tank top. When I had enough of being pawed at by various women and barraged with enough questions about my fighting style from various men, I snuck out back for a smoke.

I climbed up the half dozen stairs that brought me level to the street, jumped over the side rail at the top and into the enclosed area behind the bar. It was well past two in the morning, and the street was completely devoid of traffic. Most people in this neighborhood didn't have cars, and those who might have been passing through had done so in the safer hours of daylight. There wasn't much of anyone around except a small group of guys sitting on the steps of an abandoned warehouse on the other side of the street, passing a bottle in a brown paper bag back and forth between them.

*Subtle*, I thought with a snort and lit up my cigarette.

The back part of the bar was supposed to be used just for deliveries and taking plastic bags brimming over with bottles to the dumpster, but since it also connected to the locker room, I found it convenient to come out here to smoke, away from the crowds that gathered outside the front doors. The area was surrounded by a chain-link fence, which was not unlike the one that made up the fighting cage inside. There was a large poster on it, displaying a picture of me advertising fights twice a week.

*Takedown Teague*
*Cage Fights*
*Tuesdays and Fridays 10PM*

I leaned against the chain-link fence next to the poster and wrapped the fingers of one hand through the holes. I pulled against it a couple of times and listened to the rattling sound it made while I watched the fight run through my head again. I inhaled smoke and blew it out my nose, trying to mask the heavy scent of garbage, vomit, and urine in the street.

The smells brought back memories, and they weren't pleasant ones. At the time, I didn't care. I had other ways of masking the odors. Now I had to make do with the cigarette, and it wasn't nearly as effective.

My earlier thought of needing to get laid came back again, but I dismissed it. I hadn't hooked up with anyone in months, and even though my cock was starting to cringe from my hand out of sheer boredom, I really didn't want to just randomly fuck another fangirl.

"Penny for your thoughts?"

"A C-note, maybe," I responded to the man with the sleek black hair. I forced my muscles to relax. I was not going to let him get to me, not this time. I glanced at him briefly and then looked back to the street. The bare bulb hanging just outside the door to the bar glinted off the silver earrings in his left ear. "What brings you here, Michael?"

"Just checking up on my favorite nephew."

"I'm your only nephew."

"Technicalities."

I took another long draw on my cigarette and focused on the four guys across the street with their cheap bottle of booze and ratty clothes. One of them laughed loudly and shoved the guy next to him on the shoulder, which toppled the drunk over and onto the sidewalk. They all laughed as he tried to right himself again.

"Always loved this neighborhood," Michael said. His voice was completely flat and emotionless, but I still recognized sarcasm when I heard it.

"Well, housing is cheap," I said with a shrug.

"You still in that dump down the block?"

"It's convenient to work," I retorted. "Don't play games, Michael—what the fuck do you want?"

"Just your yearly reminder that you don't have to live like this." My uncle walked up behind me and placed his hand on my bare shoulder. "Just talk to him, Liam."

"No."

"It's been almost ten years."

"Fuck him," I replied. I could feel all my muscles tense from top to bottom—my shoulders, my arms, my back, my legs—all in a ripple down my body.

"You were a kid then."

"Old enough to be thrown out on the street, apparently."

"He regrets that," Michael stated.

"My ass," I growled. "He's pissed off he couldn't see into the future. That's his only regret."

Michael went silent, but I could hear his breath as he huffed it out through his nose.

"Your mother misses you."

That was a low blow, but I swallowed hard and clenched my fingers through the chain-link, refusing to respond. It didn't stop her face from popping up in my head, of course. Wavy brown hair covered her shoulders, and her bright smile made me feel loved and wanted.

Ultimately, she still took *his* side.

Michael stepped a few feet away from me and smoothed out his hair.

"Fuck her, too," I muttered under my breath. I didn't think Michael actually heard me, though. Even after all this time, I felt like shit for saying it and wanted to take it back.

"Ryan says hello." It was a slightly better topic.

"Haven't seen him in a while." My cousin was a big-ass motherfucker. He would have made a great fighter, but he went into the family business with the rest of them. No room for that kind of shit in his life. Michael wasn't actually his father. He had married a woman about fifteen years older than he was, and she came with a son. It was cool though, because up until then, I had been the only kid my age in the family.

Ryan and Michael were the only ones I still talked to at all.

"He's been pretty busy," Michael said. "Did he tell you he was going to marry Amanda?"

"I figured," I said, feeling myself tense up a bit.

"Well, she's planning the wedding to end all weddings, apparently."

"There's a shock," I snorted.

Michael laughed, which quickly turned into a sigh.

"Not going to change your mind?" he asked, already knowing the answer.

"Not this year," I replied. "I don't see 'daddy dearest' making the trek down here to talk to me. What makes him think I'm going to take the fucking subway all the way over to his office? He can park the fucking Porsche back here and come have a beer if he cares so much."

"Liam…"

"You done?" I snapped.

"I guess so," he said. He let out another long breath. "It was good to see you."

"You, too." I didn't turn around and watch him walk back inside. His appearance brought up too many shitty memories, and though I did love my uncle, his presence left me feeling uneasy.

After a few more cigarettes, I tossed the last butt toward the street and headed back inside for a bit. It wasn't long before I determined getting laid was not going to happen, given my mood and the general lack of teeth in the mouths of some of the patrons still left at Feet First come closing time. I untangled myself from one of the hornier ones by telling her I had to take a piss, went back to the locker room to grab my gym bag, and headed out the back door. Once outside, I dropped the bag, fished around for my pack of Marlboros, and lit one.

A lone car crawled by, momentarily obscuring my view of the drunk-fest that was still going on across the street. They were pretty fucking loud, which was disturbing my final smoke of the evening before walking home. Usually this was my peaceful time, the only real quiet of the night I would get before returning home and trying to sleep through the car alarms and gunshots. At least the idiots who used to fight at all hours of the night in the apartment below me finally moved out. Maybe they were evicted. Whatever it was, I didn't have to listen to that shit anymore.

A chilly breeze blew down the street, bringing some of the more glorious scents up into the air and cooling my skin. I tossed the cigarette butt through the holes in the fence and into the gutter with the rest of the trash and then went back to the door to retrieve my shirt from my gym bag.

The trip-trapping sound of women's shoes on pavement caused me to look up, and I watched a young woman come into view as she passed the dumpsters at the back of the bar. She walked quickly with her head down and a purse with a lengthy strap over her shoulder. Her long, brown hair was tied up in a ponytail at the top of her head, and she wore a pair of short-shorts, which showed off her long legs, and a tight T-shirt with the name across her chest of the bar and grill a few blocks down. I figured she was maybe five-foot-four and a hundred and fifteen pounds because I tended to size people up that way. Nice build, nice tits. She didn't look over at me at all, just kept up her quick pace down the street with her eyes on her feet.

My first thought was *fucking gorgeous*.

My second thought was *fucking stupid*.

Who walked around this area of town in the middle of the night by themselves? I mean, yeah—I did—but I wasn't a very easy target. She might as well have had a sign on her back that said "mug me". I shook my head and went back to rummaging around in my bag. When I looked up again, the sound of her shoes was beginning to fade, but that wasn't what caught my attention.

The guys across the street who had been sitting and drinking had gone quiet and were now all standing up with their heads close to one another. The guy with greasy, shoulder length, black hair turned his head to look down the street in the direction the girl was walking and then nodded before he and a guy with a backwards baseball cap took off down the side alley that ran perpendicular to the street they were on.

I'd lived in that area a couple of years, and I knew that alley intersected with another alley, which then met up with a walkway between two of the abandoned warehouses, and dumped out onto this street a couple blocks down. The last two guys in the group were heavyset with unkempt dirty blond hair. They looked like they might have been brothers. They quickly abandoned the bottle-in-a-bag and started walking quietly but quickly in the same direction the girl was going, pulling the hoodies up over their heads as they walked.

Their intent was obvious.

"Fuck," I mumbled. I grabbed my bag, ignoring the shirt that fell out of it and onto the ground and heaved at the heavy gate that enclosed the area behind Feet First. For once, the damn thing was padlocked. I growled before flinging my bag up and over the fence, grabbing onto the links with my fingers, and hauling myself over it, too. I had to move pretty quickly if I was going to catch up with the drunks and their would-be victim.

I was never one to play the hero, but some things you just didn't let slide.

# CHAPTER TWO
## Save the Girl

Stepping lightly but quickly, I moved down the quiet, empty street. There was a bend just a couple of blocks ahead of me, and both the girl and the guys pursuing her must have already passed it. I couldn't see anyone else on the street at all though someone could certainly have been hiding in the shadows. More than half the streetlights were out here—no one ever seemed to bother replacing them—and you couldn't see the moon or any stars. The light pollution from deeper in the city was the only thing keeping the streets from being completely dark.

I moved a little faster, making my way around the curve in the street.

I saw them then, and I was correct in my initial assessment of their plans. They had already caught up to her—two in the front, two in the back. The one with the baseball cap and the greasy one were behind her with their arms held out a little to keep her in place while the two brothers shifted back and forth in front of her. They had her surrounded and were moving slowly, herding her toward the walkway between two buildings.

"Hey, baby," the blond brother with the darker colored hoodie purred. I was pretty sure it was the one who had shoved his buddy down in the street earlier. "Relax. We just want to have a little fun."

"Yeah, you know," the kid in the backwards baseball cap said, "invite you to our little *par-tay*."

I couldn't stand it when people talked like that. It didn't make them sound cool; it made them sound like morons.

"Leave me alone!" The girl slung her bag off her shoulder and held it in both hands, as if she might try to use it as a weapon.

The group laughed and closed in on her. One of them reached out and grabbed the large bag, wrenching it from her hands and spilling the significant contents all over the street. The guy with greasy black hair reached for her then, grabbing her by the tops of both arms and pulling her backwards as she cried out.

As if anyone around here would even notice or care if they did hear her screaming.

The guy in the hoodie stepped forward and began to reach for her. I dropped my own bag, no longer concerned with a silent approach, and raced down the street. They were far too occupied with their captive to notice me anyway, and I managed to get right behind the one grabbing for her.

My hand grasped the top of his head, clenching the material of his sweatshirt and his hair as well. I yanked him backwards and off balance and then released him as he fell on his ass with a thud. Changing my stance, I leaned over and let my foot fly out, catching another one in the side. I heard a distinctive crack as my booted heel came into contact with his ribs.

I turned my eyes to the greasy black-haired guy who was taking a few steps backwards, still holding the girl tightly and shaking her, as if threatening her would keep me away from him.

"Hey, man!" They were all the words I allowed to leave his

mouth.

I stepped forward quickly and grabbed the girl by her ponytail. She cried out again, but I couldn't pay attention to that as I pulled her face toward my chest and punched at the space over her head to land three knuckles right against Greasy's trachea.

He released her arms immediately and grasped at his throat.

Spinning to my left, I kept the girl close to me for a moment and then shoved her off to one side before turning to the next guy who was coming at me. She cried out in surprise, stumbled, and ended up dropping to the street, but I couldn't really think about that. I knew she wasn't seriously hurt and was out of the way; that was all I needed.

The asshole with the backwards cap and the moronic ghetto-speak took a swing at me, which I easily ducked. He was still drunk enough that he almost knocked himself right over onto the street, but I caught him. I grabbed him by the collar and pulled him up close enough to slam my palm into his nose. I heard a snap just before I dropped him to the asphalt.

I quickly looked around me and saw two of the guys running off down the alley. The one I had just dropped to the ground was whining and moaning about his nose, and the last one—the one I had grabbed first—was heading in my direction.

He was, without a doubt, the instigator of all of this. My eyes narrowed as he approached and swung out wildly as if he didn't even know where I was. I sidestepped and backed up—letting him come at me again. After a couple more swings, he seemed to be pretty much out of breath. That's when I pounced.

Before I even touched him, I was in the zone though I never felt disconnected like some guys said they did during a fight. I was always completely focused; I just felt *different* at the same time. Everything seemed brighter even in the dim light coming from the one streetlamp at the end of the block, in sharper focus, and alive.

Every muscle was poised, ready for my command. Every synapse was prepared to fire at my will.

Spinning around, my boot connected with the side of his head. Before he had the chance to fall backwards, I reached out and gripped his hoodie in my fist, twisting the fabric right under his neck around in my fingers. I could feel the string for the hood against my thumb as I pulled him up closer to me and slammed my other fist into his gut.

The air rushed out of him in a fragrant gust. He slumped toward me, but I held him out so I had better access to punch his kidney next. Then his face. Then the top of his arm. Then his face again.

He was screaming and crying at this point, begging me to let him go. For a minute I couldn't understand why he didn't tap out, but then I realized he didn't know the rules. I released my grip with some effort—the knuckles had tightened up and ached when I straightened my fingers—and he dropped to the ground in front of me.

A moment later he was up again, turning and fleeing down the street with sideways-slouched, stumbling steps.

For a second I was confused. There wasn't any cheering, and no one was grabbing my wrist to hold my hand in the air. I was just standing in a deserted street with my heart pounding in my chest and my breaths coming out in heavy pants into the night air. The cool September breeze no longer chilled my skin even as it collided with the sweat covering my chest and back. Then I remembered what I was doing and that the street wasn't completely deserted.

I turned to the girl on the ground.

She was staring down the street in the direction the last of the attackers had run. A few feet away from her was the discarded purse —if you could really call it that—lying on the ground with the contents all over the asphalt. Whatever it was, it was too damn big to be a purse. Yolanda always carried those tiny little things that fit in your hand, but this one looked like you could fit a whole Butterball turkey in it.

My hands were still a little shaky. The fight hadn't lasted more than about a minute and a half, and I had way too much built-up adrenaline. All my muscles were tight, and my hands were still clenched into fists. The desire to beat the shit out of something hadn't ebbed nearly enough in such a short amount of time, and all the energy from my arms and legs seemed to back up into my brain.

I had an instant headache and wished there were a twenty-four hour gym somewhere close-by. As it was, there was only one place for me to vent my building energy.

"What the fuck is wrong with you?" I heard myself shout. My hands continued to tighten into fists as the girl startled and gasped, and her wide eyes focused on me.

"I was just walking home…"

"In this neighborhood? At this time of night? Do you have a fucking death wish?"

I really had no idea why I was shouting at her. I just couldn't believe how fucking stupid she was. Everyone knew how dangerous this area was in the daytime, and now it was past two in the morning. The fact that this obviously young, attractive girl—well, far more than just *attractive*—was wandering around this area in the middle of the night pissed me off.

"You know, if I had come out of the bar two minutes later or happened to have my back turned when those guys started after you, you'd be getting double-teamed in the alley about now!"

Her face went pale in the light of the distant streetlamp, and she looked a little sick. That didn't seem to stop my mouth, though.

"Are you just stupid?" I probably would have gone on, but she wrapped her arms around herself and glared up at me.

"Stop yelling at me!" she screamed. She turned away, but I saw her reach up with the back of her hand to swoop underneath her eyes.

Shit.

I turned slightly away from her and practically bit down on my tongue to keep myself from saying anything else. I brought my fisted hands up against my stomach and tried to pull the tension inside of myself, work through it, and calm down. I could hear her crying combined with choked breaths and sniffles.

"Fuck," I mumbled under my breath. I was starting to come off the fighting high I had been on—the tears might have helped with that—and my stomach felt tight.

After three long, deep breaths, I looked back to the girl on the ground and saw her frantically rubbing at her eyes and cheeks. She didn't look at me as she reached out and pulled her mostly empty bag close to her. She looked inside and then looked around her at all her things on the ground.

"Sorry," I mumbled. I wasn't all that great at apologies, and I figured now wasn't going to be much different. I'd obviously upset her with all my shitty comments, though. "I didn't mean to...I just..."

I stopped talking. I didn't know what to say, and I felt bad about yelling at her. She looked at me all red-eyed with tears staining her cheeks.

"Just don't do that shit anymore." I let out a big sigh.

She nodded once and then reached out to grab something off the ground near her and shoved it back into the bag. From the amount of stuff scattered all over the street, my estimate on the size of the so-called purse wasn't too far off. There was an umbrella, a little flashlight, a bunch of tubes and bottles, and at least a half dozen pens. As I looked around some more, I saw a small notebook, a paperback book, keys, a bottle of hand lotion that was nowhere near travel sized, a stack of tissues wrapped up in a Ziploc bag, two sets of earbuds, and a checkbook. There was also a whole pile of ponytail holders, bobby pins, and those little hair-holder-things that looked like teeth.

There was shit from her bag from one side of the fucking street to the other.

She started crawling around, gathering it all up, and cramming it back inside, which gave me a fabulous view of her ass in the short-shorts style waitress uniform the place up the street usually demanded. I could kind of see how she might have thought she could use the bag as a weapon—there had been more stuff in there than really should have been able to fit. I looked around on the ground to see if there was an actual kitchen sink, or at least part of one, but I didn't see anything metal. There was something that looked like a small rock, though.

"How do you even carry that thing around?" I asked.

"What?"

"That...that purse-bag-thingy there," I said, pointing and shaking my finger at it. I wouldn't have admitted it, but the whole idea of the thing scared me, and I wasn't sure why. I felt like if I got too close to it I might get sucked in, never to be seen again. "It's insane."

Her eyes became little slits as she looked up to me.

"There is nothing wrong with my purse!" she growled.

"It's huge," I said.

"It has everything I need in it."

"It has everything you and ten of your friends could need for a week," I replied with a laugh. "I know there are people who carry Chihuahuas in their purse, but you could fit a Dane in there."

"Don't be ridiculous."

"Okay, a decent-sized schnauzer, then."

I got another glare, but this time it sort of made me smile. As the corners of my mouth turned up, I couldn't help but take it further.

"A pair of poodles?" I asked. "They could sit under the umbrella and read to each other from the book."

"Not really." She seemed to be actively trying to keep her frown on her face now, and her tone had definitely changed.

"I bet there are lost works of art in there," I teased. She just shook her head. "Undiscovered sonnets."

"You are very strange," she said, but she had cracked a bit of a smile.

"I could be a lot worse," I said. She went silent as she looked back down the street and a shudder ran through her body. "I'm gonna get you home, okay?"

"Home?"

"You live around here, right?"

"Um...well, yeah," she stammered. She looked in the direction she had originally been walking.

"I could walk you home," I suggested. "Make sure...well, just get you home."

"How can I trust you?" she said cautiously.

"Trust me?" I asked, trying to decide if I was offended by the very notion that I was somehow not trustworthy. I mean, I had certainly just saved her from a rough night, and most likely a whole lot worse than a little pushing and shoving. I raised both brows at her. "Well, if I was going to rape you and kill you—which was probably their plan—I would have just insisted on going *first*, not chase the other guys away."

Her eyes went wide, and she dropped whatever she was holding onto the pavement. She quickly scrambled after it while I ran my hand through my hair and tried to get myself back together.

"Sorry," I muttered again. I closed my eyes and rubbed my fingers into the sockets before looking back at her. "I think, all in all, you're better off with me than you are by yourself."

"Better the evil I know?" she responded with a smirk. The look and the tone of her voice didn't match her eyes, though—there was fear there. It was entirely possible I was a bit too blunt, but that shit was also true.

"Something like that, but you don't know me, either." I smirked right back.

"You're my hero," she said but seemed to immediately regret the words. She looked away from me, and her throat bobbed as she swallowed.

She had a beautiful neck—long and pale. I could see the outline of her carotid artery as it pulsed just under her skin. Her heart rate was still a little higher than normal, and I wondered if I was the cause of her current fear. I tried to put her at ease, at least as much as she could be at ease in the dark street with a guy she didn't know minutes after she was attacked.

"I'm not going to hurt you," I told her. She nodded but didn't look up. "I'm just going to make sure you get home safely, okay?"

"Okay," she said flatly.

I wondered if she was going to go into shock or something. I definitely needed to get her behind a locked door as quickly as possible so she could relax again. I hoped, since she was walking, she wouldn't have too far to go.

"Where do you live?"

"Just around the corner," she replied as she collected the last few items from the pavement and added them to the collection in the monster-bag. "A few blocks to the left. You don't have to go out of your way—"

"I know the area," I interrupted. "I'm walking you home."

I wasn't asking anymore, and she didn't try to fight it. I picked up my gym bag, and she picked up her purse. I thought about putting a shirt on, but then I remembered I had dropped it back at Feet First. Considering Yolanda's comment about how it smelled, maybe that was for the best. Besides, I was still warm from the exertion, and it wasn't more than a ten-minute walk home.

I grabbed a couple of the other items that had been hanging out near my feet—packets of salad dressing, a tube of lipstick, and something else round—*shit*, a fucking *tampon*—and handed them to her without meeting her eyes. She took them quickly, mumbled a thank you, and shoved them into the huge, practically overflowing handbag.

She stood up and looked at me, and her eyes got big again.

"You got hurt!" she said as she lifted her fingers up toward my temple and then pulled away without touching me.

I reached up and felt the little cut above my eye and snickered.

"They didn't touch me," I assured her. "That was from work."

"Work?"

"Yeah, I'm a fighter."

She paused and her eyebrows screwed together.

"A what?"

"A fighter," I repeated. "You know—two guys in a cage beating the shit out of each other."

"In a cage?" she asked with disbelief.

"Yep." I stated it simply and without making a grandiose noise out of the final consonant because that would just sound stupid.

"For real?"

"Yeah, for real." I laughed.

"I thought that was just on TV."

"We all have to start somewhere," I muttered.

"Sorry," she said. She wrapped the strap of her bag around her neck and shoulder.

"What for?"

"I didn't mean to be…insulting."

"I'm not insulted."

"Oh…well, okay then." She ran her teeth over her bottom lip and looked down the dark street. I was pretty sure she shuddered a little.

"Let's get you home," I commanded as I started walking.

She nodded, and I walked next to her as she headed off in the same direction I usually walked home anyway. She kept her fingers wrapped around the strap of the huge bag and continued to stare at the ground as she walked.

"Don't do that," I said.

"Do what?" Her eyes met mine for a moment.

"Look at the ground," I said. "You aren't paying attention to your surroundings, so it makes you an easier target."

"Oh," she responded. At first she looked right back to the ground again, but then she seemed to process what I had said and held her head a little higher.

"Where are you from?"

"What makes you think I'm not from here?"

"You aren't from the city," I stated.

"Is it that obvious?"

"Yes," I snickered. "Girls from around here know better than to walk alone, except the hookers, but that doesn't seem your style."

She glared at me out of the corner of her eye.

"I'm from Maine," she said with a tone that told me I had just about reached my question quota.

"You're a long ways from home," I said. "How long have you lived here?"

"Two weeks," she answered. "I'm going to school here."

"You got a name?" I asked.

"Of course I have a *name*," she replied, rolling her eyes. "It's Tria. Tria Lynn. You?"

"Liam Teague," I told her, and I held out my hand. She took it, shaking it briefly before she nearly tripped over her own feet on the flat ground. "I hope you don't chew gum."

I laughed at my own joke.

"Very funny," she snapped back. "I'm not overly... coordinated."

We walked the next block in silence. I felt kind of bad for picking on her, so I tried another approach.

"So what are you studying?"

"Economics."

"Really?" I narrowed one eye at her.

"Why is that so surprising?" she asked, obviously displeased with my reaction.

"I dunno," I responded with a shrug. "Just not what I expected."

"What did you expect?"

"Um…teaching? Maybe nursing or physical therapy— something like that."

"Why, because I'm a woman?"

"Uh…um…" I didn't really know how to respond to that. I wasn't really sure why I thought she would say something else; economics just didn't seem to fit. "Well, why economics?"

"Because I don't understand why some people have a ton of money and others don't have anything," she said simply. "It doesn't have anything to do with how hard they work. I thought if I learned more about it, it would help me understand."

I laughed again.

"I'm not a comedian," she growled. "Stop laughing at me."

"I'm not." I shook my head. "I mean, I am, but…not like that. It's just…weird."

"I am not weird!" she yelled as she stopped in her tracks and snarled at me. "It makes perfect sense, and maybe you have just been hit in the head too many times to understand anything other than punching people, but I really don't see how your opinion ought to matter to me!"

"Whoa!" I called out, stopping and turning to face her and holding my hands up in surrender. "Easy there! I just…shit…I just never heard of anyone wanting to study something like that. It's cool."

Her look softened but remained wary, so I turned it around on her.

"And now you have insulted me," I told her.

"What? How?"

"I have not been hit in the head too many times—I fucking win."

I grinned at her before I started walking across the street. She rolled her eyes again, but continued on beside me. We were quiet now with her speaking up only when we made a turn to the right and crossed another dark street.

"This is my street," she said.

I felt an odd tingle run through my arms but didn't respond.

Tria stopped in front of a three-story apartment building with faded brown paneling that tried to give it some sort of Tudor flair but failed miserably. There was a barred door painted black with one of those keypad security systems attached to it. The windows on the ground floor also had bars though the ones higher up didn't. I glanced up the fire escape stairs next to the door and saw a black-haired girl swinging her legs and smoking a cigarette. The ash flicked out into the air and landed beside me on the chipped sidewalk.

"This is where you live?" I tried to stop from smiling too much. I mean, what were the odds?

"Yes," she said. Her tone was dark. "It's not as bad as it looks from the outside."

"Heh." I snorted. "Yes, it is."

I reached forward and gave the barred door a good yank. It opened immediately, even without entering a code or anything. Bullshit security system hadn't worked in at least eight months. Tria kind of glanced at me sideways as I held it open and made a grand gesture with my arm.

"After you," I said.

"It's supposed to be a secure building," she said. "They said they were going to be getting that fixed soon."

"Yep," I replied, "that's what they tell ya."

"I'm not really supposed to let anyone inside the building." She looked off to the side, like she was afraid to send me away while looking me in the eye.

I chuckled.

"You aren't home yet," I told her. "I said I would walk you home."

"It's just inside," she said.

"First floor?"

"Yes."

"What number?"

Her jaw tensed and she continued to look away from me. It looked like she was focusing on a stack of broken up pieces of brick lying in a haphazard pile near the entrance to the apartments. She glanced up at me before blowing out a big gust of breath.

"Fine," she grumbled. "Come on in."

Tria led me to the fourth door on the right, which had faded, not-really-brass numbers tacked up on it. Number 142.

I laughed in one quick burst.

"You live here?"

"Yes," she said as she fished around in her purse for keys.

I had been wondering if my nights were going to be a little quieter, and now I had my answer. I chuckled softly to myself.

"Why is that funny?"

I shook my head as she glared at me.

I started to consider the reasons it was funny, but the reasons that all of this was *not* funny popped into my head instead. They were especially obvious as she continued to fumble around for her keys with her head practically buried in her monstrous over-the-shoulder bag.

I mean, she had just led a perfect stranger—hero or not—right to her door.

"Tria…" I shook my head a little to try to keep my cool. I started counting on my fingers. "One, stop being so trusting—this ain't the small town you grew up in. Yeah, I'm not one to rape you in the street, but that doesn't mean I'm not the kind of guy who would get you back somewhere private and do the same. Two, get your keys out *before* you get to the door. Hold them in your hand—like this."

I grabbed her wrist before she could move and pushed a little, rubbery, lobster-shaped keychain against her palm. Then I positioned the keys on the ring between her fingers.

"Go for the eyes," I said. I raised her hand up with mine and wrapped her fingers into a fist. The keys jutted out between her fingers, turning her hand into a fairly impressive weapon. "Third, don't fucking walk on that street at night by yourself. Get a fucking ride. Someone where you work has to have a car. Fourth, look where you are going, for Christ's sake. Get your head up like you know where you are going and what you are doing even if you don't. Fifth and final—let me know if you need anything. I'm right above you in apartment 242."

With that, I turned and left her, mouth agape, in front of her door while I headed for the stairs at the back of the hall. I could feel her eyes on me, and found myself compelled to look back one more time and grin at her before I headed up the stairs. She pursed her lips, but they quickly spread into a smile just before she entered her apartment and closed the door.

I was never one to get attached, but I had the feeling I'd be seeing her again.

# CHAPTER THREE
## *Make the Move*

My apartment was way too quiet, and I had too much pent-up energy to even consider going to sleep. I took a quick shower and pulled on a pair of sweats, commando style. I was just about out of clean underwear, and I fucking hated doing laundry. The refrigerator called to me, but when I opened it, I was not particularly impressed with the contents. The only thing that interested me mildly was the six-pack of Guinness, but I wasn't in the mood for beer.

My hands began to shake a little. It was probably the pent-up energy from the brawl. I wished it were easier for me to calm down after such things, but any change in my routine usually ended up being a little dangerous for me. Though it has been years, the desire to slip up never really goes away.

I shut the door to the fridge and looked over the small, four-room apartment. Every room could be seen if you stood between the kitchen and the living room and looked past the small opening to one side that led to the single bedroom and bathroom. It wasn't pretty, but...

Well, *but* nothing. It was a dump. The whole building was. It did fit the unique qualifier of being a place I could afford though, which wasn't much. Most of the apartments in the building were advertised as furnished, which was an overstatement. I had gotten a deal on mine because the previous dude took most of the furniture with him the night he disappeared. I had to supply my own, but the rent was lowered to make up for it.

Most of the living room furniture came from Freecycle.

The mattress had been new when I got it, at least. I'd splurged a bit on it when I moved in, deciding I could make up for its cost by eliminating the box spring and a frame, so it's not actually a proper bed. It just sat on the floor of my bedroom next to a little nightstand made of cinderblocks and plywood.

Still, it was better than squatting in an abandoned building or living out of car. I tried to remind myself of that on a regular basis.

I walked over to the gym bag I had discarded by the door and pulled out my cigarettes. Clambering over dirty laundry on the bedroom floor, I hauled the window open and threw my leg over the sill. Right outside was a ledge of decent width, so I could make my way over to the fire escape.

On one side of the three-foot by six-foot platform was a miniscule woman of completely indeterminate age. If you just looked at her size, you'd think she was about twelve, but her eyes were a whole different story. They were deep and dark and gave the impression they'd seen a lot of deep and dark shit. If you judged her by her eyes, you'd think she was a hundred. If someone asked me to really guess, I'd probably say she was in her thirties, but that was still a guess. Her hair was a mess of spiky black tangles, and I kind of doubted she owned a hairbrush.

"What's shaking, Krazy Katie?" I wasn't expecting a response and didn't get one as I dropped down on my ass next to her and lit my cigarette.

Krazy Katie lived in the apartment next to mine and had been in the neighborhood longer than the nine years I had been here. She didn't really say much of anything, let alone talk about herself, so I didn't really know much about her. The assumption was she was on disability for whatever the hell was wrong with her head, living here in the half of the apartments dedicated to Section 8 housing. She spent almost all her days and nights sitting on the fire escape and chain smoking.

Every once in a while, she'd start yelling predictions about the future at people on the street, and the police would get called. That always stirred shit up and had even been pretty damn entertaining more than once. Most people just ignored her, but I sometimes kind of liked talking to someone who almost never said anything back, and she didn't seem to mind me sitting out here with her.

I never knew what she would be doing when I crawled out the window. Sometimes she'd make a lot of strange sounds. Sometimes she'd spend the afternoon pushing her finger into each and every hole in the fire escape grate, one-by-one. Sometimes she'd take off her clothes and just lie up there in her underwear until the landlord or police made her put her clothes back on. Sometimes she ditched the underwear, too.

Tonight she was stacking cigarette butts into a little pyramid of sorts. She had done this before, and at least her timing was a little better. When she did it during the day and a door in the building slammed shut, they would all tip over, and she'd go ballistic.

"Pretty," Krazy Katie said. She took a long draw on her cigarette, which brought it all the way to the filter. I cringed a little at the smell, knowing what that tasted like, and shook my head.

"You saying I'm pretty?" I asked with a quiet chuckle. "I didn't know you were into guys."

She didn't respond, and I didn't try to get her to do so. I had been around her enough to know that random shit just came out of her mouth for no particular reason. I used to try to figure out what she was talking about, but I never got very far, so I didn't try any more. She could have been talking about me, the stack of butts, or the crabgrass growing in the gutter, for all I knew.

I leaned back against the brick wall behind me, then hissed and pulled away. It was damn cold. I decided to sit up with my knees against my chest instead. I took a long draw on the smoke and watched the ash fall between the holes in the grate below me. Krazy Katie lit up another cigarette off a little butane lighter she kept shoved in the center of her bra and actually looked at me for a minute. As soon as I looked at her, she looked away. She never looked me in the eye.

I shivered a little, wondering if it would be warmer inside than it was outside. I concluded it was probably about the same. At least inside, there was a blanket on the bed and no wind. I sucked down my cigarette and started to climb back inside.

"Don't stay out here all night, Krazy Katie," I said on my way in. "And eat something, for Christ's sake. I'm afraid you'll fall right through the grate."

She didn't respond or even look at me.

Rubbing at my eyes, I clambered onto the queen-sized mattress and dropped onto my back. I sighed heavily and pulled the sheet and blanket up to my chest before I rolled over to my side. It was too cold to sleep comfortably but too warm to actually crank up the heat. I had already had the electricity turned off once when I couldn't cover the bill. Now I tried to economize as much as possible on heat and lights.

Physically I was exhausted, but my mind wouldn't turn off. Images of the girl in the street with her ridiculous purse-slash-Bag of Holding ran through my mind.

*Tria.*

She just didn't seem to be the kind of person who would be

living in this area, working at that nasty bar and grill, and having a bunch of guys ogle her for tips. And studying economics? Really? Who does that, other than the Northsiders and their high society business and bullshit majors? People didn't study economics because it sounded interesting—they did that because Daddy told them that's what they needed in order to take over as CEO.

*"Just your yearly reminder that you don't have to live like this."*

"Fuck you, Michael," I mumbled into my pillow. I told my mind to shut the fuck up as I brought the blanket up a little higher and dropped off to sleep.

Still bleary-eyed, I laced up my running shoes and carefully locked my apartment behind me. I couldn't help but glance at apartment 142 as I went by and realized I was kind of hoping to run into the new neighbor as I took off for my mid-morning run. It had been a week since we met in the street, but I hadn't seen her again. Sometimes when I would get home, I'd see her lights on but never actually saw *her*.

I took off running across the street, checking for cars as I went. It was good weather for running, at least. It wasn't as hot as it had been just a few weeks ago. I turned left and headed out of the neighborhood on my typical route.

My usual three-mile run took me out of the slums and into an industrial district. There were a lot of warehouses and factories that had shut down in the recession, but a few were still open. I knew at least a couple people in my building who sometimes got work in one of them, but the layoffs were frequent, and they'd be right back on welfare a few months later.

At least I wasn't that bad off.

I had a good deal working for Dordy and Yolanda. I got paid a hundred a fight, win or lose. If I won, I got more. Fighting twice a week put me at just enough to live on and not much more. I could make rent on my crappy apartment, feed myself, and pay for the utilities. I usually had a little left over for smokes and weekly pizza delivery.

I did better than a lot of people I knew, and having any extra money was dangerous for someone like me.

Thinking about my own livelihood made me wonder just how Tria was doing. She had only been around a few weeks; she had told me the night I met her. I wondered how she was adjusting to school, work, and living in a shit neighborhood that was probably very unlike whatever she had at home.

There was a scrawny little tree surrounded by the only patch of real dirt for a mile in any direction. It was the spot that marked my halfway point. I circled wide and then at a slightly faster pace headed back in the direction of my building. Once I crossed the street, I checked my time and walked around the block to cool off before going back inside to down three large cups of water.

I looked over at my hand-me-down rowing machine in the corner of the living room and sighed. I didn't work out much on fight nights. I'd run early in the day to loosen up but keep myself from doing too much right before a fight. Tonight was going to be a challenge night, too, which always took a lot out of me.

There wasn't shit to watch on television, and I wondered why I even bothered to steal cable from Krazy Katie. Not that it was really stealing from *her*; we just kind of…shared it. I brought her smokes when she ran out, and she didn't respond when I asked her if she minded if I strung another line through our windows. She let me in to do it, so I figured it was okay with her, at least.

Boredom set in, and I was starting to sweat just a little. I ran my hand over my face. My fingers were trembling, and I glanced down at the aging marks on my arm. Boredom was a dangerous mindset, and I had to get myself moving before temptation became more than just an itch in the back of my head. As long as I kept moving, I wouldn't go searching.

I grabbed my gym bag and headed to the bar early. Dordy and a kitchen chick named Stacy were there, serving a single customer whose name I couldn't remember, but he was a regular and always hammered. Phil? Peter? Some "P" name, I thought. It was still too early for the after-work crowd to start showing up yet, so he was on his own, muttering bullshit about the upcoming presidential election.

"Hey, Teague!" Dordy called out as I walked in. He rubbed at the inside of a pint glass with a towel. "You're early."

"Bored," I announced. "Figured talking to you was better than talking to myself."

"You ordering?"

"If you'll spot me from tonight's take."

"No problem," he said.

Dordy didn't carry anyone on credit—no fucking way. He let me get by with it on the day of a fight, though, since he would see enough at the door to make it worth his while even if I didn't show up and he had to jump in the cage himself. The day before a fight, I'd be shit out of luck, but fight days were okay with him.

"Scotch?" Dordy asked.

"Veggie Burger?" Stacy asked. The large, grandmotherly woman stocked them just for me.

"No scotch—just the burger and a beer. Thanks." I sat down on one of the stools nearby while Dordy drew a Guinness from the tap. I hung out and had a couple drinks while people slowly began to trickle in. The early ones knew who I was and would come over to make small talk before the crowd arrived. A couple hours before the fight, Dordy's bouncers, Gary and Wade, waltzed in. Gary was just freaking huge height-wise. He had long, grey whiskers hanging from his chin down to his collar and was shaved bald. Wade was a little older, also bald, and used to train for MMA. He wasn't as physically intimidating, but he was definitely the more dangerous of the two. Gary couldn't fight for shit, but he was big enough that he rarely ever had to do anything other than stand up straight to get a patron to behave.

"Takedown fights again!" Gary roared in greeting. I fist-bumped him, then went back to nursing my beer. A few minutes later, Wade cocked his head to one side to point at the door, and I followed him out for a smoke.

"Word on the street says you fucked up some guys on your way home the other night."

"Oh, yeah?" I said, raising my brow as I lit up. "Who said that?"

"One of the guys you fucked up."

I laughed and took a deep drag.

"He came in here last night saying Takedown Teague broke his nose," Wade told me. "He thought that as his employer, Dordy ought to pay for it."

"Oh, yeah?" I said again. "What did Dordy do?"

"Had me break one of his fingers."

That had me nearly in tears.

"So what's the deal?" Wade asked. He blew smoke out of his nose as he talked. "You don't get enough fighting as it is?"

"They were fucking with some girl," I told him.

"You in the business of saving damsels in distress now?" He snickered.

"That shit ain't right," I said. "They didn't need to be messing with her."

"Who is she?"

"Just some girl," I said with a shrug. "I hadn't seen her before that night. Turns out she lives in my building, though."

"No shit?"

"Yeah. Remember the couple I was always bitching about? The

ones who would fight and scream all the time?"

"Yep."

"They're gone, and she's in the apartment below me now."

"That ought to help you sleep better," Wade replied.

"Amen to that shit," I agreed.  I thought about the dude whose nose I had broken.  "I wonder why Dordy didn't mention that."

"Because he wants to hold it over your head later," Gary said as he stepped out from behind the front door and joined us for a smoke. "Did you fuck her?"

"Who?"

"The bitch you saved."

"No."  I scowled at him.

"Well, what's the point, then?" Gary asked.  He grinned a ridiculous grin and winked at me, but I didn't find anything funny about his comment, and he caught on to that and tried to make a serious face.  "Who is she?"

"I don't know," I said.  "If you wanted the whole fucking story, why didn't you come out sooner?"

"Dordy had me hauling beer from the delivery truck," Gary replied.  "Are you going to see this girl again?"

"I don't know," I said again.  "What's with the fucking twenty questions?  It was some random chick who is obviously so fucking stupid, she would walk through this neighborhood at night by herself.  I beat the shit out of a couple drunks and then walked her home.  I don't know her.  She lives in my building and works at that greasy spoon place with the big screen TVs.  That's all I know, bitches."

"Fin's?" Wade asked.

"Whatever it is," I said, knowing full well that was the name of the place.

"They got a new brunette waiting tables there," he said.

"That might be her," I said.  "She said she moved into town a couple weeks ago."

"Pretty little thing—hair in a ponytail?"

"Could be," I shrugged. "Sounds like her."

"I know who you mean," Gary said. "Nice, pretty mouth, too. And with that ponytail? Mmm…"

I rolled my eyes.

"Just makes you want to wrap it around your wrist and go to town!" Gary put his hands in front of his crotch and moved them back and forth in front of him, as if he were bouncing a basketball on his dick. His hips moved suggestively.

Wade just shook his head.

"Don't make me fuck you up," I threatened. I tossed the butt of the cigarette beyond the ashtray on the sidewalk and into the gutter before turning around and walking back inside.

There wasn't a scheduled opponent for me tonight, which meant it was a challenge night. Anyone in the bar was free to challenge me in the cage, and anyone who made it past five minutes without tapping out won a hundred bucks. On top of my normal hundred a fight, I received an extra ten bucks for each guy who didn't last.

I was on number six, and he was the first of the night to make it past three minutes.

He swung and hit me in the gut as I danced away. I had landed several good blows on him, but the dude was fast and wiry. He landed one good one that knocked me down and slammed my head on the ground, and the fight hadn't been completely in my favor since. I couldn't seem to get a grip on him long enough to get him in a hold and choke him to unconsciousness. I was getting a little frustrated. It wasn't often an amateur managed to last this long with me, and it pissed me off.

I decided to stop fucking around and just beat the guy.

We had spent the past two minutes smacking and just trying to get a hold of each other, and he seemed surprised when my tactics suddenly changed. I just dove at him, ignoring tactics and his fists as they came at my face. He tried to move back and away, but I shoved with my shoulder and pushed him up against the corner of the cage. I could still feel his hands punching at my shoulders, but it didn't matter anymore—I had him where I wanted him.

Using my head, I slammed against his sternum. He cried out, stunned for a moment, and then gasped as my knee connected with his gut. I hit him with my forehead again—this time in the shoulder. It hurt like a bitch, and I would pay for it later, but it worked. Then I stomped on the top of his foot. His grip on me faltered, and I turned him around and slammed him against the cage.

Now that I had my arms around him, I wasn't about to let go even as he pounded on my shoulders and back, trying to get away. I wrestled him to the floor of the cage and knocked his head against the ground a few times, then started throwing actual punches.

He tapped out a few seconds later, but it was enough to break five minutes.

I was annoyed to realize he had lasted so long, but he deserved it. Dordy was going to be pissed off, though. I hoped I would still get the fifty I earned from the last few fights. When he and I first worked out our business arrangement, he would take it out of my pay when one of the guys from the bar won.

Helping the guy back on his feet, I shook his hand and dusted him off a bit. Yolanda led him out of the cage door and announced I would be back on Tuesday to fight some guy from across town. My ears were ringing, and I could barely focus on the crowd as I headed to the locker room.

I rubbed at my head a bit. The last guy had gotten me pretty good a couple of times, and the face in the mirror was kind of a mess. I was cut above both of my eyes, one cheek, and my lip was busted open. Blood smeared my chest and my forearms.

"You okay?" Yolanda's voice came from behind me. "You took a couple good smacks."

"Ears ringing," I mumbled. "Need some air."

"Let me check you out first," Yolanda insisted.

"Fuck you," I growled as I headed for the back door. I felt her slip around me just before she popped up in front of me and shoved me backwards with both hands on my chest.

"I'm going to check you out," she said through clenched teeth. "If and only if I decide you are okay will you go out for a smoke. Got it?"

Closing my eyes and huffing breath out my nose, I turned around and dropped down to the bench next to the lockers. If I was going to admit it to myself, I was a bit dizzy. Besides, I had a sneaking suspicion Yolanda could kick my ass if she wanted to.

"Fuck you!" I cringed and yelled as she shined a little penlight in my eyes.

"Stop being such a baby," she said. She had gone back to acting all soft and mothering again, which was kind of funny for a chick who was always watching me move around naked. What was the opposite of an Oedipal complex? Electra? Nah, I had something backwards. Yolanda was more of a lioness. Or was it a cougar?

Maybe I did have a concussion.

I let her poke around at the back of my head, which was pretty tender but didn't make me see spots or anything. Then she asked me a bunch of bullshit questions until I got pissy.

"Come on, Yolanda," I whined. "I wanna smoke. I'm fine."

The dizziness and ear-ringing were gone, and I did think I was okay. Yolanda either agreed or was tired of arguing with me because she let me up and watched me head out the door. I stomped up the stairs with my head throbbing in my temples, still ticked off that the guy lasted as long as he did. Overall, I was not in a good mood.

When I got to the top of the stairs, I immediately saw a figure leaning against the outside of the fence and looking back and forth down the street quickly. Each time the head turned, a long brown pony tail bobbed around, and strands of hair got caught in the chain links. If the short-shorts and Fin's logo on the shirt weren't enough to go on, the gigantic, evil handbag gave her away.

"What the fuck?" I snarled through the fence.

Tria startled and looked at me, turning quickly on her heel and holding up her keys clenched in her fist. I tilted my head to one side and raised an eyebrow at her. What was she going to do, wave them around at me from the other side of the fence?

"I'm pretty sure that was not meant to take the place of a ride," I said, nodding toward the keys in her hand.

"You scared the shit out of me!" Tria yelled. She adjusted the mega-monster purse on her shoulder and ran her hand through her hair. "The girl who was driving me got another job. She just walked out today, and there wasn't anyone else on my shift with a car."

"So you're walking down this street again?" I yelled. I slammed my palms into the chain links, making the whole side of metal rattle. She jumped away, stammering.

"I...I..."

I didn't give her much chance to finish. I was livid.

"After what happened the last time? Seriously, Tria?" I paced over to the edge of the building and back to the fence again. My fingers wrapped around the links and yanked. "You do have a fucking death wish, don't you?"

"I do not!"

"Then why are you being so stupid?" I screamed. I planted my feet right where they were, and my heart thumped audibly in my chest.

"I was trying to find you!" she yelled back.

"Well, why didn't you come in the fucking bar?" I tossed my hands up into the air. "Is there not a big ass poster right there in your face saying exactly where I am on Friday nights?"

45

"I tried," Tria said with a glare. "The bouncer wouldn't let me in."

"Why not?"

"I'm only twenty," she said with a shrug.

There was something about that news that flipped a switch in my head. I knew she looked young, but I didn't realize *how* young. The idea that she was out here on her own, trying to make a go in this place without even being old enough to get into a bar killed my anger and made me feel something a little odd as well. Respect? Maybe even pride?

Whatever it was, it also hardened my dick.

"Jesus Christ," I muttered. I turned away from her and ran my hand through my hair, trying to get my dick under control before it made itself known through my shorts. I cringed as my fingers came across the tender spot on the back of my skull. At least the sharp pain killed my erection.

"You're hurt," Tria stated. I didn't look up, but I could hear her hands grasping the links of the fence.

"All part of the job," I responded. Turning around to look at her again, I could see concern in her eyes. I remembered what my face had looked like in the mirror, and I knew what she was seeing appeared a little crazy. I looked worse than I really was.

"Why?" I heard myself ask as I moved back to the fence that separated us. "Why did you come looking for me?"

She looked away, her neck craning to the side a little as she looked down the street.

"I was hoping…maybe…maybe you could walk me home?" Her voice quavered as she looked back at me. Our eyes met through the links, and my knuckles tightened around the little metal bits between my fingers.

I swallowed once, trying to understand why my heart was still pounding so forcefully in my chest. My appearance right now was probably as frightening as anyone on the street, but she was still asking me for help, just like I had told her to do the week before.

I moved my eyes somewhat involuntarily over her form—slender, young, beautiful, and in need. I ran my tongue over my lips, tasting blood, as these thoughts echoed through my head. My chest rose as I inhaled slowly.

She just looked far too tempting.

Another set of words that described her ran through my head: *easy target.*

I didn't like those words so much, not just for me, but for anyone around here. She had no fucking idea what she was doing or how to live in the city—that much was obvious. If she did, she would have told Wade or Gary at the door that she was twenty-one and just forgot her ID. They would have let her in. She also could have pushed her boobs up a bit, and they would have forgotten to ask altogether. Worst case, she could have said she knew me, and they would have allowed her in, too.

And here she was again, hanging out in the back street behind the bar not fifty feet from where a group of guys had been waiting to ambush her a week ago. Granted, she had learned—she was on alert and holding her keys right—but still, her precautions wouldn't have done much if someone decided they really wanted a piece of her.

And yeah—guys definitely wanted a piece of that.

"Liam?" she said quietly. I focused on the movement of her lips, and images similar to the one Gary had conjured up with his bobbing hands and thrusting hips came to mind. "Would you?"

"Would I what?" I responded.

"Walk me home?" Her voice was small and scared, and it brought out something primal inside my gut.

"Yeah," I said with a quick nod. "I can do that."

I was never the outdoorsy type, but I started walking her home every night after that.

# CHAPTER FOUR
## Find the Step

I walked slowly back and forth in front of Fin's Bar and Grill and watched people smelling like grease walk out of the place. Just the smell of greasy food made me feel a little sick—there was no way I'd ever actually eat in such a place. I couldn't even bring myself to walk through the front door.

Tria bustled out just as I finished my cigarette. She was trying to walk and find something in Godzilla's Clutch Purse at the same time, which made her trip on the step as she was coming out the door. I tried to keep from laughing out loud.

"One of these days," I told her, "you are going to stick your hand in there, and it will get lost in all that shit. You'll never find it again."

Tria sighed and tilted her head at me. She pulled her hand out and held up a little tube of lipstick or ChapStick or gloss or something—maybe all three—like it was some kind of trophy. She put it on with exaggerated flair before dropping it back into the bag.

"You just don't understand," she said.

"I hope I never do," I admitted.

"Wow...who would have thought?" she said under her breath. Her eyes darted over me.

"Thought what?" I asked, looking down to see if I had pizza sauce or something on me.

Tria's cheeks tinged with red.

"That you owned a shirt," she said with a small smile as she looked me over again. "Well, most of one, anyway. I've never seen you in one before."

"Heh...I guess not." I reached up and fiddled with the collar of my plain, black T-shirt with the sleeves sliced out of it, leaving it mostly open down the sides. I never thought much about what I was wearing. Most of my clothing came from secondhand stores.

We fell in step together, moving without a lot of rush down the sidewalk and across the street. It was Wednesday, and I wasn't working, but Tria had gotten off late *again*. She was supposed to get off before the place closed, which was one in the morning, but she always seemed to get stuck doing something else until closing time. It was only a twenty-minute walk, but she'd be so late, we usually wouldn't get back to the apartments until two thirty in the morning. This night wouldn't be any earlier.

I had given her a bunch shit about hanging out for so long behind Feet First the week before. It wasn't much safer than the street. Apparently, she thought she would be "close enough" to me that it would be okay, which set me off pretty bad. I took her around front and introduced her to Wade and made her promise to come inside when I was working on Friday.

"So who made 'patron of the evening' tonight?" I asked.

"This guy with a big green Mohawk," she said immediately. "He's a vegetarian and wanted me to get the chef to make something special for him since there wasn't anything vegetarian on the menu outside of fries and onion rings. It's a *bar*, dammit—not a four star restaurant! We don't serve pasta primavera! We don't even have spaghetti!"

"*I'm* a vegetarian," I said with a sideways glance at her.

"You are not," she said with a roll of her eyes.

"I most certainly am."

Tria looked over at me, trying to determine if I was making this up or not.

"Really?"

"Really," I replied. "Since I was about seventeen."

"How old are you now?"

"Twenty-six."

Her lip disappeared behind her teeth for a minute.

"So why did you become a vegetarian?" she asked.

"Nope," I said. "You grilled me about cage fighting last time. It's my turn to annoy you with questions."

"Ugh!" Tria groaned, and I laughed.

"Why did you decide to move here?" I asked. I shoved the tips of my fingers into the front pockets of my jeans and kicked a chunk of cement into the center of the road with the toe of my tennis shoe.

"I told you—I'm going to school."

"Yeah, but why *here*?" I asked.

"Hoffman College gave me the best deal," she said with a shrug. "Aside from the financial aid and scholarship, they have a service that will come and pick me up to get to classes."

"You're going to Hoffman?" I tried not to sound too shocked.

"Yes," she affirmed. "Why?"

"You just hadn't mentioned it before," I replied nonchalantly as images of the tall brick buildings filled my head. I remembered the ladies in the alumni center who would always give me candy when I accompanied my mom on one of her visits. "It's a pretty small school."

"That's one of the things I liked about it," Tria said. "It's actually family-owned and gives more money in scholarships than other programs. The econ department is really well known as well."

51

There would be no argument there—Hoffman College was quite well known for a few of their programs. I hadn't really heard about the economics department before, but I also didn't pay much attention to that shit when I was a kid.

We continued along the sidewalk past the back side of Feet First and around the corner toward our street. When I looked up, there were two guys heading toward us, and I heard Tria let out a long breath. Glancing over at her, I could see the muscles in her arm tense as her fingers gripped the strap of her bag, and she moved a half step closer to me.

I was pissed that they had scared her even though I knew they were only walking at this point. I looked ahead, trying to determine if I had ever seen them before, but they didn't look familiar. They certainly weren't part of the group that went after her a couple of weeks ago—I was sure of that.

With a quick side step, I moved behind Tria to stand on the other side of her so the two guys would pass us beside me, not her. They didn't even stop their conversation as they walked by, but Tria relaxed immediately after they passed.

"Thank you," she said quietly.

"No worries," I replied. She was still gripping her purse tightly. "You okay?"

"Yeah," she said. "Just remembering."

"Well, don't," I suggested. Tilting my head to look over at her, I offered her a goofy half smile. She returned one of her own, so the desired effect was attained.

"Thank you," she said again. "I mean, for the other night. I don't think I ever really properly thanked you."

"You were kinda in shock," I reminded her. "Don't worry about it."

"You didn't have to do that," she told me. "You didn't have to go after those guys and risk yourself for—"

I interrupted her with a sharp laugh.

"Risk myself? With those douchebags? Hardly."

"Still," she continued, "you got into a fight for someone you didn't even know."

"I like fighting," I told her. "I like to beat people up. It's what I do for a living, you might recall."

"I remember." She sighed and her nose wrinkled up a bit. "The point is still the same—thank you for rescuing me."

"I was in the neighborhood." I shrugged and offered her another half smile. She looked back down at her feet and shook her head a little before looking back at me. Her large brown eyes darted back and forth between mine.

"And for doing all of this," she said with a wave of her arm. "You don't have to do this—walk me home every night, especially when I get off so late. I wasn't expecting you to do this, but I'm not even sure if Stan is going to hire another server at this point, and—"

"Tria, don't worry about it," I told her. "I only work two nights a week, and I stay up late every night. If I wasn't doing this, I'd be sitting in front of the TV, trying to figure out why people watch the shit that is on there."

Tria snickered.

"You're still going out of your way," she said, looking up at me again. "And in the middle of the night, no less. I appreciate it."

I just shrugged again, not yet willing to admit to myself, let alone her, that this little walk of ours was quickly becoming the highlight of my nights. I was kind of disappointed she didn't have to work the next day.

"Why did you pick this area to live in?" I asked.

"Fin's offered me the job," she said. "School isn't too far away to use their transportation service, and I needed the work. I didn't have much experience when I filled out job applications, and no one else even called me back for an interview. Everyone seems to be looking for a job, and there don't seem to be enough to go around."

"Can't argue with that," I said. "I keep hearing that the economy sucks, and whatever politician you are talking to, it's the other one's fault. I assume you are going to fix that after you graduate, right?"

"I'll be happy if I can at least makes some sense out of it all," she responded.

We made it to the apartment entrance, and I glanced up to see Krazy Katie lying on her back on the fire escape. She had her legs straight up in the air and was doing a bicycle peddling exercise or something.

At least she had her clothes on.

"You'll never get anywhere on that bike!" I called up to her but didn't get a response. I laughed quietly as I jerked the door open and let Tria go in first.

"Who is that?" she asked.

"Krazy Katie," I replied. "She's the resident psycho. Every apartment building needs one."

"What is she doing?"

"Who knows?" I laughed. "She's a nut. Harmless enough, but still a nut."

Tria slid her key into the lock and opened her apartment door. She turned back to me then, and I became increasingly aware of how close we were standing, even though we weren't actually touching. That made me realize I had only actually touched her twice—once when I yanked her back against me and away from a thug and then later that night when I showed her how to hold her keys.

Her eyes were on mine, but I couldn't understand her expression. It seemed to be a combination of apprehension and wonder, but that didn't make any sense. Mostly I noticed the shimmer of the lip shit she had put on earlier, which was emphasized as her tongue darted out over her lips.

My hands began to feel a little clammy, and I didn't know where to put them. I considered leaning against the frame of the door, but it didn't feel right, so I ended up shoving the tips of my fingers back into my pockets again.

I swallowed, trying not to focus on either her mouth or the area where the pale skin above her breasts was exposed. I pulled more oxygen into my lungs and realized I experience a similar feeling right before a fight starts—anticipation, excitement, and something else deeper and unnamable.

"Thanks for walking me home," Tria said softly. Her eyes didn't leave mine, and I wondered if her cheek felt as soft as it looked.

"You're welcome," I replied simply.

"Good night," she said. Her face flushed, and she used her tongue once more to stroke her lips.

"Night."

She turned slowly and moved across the line of the apartment door, and whatever had been going on in my head abruptly stopped when her eyes moved from mine.

I didn't sleep well that night. In my head, I blamed the cold and figured I would have to turn the heat on by the end of the week.

I was never one to face my emotions, but I knew I was already in deep.

# CHAPTER FIVE
## Question the Motive

"Just let her in, and don't fuck around."

"Hey—it's not my fault!" Gary tossed his hands in the air. "I didn't know who she was, and she pulled out an ID that said she was underage! Shit, dude…"

"You'd seen her before, asshole," I growled. "You knew who she was."

"What, 'cause she brought him a basket of onion rings once?" Wade grinned. "Dude, I never saw any higher than her tits when you brought her over here."

I took a step forward, about ready to beat the shit out of him. Two minutes after he walked in the cage, I'd already pounded the fucker who came all the way across town to challenge me. I had plenty of energy left and balled my hands into fists as I moved toward the bouncer.

"Easy, Teague," Wade said. He held his hands out in front of him, surrendering. "I'm just messing with ya. I'll point you out to her as soon as she shows up."

"You do that." I snarled.

I was in a shitty mood; there was no doubt about that, but I couldn't pinpoint a cause. I won the fight without a lot of trouble and barely a bruise, so that wasn't it. Yolanda was getting on my nerves, but I also knew she wasn't doing anything she didn't normally do. Her usual banter was just pissing me off.

If I were going to admit it, I would have had to say I had been feeling tense since I dropped Tria off two nights ago. It started the very next day after a shitty night of sleep. I went for my usual morning run and found myself walking a little slower past her apartment both before and after my run, kind of hoping she would suddenly walk out, but she didn't. I also started taking smoke breaks just outside the building instead of on the fire escape with Krazy Katie just in case Tria came out the door or maybe back home from a class or something.

That didn't happen either.

I had no fucking idea why I was even doing these things. Normally, if I wanted a girl's attention, I just did a little flexing, let her feel my abs, and then asked her to come back to my place to fuck, but that just didn't work in this situation. For one, my place was just too damn close to hers and asking her to come upstairs with me seemed weird. Besides, Tria was a small-town girl, and she didn't seem like the "just fucking" type. I didn't do relationships—never, ever again—so there was only one thing I was interested in, and I was always honest about that.

I definitely needed to get laid.

This brought me to the next conundrum—if I did do the casual sex thing with Tria and it didn't work out, she'd still be right there in the building, and she would still need someone to walk her home. The idea of her walking by herself brought out a seriously pissy side of me that wouldn't have anything to do with the very thought of it. If I did something to piss her off, who was going to get her home safely?

Not that fucker who employed her, that was for sure. He hadn't even managed to post the position for a new server during her shift yet.

I dropped my ass onto a bar stool and accepted a beer from some random fighting fan. He was going on about the details of the fight while the chick he was with eye fucked me under the pretense of checking out my tats. I alternated between watching the door and watching the time, knowing Tria was due soon. She finally appeared at the door. According to my internal clock, it was hours. The actual clock on the wall said it had been only ten minutes. I jumped up without excusing myself and moved through the crowd to meet her.

"It's about time!" I growled.

"I just got off work," she explained. She shoved her hand into the Titan's Knapsack and pulled out a bottle of hand sanitizer and rubbed a bit around on her palms.

"I'm going to have to come and meet you there," I grumbled. "You probably shouldn't be walking to this place on your own, either."

"It's a block away, and there are people all over the street out front," Tria pointed out. "The streetlights all work out there, too. I was fine."

"This time."

"You said you were obligated to hang out here until two," she reminded me.

"I am. I could still sneak out for a few minutes—take a smoke break and a walk. No big deal."

"No," Tria said. She shook her head as she crammed the bottle back into her bag. "I never seem to get out of there on time, and you already do enough. I don't want you getting in trouble for me."

"Whatever," I grumbled. "There's a half hour left before I get paid and can get out of here. You want a drink?"

"I'm not twenty-one," she reminded me.

"You must be," I said with a smile. "Otherwise you couldn't get in here."

Tria rolled her eyes and followed me as I moved back through the crowd, which was starting to thin out a bit. We made our way to the edge of the bar where I liked to hang out after fights. It was a good combination of a place where people could see me and come up to talk but also a little bit sheltered so people didn't get too crazy on me. It didn't happen often, but every once in a while, I'd get a nutty fan or a fighter who wasn't happy about losing, and they'd make a scene.

I stopped and turned back around to face her and saw her eyes on the cage. I stood up a little straighter as she looked it over, and an odd sense of pride came over me along with a touch of apprehension. I didn't have a clear sense of what she thought about cage fighting, and she wouldn't be the first chick I had known who hated the whole idea of it.

"Pretty cool, huh?" I gave her a half smile and raised my eyebrows at her. My heart was pounding, and I felt a slight chill against the naked skin of my chest.

"That's where you fight?" Tria asked and she stared wide-eyed into the enclosed space.

"Yeah, it is," I replied. Something about her tone seemed off, and I took a slight step away from her. I leaned on a nearby barstool and watched her, feeling a little wary all of a sudden. "What do you think?"

"I thought it would be...bigger," she said. "There isn't even any room for you to move in there."

"There's plenty of room," I told her. "I can move around pretty easily in tight places."

The words were out of my mouth before I could stop them.

"Nice." Yolanda piped up before I could try to take back the words. She walked out from around the edge of the cage and came over to us. "Liam's finally admitting size matters, huh?"

I glared at her.

"Not something I've ever worried about too much," I replied coldly. My earlier annoyance with her returned, and I cocked my head to one side as I looked up at her with a "what the fuck do you want" expression.

Yolanda wasn't fazed. She looked from me to Tria and back again.

"Is this her?" she asked. "The girl whose virtue you saved?"

Tria looked away for a minute, and I couldn't see her face. I found myself taking a step forward—angling myself between Tria and Yolanda. I surveyed the whole room, taking my first really good look at the place since the first day I walked into it. The lights were dim, which only barely masked how shabby everything was inside. The barstools were frayed, and the felt on the single pool table was almost completely worn out. The people who frequented Feet First looked like people who came to drown their sorrows because that's who they were. They were as shabby as the interior of the bar, and most of them were way beyond casually drunk.

"This is Tria," I said. My voice was monotone, and I narrowed my eyes at Yolanda as I spoke. I didn't like the way she was sizing up Tria as if she were a target.

Tria was a small-town girl trying to get herself an education and somehow make the world better. I didn't think she had much more of a chance of achieving that shit than a lightweight did against me, but I couldn't help but admire her spirit for trying. Yolanda was a whole other story.

"Hi, Tria," Yolanda said. She didn't take her eyes off me, though. Her expression matched mine, and she even went as far as to raise an eyebrow at me.

I mouthed "fuck you" at her, but she ignored me and turned to Tria.

"I'm Yolanda. Welcome to Feet First, but you are a little late to see my man in action here."

"I was…um…working earlier," Tria said, stumbling over her words a bit. "I just got off."

Yolanda snickered and reached out to run her hand over my chest.

"Wouldn't be the first time that happened to a woman around Takedown." Yolanda smirked. She looked back at me and put a hand on her hip. "I put your winnings in your bag and locked it in your locker. I'm outta here. See you tomorrow?"

"Yeah," I said with a curt nod.

Yolanda sauntered through the crowd and out the front door, and I looked back at Tria, wondering what she was thinking. The look on her face told me nothing, but her words made it clear.

"So that's your girlfriend," Tria said matter-of-factly. "She's really pretty."

"She's not," I said.

"Are you kidding? She's beautiful."

"She's not my girlfriend." I clarified. "Yolanda's a fighter, like me. Well, she was before she fucked up her knee. We still work out together on the weekends."

"I see." Tria didn't sound convinced.

"She's been in the cage a lot longer than me," I said. I didn't know why it was important to me that she understand there wasn't anything between Yolanda and me. "She helps me train. That's it."

Tria just nodded and glanced around the bar again. She hadn't touched the bottle of beer sitting next to her.

"So, why 'Takedown'?" she asked as she looked back in my direction.

I laughed.

"Um, well," I started, "it's not much of a story, really."

Tria looked at me expectantly.

"Okay, when I first started fighting here, Yolanda told me I needed a catchy nickname of some sort. We toyed around with a few and figured "takedown" fit well with my name and sounded pretty tough." I stopped and looked around, wondering if this was something I really ought to be advertising to the world, but most of the world had already departed—either in mind or body. "There's a lot of theatrics about it, ya know? People remember catchy names."

It all sounded kind of dumb when I explained it.

Tria blinked a couple of times.

"So, I started going by Liam 'Takedown' Teague."

"You were right," Tria said.

"About what?" I asked, confused.

"That isn't much of a story."

We both laughed.

Most of the crowd was pretty much gone, so I said goodbye to Dordy, grabbed my gym bag, verified the cash inside was right, and then we headed off down the backstreets and toward home. Tria seemed quiet and thoughtful, which kind of drove me crazy because I had no idea what she was thinking.

"So, what's your impression of Feet First?" I asked.

"It's...interesting," she said noncommittally.

"That's it? Just interesting?" I pressed for a better answer. "What kinds of places do you usually hang out at?"

"I haven't spent a lot of time in bars, really," Tria admitted. "I don't have much to compare it to."

"I thought every small town had at least one bar," I said. "Did yours skip that little facet of entertainment? Had to be a really small town."

Tria laughed quietly.

"I grew up in a trailer park outside of town," she told me.

"So, like those little rows of houses all shoved up next to each other?"

"Not exactly," she said quietly. "Everyone lives in those mobile homes, and it's really more like a campground."

"Bet you had a great view of the neighbors." I grinned when she scowled at me. When she didn't answer, I tried another tactic. "What did your parents think of you moving all the way from Maine to here?"

"Well...um...my parents split up when I was a baby," she said. "I've only seen my mom a couple of times since then. Dad died when I was six."

"Oh, shit...sorry." I suddenly felt like an absolute ass.

"It's okay," she replied quietly. "It was a long time ago. Mom's kind of a basket case, so I was raised by my dad's friends."

It seemed like she was going to say something else, but she didn't. I considered pressing, but her mood had darkened a little. I decided to lighten it up.

"What's your favorite color?"

"My favorite color?" she repeated. "What kind of question is that?"

"A normal one," I said. "Well?"

"Yellow, I suppose," she said. Her cheeks tinged with pink, and I wondered what about the color yellow would make her blush.

"Why yellow?" I urged her to answer.

"It's bright, like the sun in the summer," she said quickly. "Yellow is warm and inviting. The sun makes the trees grow tall. It's so hazy here all the time, and there aren't any trees. I haven't seen a single tree in this neighborhood though there are a few planted on campus."

"There's one," I said. "It's a few blocks away."

"A tree?"

"Yep."

"Where?"

"It's about a mile and a half down, actually," I told her. "It's in an area that used to have a park in it when all the factories were still in business. I think it was set up for people to go eat their lunch or something. I go past it every day."

"Every day?" she repeated.

"Yes, *every day*," I mocked. She glared at me. Her expression made me grin—she was such a tiny thing but definitely had a temper to her as well. Even though I was still aware of the shitty closed-up storefronts, broken glass, and vulgar smells around us, everything else seemed to fade into the background as I talked with her. "I run in the mornings."

"Do you work out every day, too?"

"Uh-uh," I said as I shook my head from side to side and tapped my chest with my thumb. "I'm performing the interrogation here."

I eyed her as I pulled a cigarette out of the pack in my pocket and lit it.

"You got a boyfriend back home?"

"No," she said bluntly.

"Oh." I didn't really know what to say about that. She didn't offer anything else, and again I got the idea I should find another subject. "Favorite flower?"

"Seriously?"

"Just tell me!" I snapped.

"I don't know…um…orchids, I guess." She reached up and pulled the band out of her hair, which then fell around her shoulders. "They're so complicated. You can look at them for an hour and keep seeing new parts of them."

"You could look at a flower for an hour?" I snickered. "You need cable TV."

"I can barely make the bills as it is," Tria replied. "No way could I add another forty bucks a month on top of it."

"I've got cable," I told her. "You could come watch a movie with me or something."

She glanced away, and I knew I had said something wrong. Shit, it had probably sounded like I was coming on to her. I hadn't meant it that way—not really.

Had I?

"My mom always taught me to share." I started babbling to make up for what I was sure was a faux pas. "Since I share it with the neighbor, I could also share it with you, ya know? I mean, what else are big brothers for, right?"

I had no idea where that shit came from.

"Big brother?" Tria repeated. Her brow furrowed, and she brought her hand up to chew at the edge of her thumbnail.

"Yeah," I said with a nod. I smiled, hoping it looked friendly and not incestuously creepy. "That's kind of what I'm doing here, right? Helping you out and shit, like a brother would?"

"Yeah," she said. "I guess that makes sense."

She smiled then, and my heart sped up a bit when she turned it on me. I smiled back but was pretty sure my smile didn't light up my face the way hers did. I was already regretting what I said, especially given her reaction to it. I looked away and down the street, somewhat surprised and not entirely happy to see our building looming closer and closer with each step. We were at the door less than a minute later, and right after that, we were standing at the door to her apartment.

Again.

"So what time do you work tomorrow?" I asked.

"Six to closing," Tria said. "I should be done by one thirty, but that doesn't seem to be happening lately."

"I should be done with my workout in the afternoon," I said. "I could walk you to work."

"It's still light out then, Liam," Tria said with a shake of her head. "I can't take up all your free time."

"I told you, it's this or cable. Besides, walking is a decent cooldown after a long workout. I could use it."

"Are you just saying that?" she asked. She stared at me through narrowed eyes.

"Mebbe," I responded. I grinned and glanced away. "Really, I have nothing to do tomorrow evening."

"No hot date?"

When I glanced at her face, she was already looking away, her cheeks red. She took a slow breath and blew it out through her nose.

"Sorry, I'm being nosy." She reached up and gathered her hair together in the back as if she was going to put it back into a ponytail again. Then she released her hair, and it collapsed in waves around her shoulders as she shook it out vigorously.

"No worries," I said, swallowing. "No, no hot date."

"Well, all right then," she said quietly. "If you don't come up with anything better to do, I'll probably leave around five thirty or so."

"I'll see you then."

"Okay." She turned and went through the doorway, her hands gripping the frame a little too tightly. "Good night."

"Night."

With long strides, I took the stairs two at a time until I hit the landing for my floor. I knew I wasn't about to go to sleep, so I didn't even bother changing. I hauled my ass out onto the fire escape and tossed my legs over the side. I set a half-full pack down beside me and lit the first one.

"What's up, crazy bitch?" I asked.

Krazy Katie didn't respond. She didn't even acknowledge me at all. She was leaning forward with her head against the grate, making little waffle marks all over her forehead. Her stare was intense, but I had no idea what she was looking at. I leaned back on one hand and smoked with the other one, enjoying the slightly warmer air and wondering how much longer I was going to be able to get away with no heat in the apartment.

"Things are warming up," I heard myself say.

"Needs more," Krazy Katie said.

"I'd be happy to turn the clock forward to spring," I told her.

Krazy Katie's head snapped in my direction, and she glared at me for a second. Her eyes were dark, wild, and totally unnerving, even to a guy who had about a hundred pounds on her.

"What?" I asked, my voice a little quieter. "You want me to turn time backwards instead?"

"All men are idiots," Krazy Katie proclaimed. "She's gotta find the one with the level of idiocy she can put up with."

"Who?"

Krazy Katie shoved her hand inside the front of her shirt and began to rummage around inside her bra. She pulled out her lighter and quickly lit another cigarette but didn't answer me.

"Who?" I said again, but I got nothing in return. I shook my head and decided maybe I was a bit tired after all. I tossed the butt over the edge and crawled back in my window, nearly killing myself on the overgrown pile of laundry just inside.

I should've cleaned up the apartment a bit, but I didn't. I found myself looking at the dresser in my bedroom. More specifically, I stared at the bottom drawer. I knew what was in there though I never opened it. I wasn't even sure why I kept that shit. I should have thrown it out long ago.

I had to pry my eyes away from the drawer and take a few long breaths. I tightened my hands into fists, which wasn't very helpful. In my mind, I could imagine myself wrapping a bit of plastic tubing around my bicep and curling my fingers to make a vein show up a little better.

I shook my head sharply to rid myself of that thought.

Forcing myself to move away from the bedroom, I opened a beer, talked at the television for a few minutes, and then headed for the shower. Once I started lathering up, my cock decided he needed some attention. Since I wasn't actively seeking any of the female kind, he had to settle for my hand. He complained a bit—I have a stubborn, moody cock—but once he figured that was all he was going to get, he sprang to life.

I sighed heavily as I leaned against the cold, broken tiles and slowly stroked myself into a full erection. I skimmed the darkened head with my palm and closed my eyes. For a while, I didn't have anything in particular in my mind—just the basic, general, physical feeling of skin-on-skin. After a minute or so, dark brown eyes kept entering my head and trying to get my attention. As soon as I allowed myself to focus on them, I knew exactly whose they were.

Tria's face flowed easily through my mind as my hand gripped my cock and pumped faster. I could see the glistening of her lips after her tongue ran over them and the pale, enticing skin just below her neck. I imagined what she would taste like—her lips, her tits, her cunt…all of her.

I nearly drew blood out of my own lip as I bit down to keep from screaming her name loud enough for her to hear me through the thin floor. A long stream of semen coated the tiles in front of me, was captured by the flow of water from the showerhead, and disappeared down the drain.

"Damn," I muttered.

After I gave myself another quick rinse, I turned off the water and wrapped up in a towel. The TV had been left on, so I grabbed the remote and hit the power button. Inside my bedroom, I yanked at the bottom dresser drawer until it opened. The drawer was devoid of clothing. The only thing inside was a small plastic box. I looked away immediately and slammed the drawer shut.

With a huge sigh, I grabbed the sweats I had worn the night before off the floor and pulled them on over my still slightly damp skin. I dropped heavily onto the bed and pretended I wasn't still thinking about her.

I was never one to harp on anything, but I had the feeling getting her out of my system wasn't going to be easy.

# CHAPTER SIX
## Meet the Ex

"Fuck!"

Falling to the ground, I growled through my teeth and slammed my fist against the floor.

"God dammit!"

My feet became entangled, and I was unable to get up. I swung one leg out, trying to unravel myself from my opponent, but I was too deeply entwined. I fell back to the floor.

"Shit!"

I punched again.

"Ow!"

And hit my own leg.

There was just no other choice—I was going to have to do the laundry before it killed me.

*Thump thump thump.*

I had no idea what was flopping around in the dryer, and I didn't care. The sound was driving me over the edge, and I was considering just going over there and hauling whatever it was out, even though it wasn't my load. I looked around at the seven other people at the laundromat, but no one else seemed to notice or care.

With two trash bags full of clean clothes at my feet, I waited for the last load to dry so I could get the fuck out of this place. I wasn't sure if it was the act of washing and drying clothes, the atmosphere of the laundromat, or the sheer boredom of waiting for the damn clothes to dry, but there was nothing I hated more than having to do laundry.

If my Uncle Michael had walked in right then and offered me a job, I just might have taken it.

"Nice ink." A leggy blonde eased herself down in the molded plastic seat next to mine.

"Thanks," I replied. I could see a wavy vine motif in green and black ink winding its way up her calf.

"Where did you get it done?"

"Emily's Body Art, across town," I told her. "She does the best tribal art, and I wanted something custom."

"It's beautiful," she said. Her hand grazed up my bicep to my shoulder, where the remainder of the tat was covered by my shirt. "Can I see the rest?"

"Sure." I leaned forward and pulled my only clean—well, somewhat clean—ripped up T-shirt over my head. Turning a little to the right, I gave her a good view of my back.

"Wow," she breathed. Her fingers skimmed over the design, and her light touch was both sensual and a little ticklish. I kept myself still as she touched my decorated skin. "Truly incredible. Bet that one cost you."

"Heh," I snickered. "More than I could really afford, but it was worth it. Emily's also has a payment plan, and I did it in ten shorter sessions to spread it out a bit."

Her hand reached my lower back and then started up the other side. It felt good, and I was again reminded of my pathetic excuse for a sex life, which had pretty much turned into twice-daily self-love sessions while thinking about my neighbor.

Fucking pathetic.

"Very nice," she said as her fingers reached my shoulder, trailed over my neck and back down to the arm where she started. As she ran her hand over my bicep, I wasn't sure if she was talking about the tats anymore.

I turned back to her with a crooked smile, and she tossed her shimmery, straight hair over one shoulder and tilted her head to the side, exposing her neck to me.

"I'm Erin," she said as she held out her hand.

"Liam." I shook it briefly, noticing how soft her fingers were.

She was a looker—no doubt about that—and probably right about my age, give or take a year or two. Her clothes said she was desperately trying to look like a Macy's girl but with a Target budget. She was decently built though a little skinny for my personal tastes. I would have no trouble holding her against a wall and pounding into her for twenty minutes. Nice long legs with defined calf and thigh muscles that would feel nice wrapped around my waist. I could definitely hit that, but I had no interest whatsoever.

None.

Did I turn gay when I wasn't looking?

Mostly I was wondering how it would feel if Tria ran her hands over my skin the same way. That thought was enticing, and I blinked a couple of times to try to drive it from my mind. That's when the buzzer from the dryer in front of me went off, startling me slightly.

"That would be me," I said quietly. I stood and grabbed the last of my trash bags, tossed all the dry clothes into it, and gave the chick one last grin before heading out of the laundromat and back to my apartment. It took freaking forever to fold it all up and put it away, and I was in a foul mood before I was even done.

"Fuck it," I growled as I dumped the last of the clean laundry into a dresser drawer and just shoved it all inside. I needed to get out and do something physical before I burst.

Wearing a pair of shorts that smelled a whole lot better than they did earlier in the morning, I laced up my running shoes and started my run several hours later than usual. It was after three in the afternoon and already hot enough to bring the sweat out of me before I had gotten through the first half-mile. By the time I got to the tree, I was a lot more winded than usual, but I pushed on.

I still wanted to bring Tria to see the only tree in the general vicinity of our apartment building. I'd mentioned it to her a couple of times during our walks when she talked about missing the greenery —and apparently the cold—of her hometown. I just never saw her during the day and wasn't going to make that trek in the middle of the night. Though our nighttime routines seemed to match perfectly, we weren't at all in sync during the day. I hardly ever saw her in sunlight.

I saw her often enough in the privacy of my shower and my imagination, though.

Turning the last corner, I saw the apartments looming in the distance and increased my speed until I hit the sewer grate that marked the completion of my three miles. There was a rusted green pickup parked right out front, and I wondered how something so old could actually still run at all. I slowed to a stop and leaned over with my hands on my knees and breathed heavily for a few seconds, then took a fast-paced walk around the block to cool down.

Returning to the building's entrance, I yanked open the front door, started down the hall, and was immediately hit with the customary sounds of a couple fighting inside. For a moment, it didn't register with me—I was still in a post-run haze and wasn't thinking clearly. The voices belonged to a man and a woman who were obviously in a heated argument in the apartment just below mine, which wasn't an odd occurrence at all.

Except *that* couple didn't live there anymore.

Tria did.

I stopped in front of her door and leaned in, trying to figure out if it was just TV noise, but I could clearly hear Tria's voice, if not her actual words, coming from the other side. Then a deeper, male voice boomed out in anger.

Already heated from my run, the rage that quickly built up inside of me made me feel as if I were going to burst into flames. I took a deep breath before knocking loudly at the door.

The voices continued, ignoring my banging. If anything, they were getting louder. My chest tightened, and the possibility that someone might have gotten in there and was going to hurt Tria was just far too likely. She was too trusting and had no street sense whatsoever. She'd open the door for anyone.

"Tria!" I screamed as I pounded my fist against the flimsy wood. I was going to give her about four seconds before I broke the fucking door down. "Tria! Open up now!"

The door fell away as my hand tried to come down on it again. I quickly pulled the punch. If Tria had been any taller I might have hit her in the face.

"Liam, what are you—"

Without a word, I moved across the threshold into the apartment and toward the figure on the other side of the room. As I started to push past, I zeroed in on a big, dark-skinned guy behind her. Before I got too far, I felt her fingers against my chest, trying to push me back.

An explosion of thoughts ricocheted around my head. Tria's soft, light touch on my sternum was the third time we had ever touched skin-to-skin. It took me off guard, and I had to stop in my tracks to refocus beyond the sensation.

The angry glare of the dude behind her reminded me why I was there.

"What the hell?" I shouted at the guy, pushing my chest firmly against Tria's hand but not enough to move her out of the way. Tria glanced nervously from me to the figure behind her.

"It's all right," she started to say before the bastard on the other side of her interrupted her sentence.

"Who the hell is this, Demmy?"

Demmy? Why the hell would he call her Demmy?

"I'm the guy who's about to fuck your shit up, that's who!" I snarled.

"You can try!" the little shit exclaimed. I would have laughed, but I was too pissed off. He couldn't have been more than eighteen, and though he was tall and decently built, he didn't stand a chance with me. I knew another fighter when I saw one, and this guy wasn't it. He didn't look right; he didn't stand right; and he didn't move right. He was probably one of those that used his height to his advantage—intimidating others with it to the point where he never had to actually raise a fist.

"Liam!" Tria's tone stopped me.

"What the hell is he doing here?" the guy said, taking a step forward. The fingers of Tria's right hand tensed against my chest as I pressed against them, and her left hand went out to push at the other guy's shoulder to keep him from coming any closer.

"I live here," I growled.

"*What!*" His eyes went dark as he turned to face Tria and started screaming at her. "He lives here, Demmy? Seriously? You shacked up with some monkey in this dump?"

"He lives in this building, Keith. He doesn't—"

"Fuck you, you little pup," I yelled. "Where the fuck do you get

76

off talking to her like that?"

"That's none of your fucking business—"

"I'm making it my business!"

"—you fucking dick. Now get the fuck away from her—"

"Get your ass out of her apartment before I—"

"Stop it! Both of you!" Tria's voice managed to carry over both of ours.

I tried to breathe through my nose to settle myself a little, but it didn't work at all. I just ended up sounding like a raging bull or something, which was fitting because I was ready to charge. The second Tria was no longer between us, I was going to rip this fucker's head off.

He glared at me for a moment before looking down at Tria.

"Who the fuck is this?" He snarled at her, and I pushed forward a bit again. The feeling of her hand against my bare chest was seriously distracting, and I had to concentrate to keep my focus on my goal—killing the motherfucker who dared talk to her that way.

"This is Liam," Tria told him, "my neighbor."

"Your neighbor." The guy scoffed. "Does he always act like this?"

"Fuck you, you piece of—"

"Liam!" Her eyes blazed into mine, adding to the heat scorching my body. What was it about angry chicks that made them look so hot? She shook her head sharply. "This is Keith, my...um...a friend from home."

"*Friend from home*," he echoed sarcastically.

I really wanted to beat the shit out of this guy.

"Yeah, he's very friendly," I snarled.

He took a step forward, and Tria ended up straightening her arms to push both of us away from each other. He grabbed her arm to move it away.

"Get your fucking hands off her!" I screamed as I headed toward him, no longer concerned with Tria's hand on me though she managed to keep the contact as I moved. Going around to her left, he was no more than two steps away. All I needed to do was to pin him down and go to town.

I was going to kill this guy.

"Please, Liam! Stop it! *Please!*"

Until she begged me not to.

Dammit.

My chest continued to rise and fall as I attempted to get a hold of myself. I took a couple of steps backward, allowing Tria's hand to fall away from my flesh. The spot where she had been touching me went cold as I glared at the stupid little intruder.

*Keith.*

Stupid name for a stupid little shit.

"You need to go," I told him. "Get the fuck out of here right now!"

"I'm not going anywhere!" Keith yelled. "We were having a private conversation—"

"Which you made public by fucking screaming at her!"

"I am not putting up with this shit." Keith tossed his arms up in the air and turned around to walk further back inside. I should have taken the opportunity to knock him out cold since he had his back turned, but Tria's hand found its way once again to my chest and tensed against my skin as if she knew what I was thinking.

I looked at her, and her wide eyes pleaded with me.

"You should go," she said. "It's okay—really."

"Bullshit," I replied. "I'm not going anywhere as long as he's acting that way."

"The way I'm acting?" Keith snorted. "Do you even hear yourself?"

"I wasn't talking to you, fucktard."

"Liam!"

"Yeah, *Liam*." Keith sneered. "Why don't you go crawl back into whatever hole you came from?"

"Keith!"

"Very clever," I replied. "Did you go all the way through sixth grade just to learn that one?"

"Demmy, you cannot be serious about staying in this dump with this idiot!"

"Keith, I'm not going anywhere," Tria said. Her voice was soft but cold. "This is my home now. I've got classes, I have a job, and I can afford it just fine. Liam's been helping me out—"

"Yeah, I bet! Helping himself, more like."

Yeah, I was going to kill him.

"Keith! That is enough!" Tria turned and moved toward him. I started to follow her further inside, but one glare over her shoulder stopped me in my tracks. "He's been a good friend. I'm just fine here, and I'm not going back home—not until I get my degree."

"That's four years, Demmy," he whined. He fucking *whined*.

"At least you can count." I sneered at him. "Now why don't you try counting the steps outside? I'd be happy to accompany you."

Tria glared at me again, and I huffed a long breath out my nose.

"Yeah, he's obviously a great guy." Keith crossed his arms over his chest. "I bet your dad would be really proud of you shacking up with—"

"Shut your mouth, Keith Harrison!" she shrieked. "Don't you dare bring my father into this!"

"Truth hurts, huh?"

"That's it," I said. I tried to keep my voice even, but it wasn't easy. "I'm sorry, Tria, but I'm not going to stand here and have you listen to any more of this shit."

"Then why don't you walk out the door and go away?" Keith crossed his arms in front of his chest.

"You are the one who needs to get out," I said. Before he could start arguing with me about it anymore, Tria said the only words I really needed to hear.

"He's right, Keith—you need to go."

"I am not leaving you here with—"

With the words she had already spoken, I didn't need any more encouragement. I couldn't take any more of Keith's bullshit. I took three large strides forward until I was right in his face. I could feel Tria grabbing my arm, but I was beyond stopping at that point.

"Say it, motherfucker," I threatened. "Say you are going to stay when she said go, because I will happily rip your dick off and choke you with it."

Half a second later, Tria squirmed her way in between us and raised her arms up to press against my pectorals. The touch of skin-on-skin, the scent of her hair just under my nose, and the closeness of her body coupled with the heat of the argument just about gave me wood.

"Liam," she said softly. "Please, Liam. Don't."

"If he leaves," I replied. I didn't look at her. I kept my eyes focused right on his. If I looked at her I might decide to let him live, and I really didn't want to do that.

"Go, Keith," Tria ordered. "We're done talking anyway."

"This isn't over," he said. He looked away from me and down at Tria before he backed away. He reached over to her couch and picked up a black jacket before heading toward the door. "And I'm only leaving because she asked me to, asshole. Don't think this is over. It isn't over."

"I hope it isn't," I said, but I was only partially paying attention to him. Once he was away, my gaze had fallen to Tria's face, and I couldn't seem to look away. "The next time, she isn't going to stop me."

I watched him leave out of the corner of my eye, feeling very self-satisfied as the door slammed shut. Tria startled at the noise, and her fingers tensed against my shoulders. She was right up against me, clad in blue jeans and a thin, green tank top. Her bare forearms connected completely with the skin of my chest. I checked over my left shoulder—just to be sure he was really gone—and sighed. Before I had a chance to go into smug-mode, I glanced down at Tria as she suddenly burst into tears.

The hands that had been pressed lightly against my shoulders moved upwards until they were wrapped around my neck, and Tria's face was tucked against my sternum as she sobbed. For a moment, I just stood there with my hands clenching and unclenching. It occurred to me that I could probably touch her now, but I didn't know where.

Without any other ideas, I tentatively brought my hands up to rest on her hips.

Damn, that felt good.

My fingers twitched right at the place where her shirt met the top of her jeans, which was riding up slightly since her arms were up around my neck. I could feel just a little bit of skin against the tip of my left ring finger, and I knew just how easy it would be to slide my hands right up her shirt from there.

I didn't.

Actually, I had no freaking clue what I should be doing. I was having a really difficult time not sporting a massive boner from the feeling of her body pressed against mine even though I knew how ridiculously rude that would be under the circumstances. At the same time, I just wanted her to feel better. I was a little afraid I might have added to her breakdown and didn't know what I should do about it.

For a moment, I wondered how she would react if I just picked her up and kissed her. I knew how totally inappropriate it would have been on about four hundred different levels, but that didn't stop my mind from playing out its little fantasy. I would bring my hand up, run it over her cheek, and stroke underneath her eye before I wrapped my fingers around the back of her neck. Then I'd lean over her, take her bottom lip and suck on it before claiming her mouth entirely.

A shudder from Tria brought me back to reality, and I tried to think of something I could say. I should probably say it's all right or maybe tell her to stop crying or something like that. Nothing that came to mind really sounded right, so I ended up saying nothing. In a lame attempt at being some kind of comforting presence, I moved my hand to the small of her back and gently patted her a couple of times, wondering if I should say "there, there" now.

Tria suddenly gasped and unclasped her hands from around my neck. They dropped over my shoulders and back to my chest, and she stared blankly at the back of her hands for a moment. Her fingers twitched, and she looked up at me quickly before opening her mouth.

"Shit, I'm sorry...I'm sorry..." She kept repeating the phrase as she wiped moisture from my chest.

"Shut up," I said softly. My hand moved back to her hip, but I didn't release her. I didn't want to. "You don't have anything to be sorry about."

"I got you all wet."

"I was all wet before," I told her. "Well, sweaty anyway. I've been running."

"Mascara," she muttered as she rubbed the side of her thumb over a tiny black smudge right next to my nipple.

She took a step away from me, and my hands dropped from her sides. The loss of contact was unsettling, and as my hands left her, it kind of felt like I was being peeled away from her—just like peeling a fucking banana from its skin.

That thought made me think of my own banana, and I wondered if he might also be considered a comforting presence.

Maybe tucked between her thighs for an hour or so would be beneficial to her mood.

Shit, I had to stop thinking like that.

"You gonna tell me what all that was about?" I asked her.

"No," she replied.

A little battle broke out inside of my head. There was a part of me that said this was private and I should mind my own business, but most of me just wanted to know if I should go after that asshole and beat him down. I didn't need much of an excuse to do so.

"You know, if you don't tell me," I said, "I'm going to come up with the worst possible scenario. If that happens, you won't be able to stop me from running after him and beating the shit out of him."

"No, don't," Tria said. She shook her head slowly. "We were just talking."

"Talking? That's some talk."

"Keith and I don't quite see eye to eye on the whole going to college thing," Tria explained. "He thought I would be just fine going to the community college near home, but I was accepted here, and I wanted the best possible education. He didn't want me to leave."

"This is the boyfriend you don't have, isn't it?"

She looked at me and then away again. Her hand swept under her eyes once more.

"We broke up right before I left."

I paused for a minute, trying to figure out if she left him or he left her. Considering he came all the way out here from Maine led me to believe she ditched him, which made me feel better.

"Okay." I was certainly curious, but I also knew anything she said was going to make me want to run after him. I'd calmed down a bit, so I was all right with not knowing right now. "You sure you don't want me to kick his ass?"

"Yes," Tria said, cracking a little smile. "Besides, I have to get ready for work soon. I don't have the time or the money to bail you out of jail."

"I wouldn't get arrested," I assured her. "I'm not stupid."

Tria looked at me with narrowed eyes but didn't press for more information.

"You want me to stick around until it's time for us to go?" I asked. "I need to run up for a shower…"

…*for more than one reason…*

I swallowed hard as images of Tria pressed against the tiles in my bathroom filled my head for a moment. She looked at me quizzically, and I rushed to continue on a less lecherous path.

"…but I could be back down here in fifteen minutes. If he came back or something…"

"No," Tria answered immediately. "He won't come back. Not today, anyway. I'll be fine, and we'll have to head off before too long anyway. I'll tell you more on our walk."

That would have to suffice.

"You sure you're okay?" I asked.

"I'm fine, really."

"I'll be back in an hour to walk you to work."

"Okay," she said. She ran her hands through her hair and let out a big sigh. "Thank you. *Again.*"

"My pleasure," I said with a smile. "Anytime you want me to beat the shit out of someone, you just say the word."

"That's what big brothers are for, right?"

"Exactly!" I answered her with a grin. My face held a smile, but inside me, that word—*brother*—made my guts twist up. Why the fuck had I ever said that in the first place?

I practically ran upstairs to jump in the shower. Before the water had even soaked through my skin, I had my dick in my hand. It didn't take more than a minute before I was grunting and spurting against the tiles.

I breathed heavily with one hand still against the cold wall. The shower and the jerk-off did nothing to sate my need to kick someone's ass or fuck my downstairs neighbor, and I wished I didn't have to wait for the opportunity to do either. I thought about finding Keith while Tria was working, but I had the feeling she wouldn't appreciate it. I had a pretty good idea she wouldn't care for her "big brother" coming on to her, either.

At least I could pound that asshole without her ever finding out. I could hang around outside tonight. If I happened to see him, and we happened to have a little confrontation… Well, that would just be a coincidence, wouldn't it?

I soaped myself down, rinsed off, and stepped out onto the threadbare hand towel that served as a bathmat. I dripped for a bit while I stared at my face in the mirror and ran my hand over my jaw. I needed a shave, so I pulled out a razor and shaving cream and stared at myself in the mirror some more while I worked on the stubble.

*Brother.* Why, why, why did I ever say that?

I had just been trying to make her more comfortable, which seemed to have the desired effect, but it had definitely become a hindrance as well. The word "brother" loomed over me when I stood next to her, wondering if I should maybe reach out and put my arm around her shoulders as we were walking or something.

Or better yet, reach down a little farther and grab her ass.

I sighed at myself, washed the leftover shaving cream off my face, and got dressed. I slipped my boots on and grabbed a fresh pack of smokes before running out the door. I didn't want my "sister" to have to wait around for me.

"So, tell me who this asshole is that I want to kill now." I made the suggestion as we headed out the apartment door and down the street.

"Please don't talk like that." Tria sighed. "Keith just worries. It's not like he was going to get violent with me."

"He's a douche," I said bluntly. Honestly, the idea he might have gotten physical with her never crossed my mind before she mentioned it. Why did she say that? Had he done that in the past? If I found out that he had, there would be no stopping me. I was ready to fuck him up just for yelling at her.

"He shouldn't have been talking to you like that," I said. "How did you hook up with him, anyway?"

"That's kind of a long story," she said.

"Start it now," I said, "and finish it on the way home later."

Tria's shoulder rose and fell with a long breath.

"Fine," she said. "But it's not exciting or anything. It just boring, small-town crap."

"I like small-town crap," I said. Tria looked at me with narrowed eyes, and I shrugged my shoulders. I didn't really know what I meant by it, either. I liked her, and she was from a small town.

She wasn't crap, though.

I shook my head, trying to drive such contradictory and confusing thoughts away. I wondered if people who lived in small towns had always lived there or if there was something about city life that made them seek refuge somewhere else.

"So, did your parents always live in a small town, or did they move there from a city or something?" I asked her.

"My parents were from the mainland," she said softly. "My foster family lives on the island."

"So what do they think of you being here in the big city on your own?"

"Well…" Tria hesitated. "My dad passed away when I was young."

"Oh, right," I said. "Sorry. I know you told me that before. What happened to him?"

"He worked on a fishing boat. On his way home one night, he stopped on the bridge to help a guy with a flat tire. It was dark, and they were too close to the road. My dad was hit by another car and killed. My parents were already divorced then. Dad had been in the army and was deployed for about two years. Mom screwed around on him, I guess, and they divorced shortly after he came home. My mom never really wanted much to do with me. She was living in Florida at the time with a new husband, and I didn't want to leave my hometown. I ended up being raised by friends of the family."

"Those are some friends," I said with a whistle. "Taking in a kid that isn't theirs."

"We were always close," Tria said quietly. Something about her tone seemed off.

"Well, what did the family friends think of you coming here?"

"Uh...well, Leo—he is like my adopted dad, I guess—was really excited and happy about me going to college, actually. No one in his family had ever gone to college, and he pretty much treated me like his own flesh and blood. That is, until I decided to come here."

"He didn't want you to leave?"

"No one really thought it was anything more than a waste of time," she said. "They are all for the education because that's something you can bring back to the community and teach everyone else, but to move away? That's pretty much unheard of. They're very intent on keeping everyone together."

"You aren't really part of the family though, right?" I really had no idea how such things worked.

"Not by blood, obviously," Tria said. "But they considered me one of them."

I thought about that for a minute and wondered if they really treated her the same way or not. How would she know?

"You have any brothers or sisters?"

"Well, not biological ones, no," she said. When she didn't elaborate, I hounded her until she did. "Leo has three kids—two girls and a boy. I grew up with all of them."

"What about their mom?" I asked.

"She died in a car accident the year before my dad."

"Wow—already raising three kids on his own and takes in another one right after his wife dies? This Leo must be some kind of saint."

"Not…exactly," Tria mumbled, but she refused to elaborate.

"So tell me about the adopted siblings," I suggested. "Were you all close to the same age?"

"Helen and Heather are both older than me. Helen's twenty-four and Heather is twenty-two," Tria said.

"And your brother?" I lit up a smoke and watched her out of the corner of my eye as she started digging around in the Grand Canyon of women's accessories. She didn't answer but mumbled something about where she might have left her lip gloss.

As she dug into the bag, she wasn't watching where she was going. She ended up tripping on the curb and nearly falling on her face. I wanted to be the one to save her, to right her before she could fall. If I were being honest, I just wanted to touch her just for a moment. Unfortunately, she managed to right herself before I could grab her and help her up.

"That purse is going to end up killing you," I told her. "Either you're going to fall into it and never be seen again, or you're going to fall off a cliff while looking for something in it."

"Don't be ridiculous," she said.

She always said that whenever I made a comment about Grand Central Handbag.

"I bet I could put a mouse in there and you would never find it."

"I most certainly would."

"You wouldn't notice it until you found nibble marks in your lipstick."

Tria groaned at my joke and pulled the bag up a little against her side as we rounded the last turn before Fin's.

"I'll see you about one?"

Tria nodded.

"Hopefully, I won't be too late. I hate making you wait for me."

"I have nothing else to do," I told her with a shrug.

"Thanks again," she said.

"No worries."

Tria smiled and turned to walk into Fin's. There was a good chunk of me that just wanted to follow her inside, greasy food smells be damned. But as she disappeared behind the entrance, I turned to head back home.

I was never one to cling, but it almost seemed to hurt when she walked away from me.

# CHAPTER SEVEN
## Stake the Claim

The walk home was interesting.

I had been thinking about our conversation most of the night while hanging out at Feet First and listening to some crappy garage band. The conclusion I had drawn was that she had been intentionally elusive about her foster family, and my curiosity gnawed at me as I waited for her to exit Fin's so I could walk her home and barrage her with more questions.

I didn't even ask who the patron of the night was this time.

"Why did that guy call you Demmy?"

"My full name is Demetria," Tria said. "I went by Demmy as a kid. I changed it up a bit when I moved here."

"New name for a fresh start?"

"Something like that."

"So, tell me everything else about this family you grew up with," I said.

"I thought I did," she said with a little shrug. She started digging around in her purse again, which I was starting to realize was some kind of distraction tactic, and I wasn't falling for it.

"You can live without that lip shit for a few minutes," I said as she looked up at me through narrowed eyes. "Tell me about your brother. What's his name?"

She paused for far longer than was really necessary. I was about to press when she finally spoke up.

"It's, um…it's Keith Harrison," she finally said. She stared at the ground as she spoke. "Keith and I grew up together."

"Keith, the douchebag, Keith?" I asked. "The one I'm going to fillet if I ever see him again?"

"Well, yes," Tria said. "Except the filleting part."

"Keith is your *brother*?" I couldn't hide my shock. It was the farthest thing from my mind, and I didn't know how to react to that kind of news. At least I understood her hesitation now. Her *brother*? She said she was six when her dad died, so she had been living with him since she was a little kid, raised as siblings, and then they end up together? How fucked up was that?

"You know, I really took quite enough of that kind of crap when I was in high school, and I don't need to hear any more of it now. Yes, we grew up together in the same house. No, we are not related by blood in any way, and yes, we dated. Deal with it!"

I turned to look at her then, eyebrows raised to meet her glare. Really, how else did she expect me to react? It *was* fucked up, without a doubt. We looked at each other for a moment before she dropped her gaze.

"Bit of testiness around that subject, huh?"

"I'm tired of being judged," Tria snapped back at me. "Especially for something that is over and done with. Was it a mistake? Yes, it was, but not because we lived in the same house."

"Did you fuck him?" I asked.

"That is none of your damn business!"

"True," I agreed. "I'm mostly just curious."

"Well, you can just continue to be curious!"

"You have a bit of a temper, don't cha?" I wasn't sure if I was disgusted by the whole idea of it, curious about how such a relationship could come about, or intrigued that she would consider a brother-figure as dating material. If she did, maybe she would consider another.

Even more fucked up.

When I realized she hadn't answered me, I found myself pressing the issue.

"So, what was the mistake?"

She sighed.

"Keith is too much like his dad," Tria said. "Even when he doesn't agree with him, he will still go along with whatever Leo says."

"What does Leo say?" I asked. She hadn't said much about her adoptive father, and I kind of wondered about that. I found whatever revulsion I might have felt disappear into interest about her life.

"Well, like going to school, for instance," Tria explained. "He was all right with me going to a local place and still living at home, but he was completely against me going out of town to get my degree."

"It's your life," I said simply.

"Leo doesn't see it that way," she said. "Neither does Keith."

"How did he react when you got accepted to Hoffman?"

Tria went quiet, and I had to ask a couple more times before I could get her to elaborate.

"I don't know how he reacted," she finally said. "I didn't tell either of them—I just left."

"Packed your bags and disappeared in the middle of the night?"

"Basically."

I whistled low.

"So they're both pissed at you now."

"Apparently," she said. "I figured they would find out where I went, but I didn't think Keith would drive all the way out here to try to bring me back."

"Does he even know you broke up with him?"

"Yes," she said. "I did that the day before I left. We argued about school conflicting with my 'wifely duties,' and I called off the wedding."

She made little air-quotes with her fingers as she spoke, but I just shook my head as I tried to make some sort of meaning out of what she was saying.

"You were engaged?"

She snorted.

"Betrothed, more like. I don't recall anyone ever asking me; they just started planning a wedding."

"That's fucked up." I noticed there was a definite theme to my thoughts about the people she grew up with.

"No argument here."

We walked in silence for a few minutes while I tried to digest all the information she had just given me. It didn't lessen the desire to break douchebag's face at all and actually kind of led me to add Douchebag's father to the list of potential targets. I considered asking for their address, but I didn't think she would give it to me. Maybe I would have to wait for one of them to show up here again, which had me wondering.

"So what are you going to do the next time he shows up at your place?" I quickened my pace a little as I guided Tria across the street. I hopped up on the curb and tilted my head to look at her.

"I don't know," she replied. She was staring at the ground again, and I wanted to harass her for it, but I also didn't want her to change the subject on me.

"Wrong answer." I shook my head vigorously. "Number one, you don't let him in. Number two, you call me."

"I don't want to drag you into my bullshit," she said with a sigh.

"Too late," I said succinctly. "And it wouldn't matter anyway—I'm putting myself in it."

"What happened to 'it's my life'?" she asked. She reached up and pulled her hair out of its ponytail.

Damn, that was distracting.

I made myself focus on the conversation at hand and not the enticing way her hair lay on her shoulders.

"What are you going to do if he suddenly decides he's going to drag you back there, huh?" I asked. There was a hot spot in my stomach, driving the anger out of my gut and into my words. "You going to say 'No, please don't' like you would have done with those rapists in the street? Ask him politely? You think that would work?"

She didn't reply.

"It's possible, isn't it?" I pressed. "He could come back here and try to physically haul you back home."

"I think that's why he came here, yes," she said quietly.

"I figured as much." I could barely speak through my clenched teeth.

The apartment building came into view, and a minute later we stopped at Tria's door.

"So what are you going to do if he shows up here again?" I asked.

"Not let him in," she replied as she rolled her eyes.

"And?"

"I don't have your number."

It was my turn to roll my eyes. Tria shoved both hands inside of Sasquatch's Satchel and pulled out a pen and an entire notebook of paper. We exchanged numbers, and I asked her why her ex couldn't seem to just drop it and move on.

"Beals is a very small town," Tria explained. "More of a village, really. There are only about five hundred people living there, and my adoptive family made a living in lobster fishing. The whole community revolves around it. I understand it to a degree. So many of the kids in the area end up moving away since the industry is regulated, and there isn't enough lobster to go around. The number of members is dwindling, and they're afraid the whole culture is just going to cease to exist someday. I know they want to protect that, but telling me I have to stay home and have babies for their sake isn't the answer."

A flash of a slightly bulging stomach ricocheted through my head, accompanied by chills and a tensing of the muscles in my lower abdomen. I grit my teeth and forced the thoughts away.

"You don't want kids?" I heard myself ask. I had no fucking idea why I asked such a question—it was a door that remained closed in my head.

"Someday, maybe," she said softly. "But not at eighteen, like he wanted."

I had to change the subject as quickly as possible, so I went for the most obnoxious thing that could have come out of my mouth—obnoxious, crass, and far too close to what I really wanted to know.

"So you were fucking him," I said.

Tria crossed her arms over her chest and narrowed her eyes.

"Look, this isn't exactly a topic I care to discuss in the hallway."

"It's not my bedtime yet," I told her. I glanced from my wrist, which didn't actually have a watch on it, to her partially opened doorway, and then back to her face.

Tria sighed, opened her apartment door wider, and made a gesture toward the inside. I was so surprised the tactic worked, I almost just stood there and stared at her outstretched arm, but my feet finally woke up and moved me forward.

The only other time I had been in Tria's apartment at all, I hadn't really paid any attention to anything in it. I had been far too focused—first on the asshole who was yelling at her and then by the act of will it took to keep from pressing my cock against her stomach while she hugged me. Now that the distractions were removed, I looked around a bit more.

The layout was exactly like mine—a small living room and eat-in kitchen with a little hallway leading to two other doors—the bedroom and bath. Her furniture was slightly better than mine since she obviously got a place that was completely furnished, but it was still pretty bland. There was a couch and a coffee table sitting across from a bookshelf with a little television with rabbit ears on top of it. The rest of the shelf was covered in books—both novels and textbooks, as far as I could tell. Next to the couch, there was a little table with a butt-ugly lamp sitting on it.

"You want something to drink?" Tria asked. "Um...I've only got water and some apple juice, though."

I couldn't stop the smile.

"Apple juice is awesome," I said. Tria walked into the kitchen to pour two glasses while I sat on the couch and looked around. There weren't any decorations or anything on the wall, but I did notice a small, framed picture of a guy in an army uniform standing with a little girl, who I figured was Tria.

I didn't get a chance to take a closer look before Tria came back with the drinks, which she set on little cardboard coasters. She stood there nervously for a moment before sitting beside me and curling her legs up underneath her.

"So?" I asked as I leaned an elbow on the back of the couch. I tilted my body toward her, pulling my leg up slightly and nearly matching her posture. I leaned my head down onto my open hand.

"I have no idea why I'm talking to you about this," Tria said.

"Apple juice will make you say all kinds of crazy shit," I informed her. I gave her a very serious look. "Chug that glass, and it'll all just flow right out."

"The story or the juice?"

"Both."

Tria snickered and rubbed her hands against her thighs. I waited somewhat patiently as she seemed to gather herself.

"This is so embarrassing," Tria said as she dropped her head into her hands. "We tried, okay? It just didn't really work."

"He couldn't get it up," I said with a smirk. "Maybe he's gay."

"That wasn't it." Tria promptly corrected me.

"What didn't work then?" I asked. I had no idea what she was trying to say, or what she was trying to avoid saying. She was obviously embarrassed by something, but I had run out of patience and wasn't going to let it go at that point. "Well?"

"He just…couldn't get it in."

Oh.

"Must be a big guy," I said. My smirk was gone.

"No, no…he's…I don't know, average, I guess. It just… wouldn't go."

"Wait…" I had a sudden epiphany. "You mean you weren't ready, right?"

"I was ready," she said defensively. "We planned it for weeks. After prom and all that trite shit."

"Maybe you said you were, but you weren't wet, were you? He couldn't get it in because you weren't into it."

Tria went silent as she stared at the corner of the coffee table where her drink sat untouched. Without the ability to read her mind, I wasn't sure what she might have been contemplating, only that she was definitely deep in thought, and I didn't want to break the imposed silence.

A couple of minutes later, she finally spoke.

"He was right," she said quietly. Her voice was strained, and the tension in her shoulders was visible.

"What do you mean? Who was right?"

"Keith," she answered. "He said there was something wrong with me; I just didn't want to believe it."

"What?" I bellowed. Tria jumped in her seat. "What the fuck are you talking about?"

"Just what you said!" she shouted back as her voice broke. "There's something wrong with me!"

"For fuck's sake," I cried, "there is not!"

"But you just said…"

"I said you weren't into it," I reminded her. "You weren't wet because he didn't turn you on. You didn't want him. That's not a problem with you; that's a problem with him being a douchebag. You didn't want to sleep with him."

"I did…" Her voice trailed off. Her tone was completely unconvincing.

"Bullshit." I put my empty glass down and turned to face her. "Maybe he said you were ready, and maybe you wanted to believe you were, but you weren't. If you really wanted it, you would have known it, felt it. Your body would respond to that, and it would have worked."

I tried not to think about how fucked up the direction this conversation had taken and reminded myself that she was still pretty young. I hadn't realized she was so naïve, but it kind of fit with the whole small-town theme about her. I didn't want to admit it, but the fact that Keith had backed off and not just…well…forced his way in was a pretty good thing.

"How do you know?" Tria asked as she looked at me. The edges of her eyes were a little red, and though I didn't see any actual tears, I could tell they were close.

"Because…well…" I had no idea how to answer that without sounding like a total man-whore. I reached up and ran my hand over my face as if that was going to help me come up with a better answer.

"Because what?" Tria pushed for an answer. Apparently she was not going to let me off easy.

"Because I know women," I said. "I know women and how they

are when they're turned on. If there's something wrong with anyone, it's him for not knowing what the fuck he was doing. He didn't know how to get you going."

I looked straight into her eyes, and she looked into mine. It felt like some kind of understanding was flowing between us, but I couldn't have put a name to it. It should have felt awkward—the whole conversation was bizarre—but it didn't. It felt right. It felt good.

"You really think it's not me?" she asked.

"It's not you," I told her definitively. I wanted to add that I would be happy to show her just how turned on she could get. I wanted to crawl right over the top of her and leave her dripping in her panties. I wanted to show her everything I could make her feel with my hands, my tongue, my...

"Do you want more?"

"Huh? What?" Her question caught me off guard, and my imagination exploded with possibilities.

"Juice," she said, nodding toward my empty glass. "Do you want some more apple juice?"

"Oh, um...no, that's okay."

Fuck.

With the conversation abruptly changed, we both sat back against the couch cushions. After about five more minutes of small talk, Tria yawned and we called it a night. I walked upstairs, stripped, and dropped face down on my bed with my hands up by the pillow. I tried to relax, but my back and shoulders were tense, and my cock was simply not going to let me sleep without any attention first, so I rolled over on my back and took matters into my hand.

I was never one to think with my cock, but I really, really needed to get laid.

# CHAPTER EIGHT
## Realize the Truth

I never worked on Saturday or Sunday, but I usually hung out at Feet First anyway. They had a couple other dudes who would fight on Saturday nights, but they weren't very good. They were lightweights, and the fights were usually quick and scrappy, which some people liked.

There wasn't nearly enough blood, if you asked me.

"Why don't you fight against them?"

Out of the corner of my eye, I could see a woman sit down on the bar stool next to mine, but I didn't turn to her. My eyes stayed on the fight.

"Because I outweigh them by fifty pounds," I told her. "I could probably just sit on them and knock them unconscious."

She giggled, and I turned my head to check her out. The long, straight platinum blonde hair was easy to recognize.

"Erin, right?"

"You remembered."

"You were the only thing worth looking at in the laundromat," I said with a shrug and a smile. Flirt mode automatically engaged as she smiled back, and I bought her a drink.

"So, how'd you find me?" I asked.

"Saw that back tattoo on a poster outside the game shop on Fourth Street," she told me. "I knew it was you, so I thought I'd come check out this whole cage fighting thing. Sorry to see you aren't up there." She nodded toward the cage.

"Not until Tuesday."

"I'll have to come back."

"I think you should."

For the next hour, we drank, complained about laundry, and stepped out for the occasional smoke. She was pretty cool, had awesome ink, and was smart enough to hold a decent conversation. She also couldn't keep her hands off my inked skin, and I was both pleasantly buzzed and horny enough to really, really enjoy it.

"So, what else is there to do around here?" she asked with a raise of her eyebrows. She slipped the longneck bottle into her mouth and poured amber liquid down her throat.

"I could show you the locker room," I said, watching her lips wrap around the bottle.

"Private locker room?"

"It is if I padlock it," I replied. I licked my lips as I watched for her reaction.

"Hmm...interesting." Erin flipped her hair over her shoulder and tilted her head as she looked at me. "I've never seen the inside of a cage fighter's locker room before."

"First time for everything," I said. "Shall we?"

I offered her my hand and quickly made my way around the cage. I nudged past Gary, who winked at me as we went by, and I led Erin down the ramp to the locker room.

As soon as we were inside, I slipped the lock through the ring in the metal plate on the door, turned, and grabbed Erin by the waist. I lifted her easily and spun us both around before pressing her back against the door and covering her mouth with mine.

She pressed her hands against my stomach and then slipped them lower to the buttons of my jeans. I reached my hands inside the back of her shirt where I found and released the clasp of her bra. Our tongues tangled together in her mouth, and she moaned as she pressed her crotch up against mine.

She tasted like lipstick.

Her hair didn't feel right. Too smooth. Too straight.

She didn't smell right, either. The scent of chemically induced roses or whatever made my nose sting.

Her hand found its way inside my boxers.

Her mouth stopped moving.

"Everything okay?" she said quietly.

"Yeah," I said quickly. "Fine…just, um…here—"

I shifted her a little, bringing her legs around my waist and grinding against her a bit.

Nothing.

"Maybe I'm a little drunk," I shrugged.

"You've had two beers," she reminded me.

I swallowed and then started kissing up the side of her neck. She wrapped her hands in my hair and tugged at it a bit.

I didn't like it.

"Don't," I mumbled. I reached up behind my head and pulled her hand down to my shoulder instead.

She looked at me with disbelief in her eyes, and I slowly lowered her to the ground. I moved in to kiss her again, but she brought up her hand and placed it against the center of my chest, holding me off.

I remembered how another hand felt against my chest, and I liked that one better.

Erin let out an exaggerated sigh.

"Look, Liam, you are totally hot, but I'm not one to pursue a

guy who obviously"—her eyes darted down and then back up again
—"isn't into me. So, let's not make a big deal out of it, okay?"

"I just…I never…"

"Shush," she said as she placed her cheap, plastic, fake nails
across my lips. "If I had to guess, there's someone else you would
much rather have in here with you right now. I can deal with that.
Maybe you need to deal with it yourself, hmm?"

With that, she reached behind her back to re-hook her bra, lifted
the lock on the door, placed it in my palm, and left.

Taking a couple of steps backwards, I plopped myself down on
the bench by the lockers and dropped my head into my hands. I had
no fucking clue what just happened. I had never, *never* had any
issues with my cock standing straight and tall for any woman I had
even the slightest interest in fucking. Never, ever, ever, not even
once.

Well, once now.

I leaned back against the cool metal for a moment, sighed
disgustedly at myself, and then started buttoning up my pants. I dug
my hands around in my hair while I wondered what the hell was
wrong with me. Even strung out, I could still get it up. Couldn't
come most of the time, but performing was never an issue. Maybe
Katie's crazy was contagious or something.

With nothing better to do, I left early and hung around outside
of Fin's for an hour until Tria was done with her shift. She was
pretty tired after hauling greasy food around for hours and didn't
have a lot to say on the way home.

If I really thought about it, I would have to admit that she'd
been somewhat uncommunicative since we had the little heart to
heart on her couch the other night, and I hoped I hadn't pushed her
too much. She didn't seem like she was mad at me, more like she was
introspective.

I was distracted myself, thinking about what Erin had said to me and wondering just how close to the truth she might have been. It made me wonder about the whole big brother thing and if I should maybe consider turning that around. I mean, we obviously weren't related and had only known each other for about a month and a half. Considering she had a thing with a guy she actually grew up with, maybe she wouldn't have an issue reconsidering the sibling status we had established.

Say that shit ten times fast.

We were halfway back, and I realized we hadn't said two words to each other.

"Everything okay tonight?" I asked.

"Hmm?" Tria cocked her head to the side to look at me. "Oh, um…it was fine, I guess. Nothing very exciting."

"No crazy diners tonight?"

"Not really," she said. "There was one who sent his food back three times, but that's not very exciting."

"He didn't like it?"

"Guess not."

That was about the extent I was getting out of her for conversation, and it was starting to tick me off a little. This was my favorite part of the day, and she wasn't at all cooperative about it. That, coupled with the generally shitty way my night had gone, was making me pretty pissy.

"What's up with you?" I demanded.

"What?" she asked, startling slightly.

"Talk to me or something!" I was practically growling at the poor girl. I sounded ridiculous, and I didn't care. "Tell me more about screwing around with your siblings or something."

Yeah, that crossed a line.

Tria glared at me, looked like she was about to say something, but quickly closed her mouth instead. She started to walk ahead of me, like she was going to escape into the building and avoid me altogether. I took a couple of quick steps and placed my hand over the door, obstructing her entry. Tria growled through her teeth and clutched at Gorilla Gucci.

I ignored the bag and its potentially frightening contents.

"Get out of my way!" she snapped.

"Fuck, Tria, I didn't mean—"

"I know exactly what you meant! I thought maybe you weren't going to be like that, but I can see you are! So get the fuck out of my way before I slap you!"

A little chill went through my body, and the boner I couldn't seem to find earlier started shoving painfully against the buttons of my jeans.

Holy shit, why did I find that hot?

"Stop it!" I yelled as my heart beat furiously in my chest. I ached to grab her, slam her up against the door, rip off her shorts, and do her in front of the neighborhood. "I didn't mean it like that! It just…it just came out wrong."

I moved further between her and the door as I took a deep breath.

"I'm sorry," I said.

"You think I'm fucked up just like everyone else in school did," she said. I didn't have to see the slight tears welling up at the corners of her eyes; I could hear them in her voice.

"Fuck, Tria. I didn't mean it that way, I swear." Well, I did think it was fucked up, but I hadn't meant to direct that toward her. "So you dated a guy you grew up with—what's it to me?"

She glanced at me, her expression telling me immediately that she didn't believe a word coming out of my mouth.

"Look, Tria," I said quietly. I reached out and placed one hand on the door frame and leaned a little closer. "I'm not going to lie to you and say it isn't a little…*surprising*. It doesn't mean I think any less of you. Besides, you aren't with him anymore. You don't even live there anymore."

"Why don't you just say what you want?" she asked. The anger was gone from her voice, but her words stung more. "Tell me I'm a freak. Tell me I'm going to hell. Tell me what a horrible person I am. I'm used to it."

"I don't think that," I told her.

"Don't you?"

"No!" I narrowed my eyes, my own ire returning. She didn't have any reason to doubt me. I had never lied to her.

She took a step back and covered her face with her hands. A moment later, she let out a loud growl, shook her head, and then looked back at me. Her throat bobbed as she swallowed, and I tried not to think filthy things about how awesome it looked.

Her shoulders sagged as she let out a long breath.

"I wasn't expecting people here to find out and judge me for it."

"I'm not judging you."

"Judgment day! Judgment day!" A singsong voice called out from above us.

"Shut up, you crazy bitch!" I yelled.

Tria snickered, and the tension between us instantly faded away as Krazy Katie threw her still-lit cigarette out over the edge of the fire escape and toward us. It dropped to the cement in front of me, and I bent over to pick it up.

"Thanks!" I said as I took a long drag off of it.

"Even she knows now," Tria muttered.

"Krazy Katie isn't going to tell anybody anything, are you, baby?" I yelled up at her. I smiled as I looked back at Tria. "Even if she did, no one would believe a word of it."

"What's wrong with her?" Tria asked quietly, as if Krazy Katie would care if she heard anything Tria said.

"I told you before—she's crazy."

"But what kind of crazy?" Tria asked. "Is she schizophrenic or something?"

"Hell if I know," I responded with a shrug. "All I can tell you is she doesn't make any sense about ninety-five percent of the time. Then the other five percent of the time, she says something you think is absolutely brilliant."

"Like what?" She looked up at the fire escape with wide eyes.

I could feel a smile creep over my face as she stared toward the fire escape. She was beautiful in the faded light from the one and only functional streetlight around, and I was thrilled she hadn't stayed mad at me. It made me feel...*giddy.*

"Like mares eat oats, and does eat oats, and little lambs eat ivy..."

"Liam!" Tria smacked me on the arm and laughed.

"What?" I placed my hand on my chest and tried my best to look shocked. "I looked it up on the internet! It's true! All of it! The lambs, the mares—everything!"

Tria shook her head and laughed again. It was a wonderful sound, and I was glad we weren't ending the night with any more talk of her ex-boyfriend-brother, Keith Harrison.

We headed into the building, said goodnight at Tria's door, and I went up to my own apartment for my date with a handful of lather and my fingers wrapped around my cock.

The following Wednesday, our walks came to an abrupt end.

I had just dropped Tria off and was already wishing it were time to pick her up again. The nights were a lot longer when I wasn't working, but she was. Stepping over the little brick border around a half-dead bunch of annuals, I hopped off the curb to cross the alley behind Fin's, figuring I'd spend my time at Feet First even though I didn't have any spare cash for dinner or a drink. I reached into my pocket, pulled out my smokes and lighter, and took a deep drag on the Marlboro. I blew smoke high into the cooling night air and then turned abruptly at the sound of my name.

"Liam! Liam, wait!"

I stopped right in the gutter, turned to see Tria running toward me, and wondered if some sort of prayer had been answered. I stepped back up onto the curb and watched her run up to me. As soon as she was close enough, I could see the tears running down her face.

Did all girls cry so much?

"What's wrong?" I asked. It hadn't been more than five minutes since I watched the door close behind her, and I couldn't fathom what could have happened in such a short amount of time.

"Stan," she gasped.

"What did he do?" My words sounded like a snarl. I was trying really hard not to yell, but if she didn't come out with it, I was going to beat his ass. I reached out and grasped her by both shoulders, making her turn to face me.

"He...he...he *fired* me!" Tria cried.

She was completely hysterical, and I couldn't make out a single syllable after that. I eventually gave up trying to understand her, bent down, and picked her up in my arms. She squealed at first but then just let me carry her all the way home while she soaked the shoulder of my shirt. Once I got her into her apartment with a glass of apple juice in her hand, she calmed down enough so I could understand her words.

"There was a new girl there," Tria told me. "I think he called her Jessica. I've never seen her before, but she had huge tits that were practically hanging out of her top, and...and..."

She sniffed loudly and rummaged around in Hagrid's Haversack, grabbing a whole mess of tissues out of it. She wiped her eyes and nose before continuing.

"He said she had more experience, and he didn't need me there anymore," she said. "He said he was sorry, and he'd keep my number just in case someone quit or something."

She turned toward me, and the look in her eyes tore right through my chest.

"What am I going to do?" she asked. "I can't survive here without a job. I just barely have enough to make rent. I have books I still need to buy for one of my classes, and they're over a hundred dollars! I can't pass the class without the books!"

"Can't you find them at the library or something?"

"They're all checked out," she said. "And I'm fourth on the waiting list."

"Fuck," I muttered. I wanted to be able to tell her the perfect solution, but I was nearly as stunned as she was. I wasn't shocked that Stan Fin made such a shitty move—that didn't surprise me because most bar owners were assholes—but that she had gone from having everything in order to being totally screwed in a matter of minutes.

"I'll have to move back," Tria said quietly. "There's no way I'll be able to make it without that job. Rent is due the day after tomorrow, and I barely have enough to pay it. I won't have enough for food, or the electric, or *anything* if I don't get tip money. But if I don't pay, I'll get thrown out."

One thing about our landlord—he didn't put up with late payments, and he didn't have any sympathy for anyone's sob story. She was completely right thinking that he'd throw her out, and he wouldn't give her any thirty days' notice, either. Leases were month-to-month, and anyone who didn't pay by the second was out on the street by noon.

"They were right," Tria said. Her voice cracked a little. "They were all right. I never should have come here. I can't do this."

"Yes, you can," I corrected. "Look how well you have already done."

"I probably would have been killed in the street the second week I was here if it weren't for you." Tria scoffed as she wiped at her eyes. "I haven't done anything."

"Yes," I said emphatically, "you have. You've been going to school, and I bet you are spending a whole lot of time studying, and you are probably getting great grades, aren't you?"

She looked at me through her lashes, then lowered her head a bit and nodded.

"So you can do it, and it's not like you got fired for doing a shitty job. You got fired because Fin is an asshole, and I just might have to give him a coupon to amateur night in the cage."

Actually, I kind of liked that idea. I wondered if he could be coaxed into it. The thought was really, really intriguing, but Tria's words took me in a completely different direction.

"I can't keep doing this, Liam," she said so softly I could barely hear her. "Not without a job, and I don't have time to find one. I'm pretty much screwed here. I have to move back to Beals."

Knowing what she said was absolutely true, and also knowing how few and far between decent jobs were around here, I couldn't really argue with her. The very idea that she would have to give up on her dream so quickly was bad enough, but adding that to knowing that if she moved back home, I'd probably never see her again was more than I could take.

I didn't think. I didn't consider. I didn't even realize what I was saying.

"Move in with me."

I was never one for impulsiveness, but the words just leaped from my mouth.

# CHAPTER NINE

## Clean the Mess

"Don't be ridiculous."

I was starting to hate that phrase.

"I'm not," I insisted. I was still trying to figure out what the hell I had just said. There was a little voice in the back of my head telling me I had asked her to move in with me, but I knew that couldn't be right. I never lived with a woman before, and I barely knew this one. I couldn't have said that.

*Oh yes, you did.*

Fuck.

I had to take it back, didn't I? But I couldn't do that. I mean— she hadn't answered yet, but I had already offered. It would be rude to take back the extended hand at this point, wouldn't it?

Why didn't I ever pay attention to all those etiquette lessons I was forced to endure as a child?

Besides, I wasn't so sure I wanted to take it back at all. Yeah, this was definitely out of the norm. There was no denying that, but that didn't mean it was a bad idea.

Of course it was. It was a fucking awful idea.

"It's the perfect answer." I felt my mouth open, and words spewed forth on their own. "You wouldn't have to find a job right away. You would still be able to get to school, and we'd only have to carry your stuff upstairs."

"Liam, I am not a mooch!" Tria insisted. "I'm not going to move in with you and have you take care of me like some child!"

"It wouldn't be like that," I said. My arms and shoulders tensed up. I was losing this battle, if that's what it was, and I didn't want to lose it. The more I thought about it, the more I wanted her with me. No matter how stupid the idea was, I wanted to figure out how to make it work so she would stay.

"Oh, really? How would it be then?" she asked, the anger flashing through her eyes.

I wasn't exactly sure what she was thinking, but I had the feeling she had the wrong idea. I was also dealing with a certain amount of pride here. She didn't want anyone to think she couldn't succeed on her own.

"We'd just be…you know…roommates. Help each other out, right?"

"Roommates?" Tria echoed.

"Yeah," I replied with a nod. "Lots of people have roommates to help with expenses. There's nothing wrong with that. I help you; you help me. Even if you paid half the rent, that would give you two months before you would need to have another job. We'd share food and shit, so that wouldn't cost as much."

"Roommates," she said again. Her tone was rather deadpan, but there was still a hint of ire underneath it.

"Right. It's actually kind of perfect for me, too. I could use the help, I guess." I had no fucking clue what I was babbling about, but it seemed to be working.

"I'm still paying half the rent, though," she said as she looked up at me. "I'm not negotiating on that."

"Sure," I said with a shrug. I really didn't care if she paid rent or not. I was just glad she seemed to be considering it.

"What about the utilities?" She was just trying to come up with excuses now.

"Don't worry about it."

"Liam." She sighed.

"Pay me back later. Whatever."

"This just doesn't sound right."

"You wouldn't have to quit school," I reminded her. "You'll have time to find a job that isn't too far away, and then you can pay me back, or we'll split the bills or whatever. It's just temporary, you know?"

Holy shit, did I really just say that?

"You know, until you're back on your feet."

"Temporary," she repeated softly.

Obviously, that made the plan sound a lot better to her, so I went with it.

"Just until you're back on your feet with a new job, ya know? You could stay in school, and you wouldn't have to go back to Maine. Once you've found another job, you can save up a bit and do whatever you want. "

Her eyes widened, and I had the feeling the tide had just turned.

"I'd pay half your rent for this next month, right?"

"Sure," I said. "I mean—that helps me out, too, right? Not at all moochy."

Tria looked up at me, and I could see her gaze darting between my eyes. Her mouth tightened a little as she kept looking at me intently as if she were trying to find the perfect answer written in my irises.

"Are you sure?" she asked.

"Positive."

She nodded slightly then, and all the tension in my body flooded out so fast I was surprised I managed to keep myself from falling over.

"So, you'll do it?" I felt the need to hear her say the actual words.

"If you are sure it's okay," Tria answered. "I don't feel good about it."

I was pretty sure I felt good enough about it for the both of us.

I had been completely right about one thing: moving all her stuff out didn't take a lot of time. It was a good thing, too. I went with Tria to tell the landlord she was moving out of her place and into mine, and I had the idea he would have been a lot shittier about it if I hadn't been there. As it was, he was very insistent she be out pretty much immediately because he needed to move another section eight family in, or he wasn't going to get something or other from the government next month. He basically gave her until three in the afternoon, or she wouldn't get her deposit back.

We didn't waste any time but went straight back to her place and got to work. Tria shoved items into some empty beer crates I brought over from Feet First, and I carried them up to my apartment —*our* apartment—and stacked them in the living room.

Our apartment.

I smiled a little at the thought as I set a crate of freaking heavy books down next to my rowing machine in the living room. Though it was staying cool outside, I was sweating up a storm going back and forth, carrying boxes between apartments. I pulled up the edge of my T-shirt and wiped it over my face, and then I headed back downstairs.

We had both agreed the best thing to do was just to get stuff moved so the landlord would have no excuse to keep her security deposit. The extra money would come in really handy if she were to get it back. I had my doubts, but I knew the landlord wouldn't return a nickel if she wasn't totally out of the place on time. Sure, there were laws about evicting people, but you had to be able to afford to take the landlord to court. No one in this building could manage that. Given that it was the last day of the month, there was no chance of leniency, so we focused on just getting everything out as quickly as possible.

"This is just about it," Tria said as I walked back in. "There are a few more things in the bathroom to pack up, but I should be able to fit them in here."

She held up the Beast Bag.

"Well, if I had known we could pack stuff in that thing,"—I grinned—"I wouldn't have bothered to bring those crates from the bar. Here, let me shove the fridge in there…"

I moved across the floor and wrapped my arms around the front of the refrigerator and acted as if I were going to pick it up.

"Don't be ridiculous." Tria sighed, but she also smiled slightly and shook her head at me. "There are two more boxes in the kitchen, one in the bedroom, and the bathroom stuff. I think that's it. I'll just need to clean everything off and then tell the landlord I'm out."

"I'll get this stuff upstairs," I said. I picked up the kitchen boxes, dropped them off on my kitchen table, and ran back down for the last bits.

Tria was already vacuuming the floors when I got there, and she spent the next hour cleaning the whole place up. She seemed to think having it nice and clean was going to make any difference in the landlord's decision to return her deposit. I wasn't so sure, but we had plenty of time before three o'clock, and it certainly couldn't hurt.

I went upstairs, grabbed two beers, and brought them back down. I popped the caps off and handed a beer to Tria, who paused from cleaning the countertop to sit and eye the bottle a bit before shrugging and having a drink.

"Better than apple juice?" I asked, teasing.

"No," she replied seriously. "Not really."

I laughed because she was right. The beer was cheap and not very good. It was cold, though, and there was something about beer and physical labor that just went together.

"Oh! I almost forgot!" Tria jumped up and opened the refrigerator. She brought out a small paper plate with two large, red apples coated in caramel. There was a big Popsicle stick shoved into the top of each one.

"What's this?" I asked.

"Caramel apples!" Tria announced. "I thought they would be appropriate, and it *is* Halloween."

"Oh yeah," I said with a nod. I hadn't really thought about it, but I couldn't argue with the date. The apples were crunchy, and the caramel was gooey and sweeter than I remembered from childhood. "This is different than the ones I've had before."

"How so?" Tria asked. She looked up at me through her lashes, appearing apprehensive.

"The caramel is different," I said. "It's...sweeter, maybe? Definitely stickier."

"Is that bad?"

"No," I replied, "I like it this way."

"Good," she said as she smiled. "I made it from scratch."

"You made caramel?"

"Yep," she said, and she licked a bit off her lip.

I could have helped with that.

"So, you really do like it?"

Yeah...I'd definitely like to lick the caramel off...

"Liam?"

"Hmm? Oh...sorry." I swallowed the mouthful of apple and tried to focus. "What did you say?"

Tria gave me a weird look and shook her head minutely.

"I asked if you liked the apple."

"Yeah! It's awesome!"

"See, I was thinking about this whole mooching off you thing," she said, but I interrupted her.

"I told you, it's not mooching," I said. "We're just helping each other out."

"Yeah, whatever," Tria said dismissively. She waved her hand around a bit, trying to make her point. "It's seriously lopsided, but I'm not going to argue about that any more. Anyway, I thought maybe I could even it up a little by doing the cooking."

"Cooking?"

"Yes," she said as she looked through her lashes again at me. I tried not to focus on her when she did that because it did funny things to my cock. "I like cooking, but it never seems worth it for just me."

"Cooking," I said again.

"You do realize there's more out there to eat besides veggie burgers and protein shakes, right?"

"Sounds kind of familiar," I said with a nod. For a moment, I wondered how she knew so much about my normal meal plan, but figured I had probably talked about it a couple of times on our walks.

Tria laughed.

"So, what do you think?"

I was still kind of focused on her sticky lips and had no idea what she was asking me.

"About what?"

"Food. Cooking. Me cook you food," Tria said in short, clipped syllables and then began to laugh. "Did you zone out on me?"

"Um...sorry," I said. "I guess I'm a little tired."

"Well, what do you think about me doing the cooking while I'm

119

staying with you?"

"I think I haven't had a decent meal since my mom was cooking for me."

"How long has that been?" Tria asked.

I went stiff almost immediately. I straightened my back in the chair and looked quickly at the window to stare at nothing. I tried to make my mind match the blank image in my eyes. I had no idea why I had made that comment. I didn't want to think about, talk about, or even broach a tangent conversation regarding my family.

"You never talk about your family," Tria said softly.

I clenched my jaw and grit my teeth. I didn't look at her, and I didn't respond. After a moment, Tria reached part way across the kitchen table but stopped moving as I sat back and pulled away.

"Long time?" she said quietly.

"Yeah," I replied. I kept staring out the window until I felt a little more in control. I tightened my fingers around the neck of the beer bottle and quickly tilted it up to my lips to drain it. "We better get this shit finished."

I stood immediately, and Tria was just a fraction behind. She seemed to want to say something else, but I wasn't going to give her the chance. I started cleaning up again, and she took the hint.

Tria wiped down the inside of the refrigerator while I gathered up the apple cores and beer bottles into a big trash bag and hauled it out to the dumpsters behind the building. After tossing the bag into the bin, I pulled out a cigarette and lit it.

The conversation about meals and the mention of my mother had left me on edge. I didn't want to go back in feeling like that. I didn't let that shit get to me because I just didn't think about it. I didn't want to be thinking about it now, either, but I couldn't help but remember the last meal I shared with my family.

*Breaded veal cutlets, mashed potatoes, and green beans seasoned with those tiny, round onions. Mom and Dad drank wine from crystal* glasses, and Mrs. Carter served crème brûlée for dessert. No one said a word while we ate, and at the end of the meal, Dad had dropped his glass heavily on the top of the carved cherry table.

"When are you going to stop moping?" he snapped.

"Douglass, don't," Mom said in a hushed tone.

"How long is he going to act like this?" He turned abruptly to her while gesturing toward me.

"I'm not moping," I replied. I shoved the spoon into the crusted top of the dessert and carved out some of the custard underneath.

"Well, what else would you call it, then?" Dad asked.

"Contemplating."

"There's nothing to contemplate," he said. He picked up the glass again and pointed it toward me. "It's over. Take care of it, and get away from that tramp."

I dropped the spoon audibly onto the plate and sat back in my chair.

"No."

There.

I said it.

I shifted my gaze to meet those of my father. The intensity was almost too much, but I managed not to look away from his fearsome glare.

"What did you just say?" he asked slowly through a tensed jaw.

"I said no. I'm not going to 'take care of it.' At least, not in the way you mean."

"How the hell else could you mean it?"

"Douglass…"

"Shut up, Jules. This is between the men here."

She cringed a bit and took another sip of her wine. She wouldn't meet my eyes.

"I'm going to be a father," I said quietly.

"Not if you expect to live under this roof." Dad sneered. "My roof, *my rules. You think you two can survive playing house together without my support? I don't think so. You have no idea what it's like out there in the world."*

*He sat back and drained his glass before setting it down next to his plate and calling for Mrs. Carter to bring back the bottle.*

*"Your father is right, Liam," Mom told me in her quiet, no-nonsense voice. "You still have a year of high school, and you can't support yourself and a family."*

*"I guess I'm going to find out," I said. My hands trembled as they picked up the maroon linen napkin from my lap and placed it on the table. I stood slowly, glanced once at my mother, and walked out of the dining room and out of the house. The distinctive thump of my shoes against the stone steps echoed in my head.*

*"If you leave here now, you will never be welcomed back!" I heard him yell from the front porch.*

*Without looking behind me, I yanked open the door to my Lexus and headed down the mile-long drive to the high brick walls and gated entrance that had always shielded me from the world outside. I drove beyond them, leaving behind everything I had ever known.*

My hands tightened into fists and ended up crushing the cigarette between my fingers. I squeezed my eyes shut, forcing the past out of the present before I opened them again and was met with the back view of the apartment building.

I saw cracked wooden shutters in need of paint and repair; crumbled bricks, litter, patchy grass, and a couple of broken beer bottles lay next to the steps of the back entrance. All around was a high, chain-link fence, which seemed to be a common theme in every aspect of my life now.

I resisted the urge to punch the dumpster. I knew from experience that I would only break a knuckle, and I couldn't afford to do that. I had to be able to work this week. Instead, I drew in a few long breaths, pulled out another smoke, and then hot-boxed it on my way back into the building.

By the time I opened the door, the troublesome thoughts were gone from my mind. Tria had finished up the cleaning and was shoving various toiletry items into Buckingham Billfold. I glanced around at the empty apartment to see if we missed anything.

"I think this is it," Tria said as she walked out of the bathroom. "And forty minutes to spare! I better get at least some of that deposit back."

"You will," I said, trying to reassure her. I had no idea if the landlord ever gave anyone any deposit back, but I could probably stop by and offer a little persuasion.

I heaved the last of the boxes up into my arms, and Tria opened the door for me. We split up long enough for me to take stuff upstairs and for her to return the key to the landlord. I dropped the boxes next to the kitchen table and surveyed the stuff.

There really wasn't much, which was good because there weren't going to be a lot of places to put it. Tria's books took up as much room as anything, and I wondered where we were going to put those since I didn't have any kind of bookcase. I considered the plywood and cinderblock nightstand I made out of shit I found lying around, and wondered if I could use similar materials to make Tria a place for her books.

There was a soft knock at the door, and I went to open it.

"You don't have to knock," I said with a smile. "You live here!"

Tria looked down at the ground, and her face flushed as she laughed through her nose.

"Well...I wasn't sure..."

"Be sure," I said. I handed her the key I had made for her and stepped back to let her in.

Tria walked in for the first time, took about two steps inside, and then stopped. She was gripping the massive purse in both hands, and I realized she was probably looking for a place to put it down, but the coffee table was covered with all kinds of crap. Aside from that, one of my jackets was lying in front of her on the floor, and there were a couple of hand weights near her feet, too.

"Um…shit," I muttered. "Sorry—I'll get it cleaned up."

I started grabbing pizza boxes and beer bottles from the coffee table and shoving them into the kitchen trash can. When I got back into the living room, I noticed a stack of magazines on the far side of the coffee table and quickly rushed over to shove several editions of *Playboy* and *Hustler* underneath the couch.

"I never really have anyone over here," I told her as I scurried around to pick up whatever was all over the floor and potentially just as offensive. "I should have thought about this before…shit…"

I kicked at the corner of the magazines to shove them further out of view and then grabbed some more dishes off the table. With a couple of plates and cups in my hands, I headed into the kitchen. Dirty dishes were scattered all over the place, too.

"Liam…um…"

"Yeah?" I called out as I started shoving a bunch of dishes into the sink so they at least weren't lying all over the counters.

"You…um…"

"What?" I asked. I poked my head around the corner and saw her slowly shaking her head.

"This place is a disaster."

I cringed as I looked around the room, seeing it as it must look through her eyes. I knew it was kind of a mess, but I never had company that wasn't someone like Gary or Wade, so I never considered how bad it really looked.

Aside from the pizza boxes, dishes, wrappers, and bottles, there were free weights lying around, a couple of less offensive magazines on the floor, and a stack of junk mail piled so high it was falling over. There were CDs outside of their cases lying around all over the floor by the portable CD player, and stacks and stacks of cases all over the place.

"Yeah," I admitted, "it is."

"I'm going to help you get it cleaned up," she said, and her tone left no room for discussion, and she hadn't even seen the bathroom yet.

The bathroom.

Shit.

Were there cum stains on the tile in the shower? Did cum leave stains?

"Yeah, I could probably use a little help," I agreed. "I'll start in the bathroom."

I shoved past her and closed the bathroom door behind me. I looked around apprehensively, feeling liked I'd never really looked at the condition of the room before. I quickly gathered up a pair of dirty boxers, a spare porn magazine, and a couple burrito wrappers. I had no idea how those had even gotten in here. I grabbed a washcloth and wiped down the sink, shower, and toilet to get rid of pee stains, stray hairs, and nail clippings. I shoved the stuff lying around on the sink into the medicine cabinet, realized she'd need some room for her own stuff, and pulled it back out again. I looked around for another place to stash razors, trimmers, and Q-tips so there would be a place for Tria's things.

Leaning back against the sink, I looked around and decided there wasn't anything worse to clean up. I swallowed and sighed in relief.

I was never one to be overly concerned with spotlessness, but I probably needed to clean up my act.

# CHAPTER TEN
## Accept the Consequences

"Well, I feel a lot less like a mooch now," Tria said several hours later. We had completely cleaned up the kitchen, living room, and bathroom. The only place we hadn't touched was the bedroom, but I had just done laundry, and there wasn't much else in there. All the trash had been gathered up, the CDs placed back in their respective cases, and the dishes washed. Tria handed me the last of the plates, which I dried carefully with a towel before placing them in the cabinet where they belonged.

"I think I'm pretty much feeling like the waste of space so far," I agreed. "I made the mess, but you cleaned up more of it than I did."

"If I didn't know better, I'd think you trashed the place just to make me feel better!"

We both laughed, and then Tria poured apple juice into two clean glasses and brought them over to the sparkling clean table.

"I'm really sorry," I said after I took a sip. "I guess I never really thought too much about how this place looked. I should have cleaned it up before you got here."

"It was all kind of rushed," Tria said. "Don't worry about it. It really did make me feel like I was contributing."

"I don't think this place looked this good the day I moved in," I told her.

"How long have you been here?"

"Quite a while," I said. "I moved here not long after I dropped out of school."

"Were you going to Hoffman?" Tria asked.

"No." I shook my head. "I never graduated from high school."

"Oh…um…I'm sorry."

"Don't be," I said. "It was my own decision."

"Why did you drop out?"

"That is way too long a story," I said. "It's late, and I have to train tomorrow."

"You're right," she said. "I'm sorry. I should have realized how late it was."

"Well, we both keep pretty unconventional hours," I said. "I do, at least. I try to get to bed at a decent hour when I know I'll be training the next day. If I don't, Yolanda will kick my ass."

"I try to keep it normal so I can get to my classes," Tria told me. "The earliest one doesn't start until ten o'clock, at least."

"That's good." I looked up at the clock on the kitchen wall. "We probably ought to turn in so you're not late or tired or anything."

We both stood, and Tria washed and dried the glasses quickly before putting them away. I had to smile because cleaning up wouldn't even have occurred to me. On a good day, I might have put them in the sink.

I led the way to the hall and toward the bedroom door. As soon as we approached, Tria reached over and opened up the door to the closet, looking a little confused. That's when a sinking feeling came over me. There was a major aspect of this whole arrangement that hadn't even come to mind. Tria stopped and looked from one side of the hall to the other as she slowly closed the closet door.

"Ah...I...um..." Tria stumbled over her words. "I'll just make up the couch, then?"

My arms felt like they were made of jelly as I realized what she meant. She had obviously thought the closet—which she hadn't had in her apartment—was the second bedroom. Much like the mess, I hadn't considered sleeping arrangements either.

"Take the bed," I told her. I couldn't believe how little I had actually thought about how this would all work out and was a little disgusted with myself. "I'll stay on the couch."

"No, Liam, no." Tria held her hand out in front of her as if she was one of the Supremes and shook her head vigorously. "I am not kicking you out of your own bed. No."

"I'm not letting you sleep on the couch," I said emphatically. All I could think about was the stack of magazines I had hidden under there now.

"Why not?" She placed her hands on her hips, and I knew from the look in her eye this was going to be a battle.

"Because it's a piece of shit," I said. "It's uncomfortable and nasty."

*And there's a huge stack of porn underneath it.*

"There's no way I'm kicking you out of your bed!" Tria was equally emphatic, but I wasn't going to budge on this one.

"You are not sleeping on the couch."

"Well, what other options are there?"

Of course, there was really only one. I swallowed, glanced into the bedroom, and then back at Tria. After a long pause, I offered the only suggestion I had.

"It's big enough," I said quietly.

"Liam, I..." Her voice trailed off. She also looked from the small bedroom, which consisted of the bed and dresser, and then back to me. At least there wasn't a shit-ton of dirty laundry around. There was only a small pile at the end of the unmade bed.

"I wouldn't..." I started to speak but wasn't sure how to end the sentence. I wanted to reassure her of...of what? That I wasn't interested in getting into her panties? Because there was no way those words could pass my lips without having dead baby angels drop out of the sky.

She wrapped her arms around herself and continued to look from the bed to the couch over and over again. Her teeth gnawed nervously at her lip, and she rocked from one foot to the other.

"You're not sleeping on the couch," I said again.

"Neither are you."

"That leaves the options a little slim," I pointed out.

"True," she whispered, "but..."

Her voice trailed off, and her fingers gripped her upper arms.

"I wouldn't..." I started again, trying to come up with something I wouldn't do, no matter how much I might want to. I eventually managed to spit out something relatively meaningful. "I wouldn't...take advantage of you. You know that, right?"

"Yes, I know," she replied. Her tone was off, and I couldn't understand what her expression meant. It almost seemed like she was disappointed, but that didn't make any sense.

"We could...give it a try." It was lame, but it was all I had. We were both obviously too stubborn to let go this time.

"Give it a try," she said quietly, and I wasn't sure if it was a statement or a question, but I swallowed past the lump in my throat and nodded.

"Okay," I said a little louder. "I'll...um...just..."

I had no idea what I was going to "um just" do.

"I'll get my things and use the bathroom," Tria said, saving me from having to come up with any additional plan, for which I was quite grateful.

Tria grabbed her purse and some clothes from her tattered suitcase and closed the bathroom door behind her. I went into the bedroom and shut the door partway while I tried to figure out what I was going to wear while sleeping.

Next to Tria.

Fuck, what had I gotten myself into? The single bedroom layout of the apartment hadn't even entered my head before we were standing in the hallway. Tria was in the bathroom, probably changing into whatever her normal sleeping attire might be, and I usually slept either nude or just in my boxers.

Hey—it saved on laundry.

Fucking sue me.

Obviously I couldn't sleep nude, and I didn't own pajamas, so I dug around in the bottom dresser drawer and came up with a pair of sweatpants I usually wore jogging in the winter. I ripped off my jeans and shirt, pulled the sweats up over my hips, and tightened the string. Then I gathered up the majority of the dirty clothes and piled them in the corner on the far side of the dresser. I tried to straighten out the sheet and blanket on the bed.

Thankfully, I always masturbated into a towel, and the sheets weren't nasty. I made sure said towel was buried under the pile of clothes.

Shit, what if I woke up with morning wood?

It was one more thing I hadn't considered, but I knew I could not freak out now. If I did, Tria would get the wrong idea and decide living here with me was a bad plan. If she did that, she'd end up dropping out of school and going back to that place and those people, and it would be all my fault for not having my own shit together.

Fuck.

Back out in the living room, I sat down on the couch and wondered what else I hadn't considered when it came to having Tria here as my roommate. The sleeping arrangements and the mess were probably the biggest issues we'd have to face. I rarely smoked in the apartment, so I could just take that outside all the time.

Fuck, what if she wanted to cook meat? The smell alone made me want to vomit. That was probably something we ought to talk about. What if she was insistent? I couldn't tell her what she could or couldn't eat, but if this place was hers as well as mine, I couldn't force her not to eat it here.

Fuck again.

We'd definitely have to spend some time tomorrow evening talking about shit like this. The changes were all so rushed. I didn't think either one of us had thought about the things that might be a problem. It would be best to work the details out in the beginning before they became issues.

A few minutes later, Tria came out of the bathroom in a pair of sweats and a T-shirt with a picture of a puppy on the front of it. I stood up from the couch, and we both walked into the bedroom together, stopping at the doorway as we tried to figure out who should go in first.

It felt just as fucking awkward as it sounds.

Once we were both in the room, we just kind of stared at the bed for a minute. Or at least, I stared at the bed. Tria was looking all around, taking in the room. It had been the least disastrous area of the apartment but was now the messiest since we had completely cleaned the rest. Still, it wasn't bad. There were clothes on the floor, but they were at least all piled up in the corner and out of the way. I didn't own a laundry hamper, so I had a decent excuse. The nightstand had a little alarm clock radio on it and a small lamp. The dresser drawers were mostly closed, and the top of it only held a couple of things.

"What are these?" Tria asked, noticing the line of trophies on the dresser.

"High school wrestling," I told her, pointing out the largest. "I was all-state my junior year. The other ones are for Akido, kickboxing, and Tae Kwon Do."

"Wow! You were really good back then, too?"

"I guess."

"You probably would have been able to get scholarships for that and go to school," she said.

I just shrugged.

"Probably could have," I agreed. It just didn't matter now, so I didn't think about it.

"Why didn't you?"

"None of that now." I shook my head. "It's late, remember?"

"Right," Tria said. "So, um…what side of the bed do you sleep on?"

"Um…" I muttered and scratched at the back of my head. "I don't know. I never thought about it. I get in on the far side, but that's usually because I go out the window to smoke before I go to bed."

"You smoke out the window?" Tria asked. "It's the second floor."

"The fire escape where Krazy Katie hangs out is right there."

"Is she always there?" Tria asked in a low voice, as if Krazy Katie could hear her through the window.

"Usually," I told her. "She's supposed to go down and see her social worker or whatever on Tuesdays, but half the time she doesn't go, and someone comes out here at the end of the week to check on her."

"You seem to know a lot about her."

"I've talked to her social worker a few times. Krazy Katie won't go near a telephone, so the social worker will call me sometimes to make sure she's all right if she misses her appointment."

"That's nice of you," Tria said.

I shrugged again, and we were back to silence and awkwardly standing around near the mattress on the floor. At least I had pulled up the blankets so it didn't look too bad, and I had washed the sheets recently during my trip to the evil land of coin-operated washers and dryers.

"I guess I'll…um…I'll sleep on this side?" Tria said, making it sound more like a question than a decision. She indicated the side closest to the door and away from the window.

"Sounds good," I replied. My own voice felt strained as well.

We walked in tandem, moving our feet carefully on the faded, beige industrial carpet. We sat down on opposite sides of the bed with our backs to each other, and we both slipped under the blanket without looking in each other's direction at all.

I just lay there with my eyes wide open, but Tria must have been exhausted after cleaning both of our apartments. I could tell by her breathing that she was asleep almost immediately. A few minutes later, I knew she was asleep because she rolled over, took the entire top blanket with her, and seemed to latch on to it with some kind of sleep-induced death grip.

A blanket hog.

I knew there was a reason I never *slept* with women I slept with.

Keeping thoughts of my past from my head was suddenly a difficult task for me. Though I usually had no problems in that department, having a woman so close to me as I slept felt strange and reminded me too much of the past. I squeezed my eyes shut, focused on the tension it created all around my face, and then opened them again, free from the memories. I sighed, pulled the thin sheet up around my shoulders, and eventually dropped off though not for long.

There were several things that made me think I wasn't really awake. The main reason was the temperature—I was warm. It was always freaking freezing in my room, and I was positively warm all over. There was also this simply fantastic scent that filled the air around me. The scent itself seemed warm, too, and clean and calming and completely feminine.

That part didn't make any sense unless I was having some kind of wet dream. I didn't fall asleep with women after sex. Usually I would just get up and go home. Something about this felt different though—not quite as dreamlike but still surreal. I was on my left side, and running all the way down my body, I could feel the heat from another form.

My eyes opened slowly, and I was met by the serene, sleeping face of Tria.

Wrapped up in my arms.

Somehow, I had managed to roll all the way over to her side of the bed and snuggle up against her. One arm was up under my head, which was right above hers on her pillow, and the other was wrapped tightly around her middle, holding her body against my chest. I could feel the steady beat of my own heart right up against her side and the warmth of her skin from my shoulder to my ankle.

Shit!

I had told her I wouldn't do anything like this, and here I was practically accosting her in her sleep. I closed my eyes for a moment, trying not to get lost in the scent that must have been coming from her hair. I remembered all the bottles she had in the bathroom at her place that ended up shoved in her purse and wondered which of the contents made her smell so good.

Praying I wouldn't wake her up in the process, I slowly pulled my arm back and rolled over to my own side of the bed. I lost most of the sheet when I moved. Tria's fingers were wrapped around the edge of that now as well. I shook my head at myself, grabbed the slight edge of the sheet I could still reach, and stared at the window until I fell back asleep.

I had no idea how long it had been since the first time I woke up. I only knew I was warm and content again. The scent was all over me, and the soft body was turned toward me this time. There was a small hand pressed lightly above my beating heart.

There was also one additional complication. I had somehow managed to get my left arm underneath Tria. Now I had her wrapped up in both arms, and she was lying with her head resting against my shoulder.

Fuck!

Very slowly and carefully, I extricated my arm from underneath her and gently placed her head back on the pillow. I shifted away and quickly moved back to my side of the bed. I was instantly cold because the blanket was still wrapped securely around Tria, and both it and the sheet were pretty much inaccessible unless I moved back to her side of the bed again. I reached up with one hand and ran it over my face.

I was never one to overthink things, but how the fuck was I going to deal with this?

# CHAPTER ELEVEN
## Keep the Distance

No matter how many times I woke up and moved away, I ended up curled around Tria as soon as I fell back to sleep. Throughout the night and into the early morning, I seemed to be drawn to the warmth on the other side of the bed. I kept moving back every time I realized I was doing it, but as soon as I fell asleep again, I moved right back to where she was.

I didn't know what to think of it.

When I woke up to daylight coming through the window, I was on top of her pillow but alone. My right arm and leg were splayed across Tria's side of the bed with both fingers and toes hanging off the edge of the mattress.

At least I had the blanket again.

Her scent still covered the pillow and the sheet though it wasn't as strong as it had been when I woke up next to her. That was assuming I didn't dream all of that shit, because I still couldn't wrap my head around why I would do that in the first place.

I rolled myself over, dropped my feet to the floor, and shook my head to clear the fuzziness of sleep. Standing up, I made a quick trip to the bathroom where my cock was refusing to cooperate with me long enough to pee.

"You won't go up when I want you to," I muttered under my breath, "and you won't go down when I want you to, either. Moody little bastard."

I flushed, rinsed off my hands, and then ran my wet hands over my head and face. The hair on the back of my head was getting a little long, and I was going to have to get it cut this weekend before there was enough there for someone to hold on to and use against me. The top was a little longer, but I always kept the back and sides pretty short.

Moving slowly out of the bathroom and through the living room, I could hear soft techno-pop coming from the kitchen. When I went around the corner, I saw my CD player on the table just a few feet from the stove where Tria was dancing around with a spatula in her hand. She wiggled her hips in time to the electronic beat and occasionally moved in to poke around in a frying pan sitting on one of the elements. As she lifted the spatula, I could see the edge of a pancake before she flipped it over and dropped it back in the pan.

I'd seen some seriously hot, naked chicks in my time, both on the pages of magazines and in person. I'd seen perfect tits wrapped around my cock. I'd seen fabulously round asses being squeezed between my hands. But I'd never in my life seen anything sexier than Tria right at that moment.

I wanted to bend her over the table right then and there.

I wanted to fuck her on the kitchen floor.

I wanted to take her on the counter.

I wanted to pull her back into bed and show her just what I could do to her.

I wanted my cock in her so bad, I could hardly see straight.

"Good morning!" Tria said as she glanced over her shoulder at me and graced me with a gigantic smile. "I'm glad you're awake! I was afraid I'd have to leave for class before you got up."

I coughed a bit, cleared my throat, adjusted my sweats to make my cock less conspicuous, and returned the salutations.

"Smells good," I said, desperately trying to keep my voice from cracking in the process. "I'm not really used to an actual breakfast—where did you get the makings for pancakes?"

Tria gave me a weird look and shook her head a little.

"The grocery store up the block," she said with a giggle.

"Oh, yeah." I reached up and scratched the back of my head, wondering how long she had been up.

"You ever been there?" Tria asked with a smirk.

"Of course I have!" I scowled at her. "I at least have the basics stocked."

"Really?"

"Yeah!" I said.

"Aside from beer and half a pizza in a cardboard box," Tria said as she started counting on her fingers, "your refrigerator contained half a stick of smooshed margarine, three bread heels in the same bread bag—which I do not understand, nor do I want to—one thawed Boca burger, and an unopened carton of almond milk."

"I ran out of cereal."

Tria laughed and went back to flipping pancakes.

The way she moved around the kitchen did something to my inner Ward Cleaver; that was for sure. I could almost see her in a pale blue dress, heels, and pearls as she vacuumed the apartment. I was quite sure the thought was sexist or maybe even misogynistic, but that didn't stop it from making me hard as a rock.

I had to sit down in the chair at the opposite side of the table and lean forward a bit to keep from being obvious as Tria placed orange juice in glasses and plates full of pancakes on the table. There were little bowls of grapes off to the side.

I didn't even know I had little bowls like that.

I realized I had hauled Tria's dishes up to this kitchen, so the bowls could have been hers. I didn't remember seeing any little bowls, but I also hadn't paid much attention to what had been in the boxes. I only noticed she didn't have much. I mean, I didn't have much of anything either, but other than her books, Tria didn't seem to have *anything*. It made me wonder briefly just how quickly she had left her former home and how accurate the "escaping in the middle of the night" scenario might be.

Tria placed a small glass bottle of fake maple syrup in the middle of the table and sat down opposite me. She watched as I covered the pancakes in margarine and syrup and took a bite.

Then another.

Then another.

Then about twelve more.

"My God, these are incredible!" I spoke only long enough to gather up more and shovel another mouthful into my face. I leaned back in the chair, groaned, and rubbed my stomach before I stabbed another one and downed it, too.

"I'm going to eat like...ten of these," I said as I wiped off my face. "And then I'm going to have to work out twice as long today."

"Watching your figure?" Tria snickered as she sipped her juice. It was good, too—lots of pulp in it.

"Well, I have to stay in my weight class," I said. "I'm right at two hundred and five pounds on most days, which puts me at the top of light heavyweight. If I gain a pound, I'd have to fight bigger guys."

"Is it really so strict?"

"In the bar, not as much," I told her. "But if anyone ever lost and they could show I was over the weight limit, it would definitely create a lot of drama, which would get me in a lot of trouble with Dordy. Yolanda weighs me before every match."

"But...you're working tonight!" Tria gasped. "What if you go over? Shit...I fucked this up already!"

"Nah," I said with a half smile. "I was at two-oh-three on Tuesday. I have room to spare. I'll weigh in at training today, and if I'm over at all, I'll sit in the sauna a little longer than normal or run an extra mile. It's all good. I can actually drop two pounds in a few hours if I need to."

"Really?" She looked at me skeptically but at least didn't seem to be beating herself up over it any longer.

"Yep."

"That can't be good for you." She scowled.

"I'm sure it's not," I agreed. "I try not to play that game too much, but I did it a lot in high school for wrestling. We did nothing but drink water and eat laxatives until we puked to drop some weight before a match."

"That's kind of sick," Tria said.

I shrugged. I couldn't argue with her. It was sick. I wouldn't go to those extremes now, but at the time, it was pretty common. I quickly changed the subject before too much of my ancient history was discussed.

"So what classes do you have today?" I asked.

"Microeconomics, statistics, and English," Tria responded. "Mondays and Fridays are my heavy days for classes. I only have two classes on the other days."

"When does that bus pick you up?"

"It's really just a van," Tria replied as she started collecting the dishes and taking them to the sink. "It should be here in about fifteen minutes."

I got up to help though I was so full I was more tempted to flop down on the couch and fall back to sleep. If anyone felt like a mooch at this point, it would have been me, so I dried and put dishes away as Tria washed them.

Once the kitchen was spotless again, Tria grabbed Medusa's Moneybag and a couple of textbooks before heading out the door. I crawled out onto the fire escape to smoke while I watched her wait for the van from Hoffman College to pick her up.

Krazy Katie was already out there, of course, and she waved, too, as Tria boarded the dark red van with the Hoffman crest on the side of it and headed off. I was surprised at the gesture Krazy Katie had made, and I looked over to study her for a moment. Strangely enough, she looked back at me.

As soon as I made eye contact, she usually looked away, but this time, she held my gaze for about three seconds.

"You should fuck her," Krazy Katie said.

"Um…what?" I had to have heard her wrong.

"You should take off your clothes, and put your penis in her vagina," Krazy Katie said. Her voice was rushed, and all the words strung together. "You should ejaculate in her, and then she'll get pregnant, and you'll have a little girl. You can love them, and then you won't be so sad. It feels good, too."

"What the fuck are you talking about, you crazy bitch?" I asked. I didn't think I had ever heard her say more than a couple of words to me, and to have her suddenly start spewing shit about fucking and babies—it was too much.

Apparently, it was too much for Krazy Katie, too, because she curled up in the corner of the fire escape and didn't say another word. That suited me just fine—I didn't need her saying that shit. Tria was in school, for Christ's sake—the last thing she needed was someone poking her fish and getting her pregnant.

I tossed the butt over the side and glared at Krazy Katie as I headed to my window.

"Don't you say any shit like that to Tria," I warned, as if it would make any difference. "She doesn't need to hear any of your fucking lunatic ranting, you hear me?"

She didn't respond, of course.

I went back inside, shoved a few things into my gym bag, and shoved any thoughts of Krazy Katie's fucked up speech out of my head. I needed to get to the gym as early as possible. I hadn't gone at all yesterday, and I wasn't supposed to work out too much on fight days.

Part of my deal with Dordy included a membership to a pretty decent gym near downtown. I had to ride the bus to get there, but it only cost a dollar each way, and I only went twice a week. If money was tight for some reason, I'd walk it, but I would be pretty wiped out before I got home.

As soon as I arrived, I went straight for the squat rack. I started with my legs, back, and triceps. I went a whole circuit three times before heading to a bench to work out my core. Once that was done, I headed back to the weight benches to do some shoulders and biceps.

I knew most of the guys there, and we shot the shit as we lifted and boasted about how many reps we could do or how much so-and-so lifted last week. It was typical bullshit but mildly entertaining as well. I was laughing at the mental image described by of one of the guys who had tried one of those exercise ball classes and rolled over onto his ass in front of a room full of chicks, which was when Yolanda came in. She was already glaring at me, and I rolled my eyes as she approached and kept my focus on the weights in my hands.

"So you want to explain why you blew me off yesterday?" Yolanda asked.

"I had shit to do," I replied. I continued to alternate hands—lifting each weight up to my chest and then back down to my hip again—and didn't look at her.

"What kind of shit?" Yolanda pressed.

"I was helping my neighbor move," I said nonchalantly.

Yolanda laughed.

"Since when are you such a do-gooder?"

I just shrugged and continued with the weights.

"What neighbor?" she asked.

I took in a long breath and blew it out my nose. I had the distinct feeling there was no getting out of this conversation with her, so I decided to just spit it out.

"Tria."

More laughter.

"So, was it a tearful goodbye when the damsel in distress moved out?"

Glancing over at her, I narrowed my eyes a little.

"No," I replied. I set the weights down and moved over to the mat on the floor for crunches. "She didn't leave the building, just switched apartments."

"Why would she do that?"

"She lost her job," I told her. "She couldn't afford that place on her own anymore. This shit really isn't any of your business, you know."

"What did you do?" Yolanda continued to question me. "Move her in with the nutcase that lives next to you?"

"No." As much as I wanted to get out of this conversation, I knew my delay tactics weren't going to work on her. Yolanda had a knack for knowing when I was stalling, and she always managed to cut through the bullshit. As I glanced up at her, I saw her arms crossed and her eyebrows raised, so I gave up. "She moved in with me."

Dead silence for at least twenty crunches.

"She did what?"

Yolanda dropped her chin and looked at me from the top of her eyes as I brought my elbow up to touch the opposite knee, then moved back to the mat, then did the same on the other side.

"Moved in with me," I repeated without pausing. Yolanda continued to just stare at me until I finally stopped and rested my arms over my knees. "What?"

"You let a chick move in with you?"

"Yeah."

"You," she stated as she pointed a finger at me, "Takedown Teague, let a chick move into your apartment."

I couldn't help but notice the other guys had gone a little quiet and were listening intently to the conversation. Fucking awesome.

Note sarcasm.

"She needed a place to stay." I responded with a shrug, hauled myself up, and headed over to the heavy bag—which was also out of earshot of the rest of the gym rats—to throw some punches. Yolanda moved to the opposite side and braced the bag for me.

"And you figured you'd just let her move in with you?"

"Yep." I slammed a fist into the bag, spun in a circle, then hit it with the other hand.

"So, you are fucking her," Yolanda stated.

"I am not." I corrected her through grunts as I punched. "It's not like that. She's not like that."

"You have a one-bedroom apartment," Yolanda said as if I hadn't noticed.

Well, I guess I didn't notice right away.

"Where is she sleeping?"

"In the bed," I said with another shrug.

"With you." The smile on her face was starting to piss me off. "So you are sleeping with her."

"We slept in the same bed," I growled before slamming my fist hard enough into the bag to knock Yolanda a little off balance. "I'm not *sleeping* with her. I told you; she's not like that."

Turning away from her, I moved over to the weight bench and sat down. Yolanda walked up to me slowly, still smiling.

"I bet your balls are the color of the sky," she said with another laugh.

"Nice," I mumbled as I lay down on the bench and braced my hands on the bar.

Yolanda moved behind me and signaled to a big guy with arms about the size of my thighs. She helped me lift the barbells up, but he took her place to spot me. As soon as she let go, I knew why—they were fucking heavy, and I had difficulty with the first press.

"What the fuck did you put on these?" I gasped.

"Three fifty," she replied. "So when are you going to admit that you're into her?"

"Fuck you." I grunted under my breath as I brought the bar to my chest and pressed up again. It was a good twenty-five pounds over my usual max, and it wasn't easy. I could barely speak. "You... trying...to kill me here?"

"You can handle it," she said. "You need to move up. You let that little shit get in too many hits Tuesday night. Need to pump you up a bit."

I lost count of the sets as I closed my eyes and forced myself into that place in my brain that didn't recognize pain. Before too long, the spotter was taking the bar from me and smiling a nearly toothless grin.

"You're getting there!" he told me.

I rolled my eyes and sat up, rubbing at my shoulders.

"Let's weigh you." Yolanda led me over to the scales. I rolled my shoulders a couple of times as I stepped up on the scale and watched the digital display crawl up. "Two-oh-four-point-seven."

"All good, despite breakfast," I said with a grin.

"Breakfast?"

"Pancakes."

"She cooks, huh?"

I nodded.

"You stay away from carbs on fight nights." Yolanda scolded me, wagging a finger in my face. "Load up only the night before.

Take it easy the rest of the day—protein and water only. I want you ready to kick ass come ten o'clock, not dragged down by *pancakes*."

I ignored her and started to head for the showers in the lower part of the gym. She followed like the kinky fuck she was. The room was totally concrete and used to be for fighters when the gym was dedicated to boxing matches. There wasn't much to it, just a few shower spigots along one wall and some rusted lockers on the other. I looked over my head at the retro sign hanging on the post next to the wall. It read "Boxers and Mgrs only—All others keep out."

"Are you my manager now?"

I took a big swig from my bottle of water, which dribbled down my chin and cooled my neck. I took a few deep breaths to relax myself and then began to pull the tape from my hands. Once that was done, I was ready for a shower. Yolanda stood there watching me while I dropped my clothes to the ground.

"Why don't you just tell me you like her?" Yolanda asked. "Or are you refusing to tell yourself?"

I flipped the shower up to warm and stepped into the stream.

"I told you—it isn't like that."

"What is it like, then?"

I turned my face into the water, then stepped back and shook droplets from my hair. Ultimately, I didn't want to talk about this, but I also knew my pit-bull-like trainer wasn't going to loosen her grip. I ended up yelling over the noise from the water as I lathered up.

"She thinks of me like I'm her big brother, you know? I'm just trying to help her out. She's never lived in a city before; she doesn't know anyone, and she's all on her own. She doesn't need my shit complicating her life."

"So you figure you'd invite her to live with you."

"I didn't know what else to do," I admitted. I rinsed, shut the water off, and grabbed one of the towels in a stack next to the shower.

"She was going to move back home—quit school and everything. I didn't want her to have to do that."

I rubbed a towel over my head and then shook out my hair again. Inside my gym bag were clean boxers and a T-shirt, which I pulled on quickly as the chilled air began to permeate my skin. I was going to have to turn the heat on this weekend; I was sure of it.

"Holy shit," Yolanda muttered under her breath. She leaned heavily on the door frame and shook her head slowly. "You have no fucking clue, do you?"

"I don't know what you're talking about."

"You want her."

"It's not like that," I repeated for what felt like the hundredth time. I shook my head again. "I told you. She just needed a little help, and I—"

"Went all 'big brother' on her."

"Yeah, I guess."

"Except 'big brother' wants to fuck 'little sister.'"

"Nice," I growled up at her. I yanked on my jeans and tennis shoes before I sat back down and started shoving stuff back into the bag at my feet. I moved my knees apart and leaned over so I could zip it all up.

"You won't even admit it." Yolanda continued to push.

I sighed and leaned back to look up at my trainer and friend.

"For the final fucking time, Yolanda," I said, "it is not like that with us. It shouldn't be like that for her anyway."

"Like what?" Yolanda asked. She tilted her head to one side and waited for me to give her a better answer. I thought it was fucking obvious.

"What she needs is not what I have to offer," I said. "Even if she were interested in me, she wouldn't be interested in the dead-end life around here. She's in school, trying to make something of herself. She's a transient. She's not looking for a fuck buddy, and I'd never get involved with someone seriously, so what difference does it make?"

Yolanda seemed to think about that for a minute before she took a couple of swift steps closer to me, kicked the bag out of the way, and stood right between my legs. She shoved at my shoulder until I was sitting upright again. With her standing and me sitting, she was just slightly above my eye level.

"Look at me!" she said sharply. Like I usually did when it came to her barking, I obeyed immediately. "You look at me and tell me you aren't into her. Tell me you don't want to be fucking her like a goddamn stud bull. Say if given the chance, you wouldn't take her in a heartbeat. Tell me her cooking fucking *pancakes* didn't make you hard as hell. Go ahead. I dare you."

I swallowed as I tried to hold her gaze. I couldn't even win the staring contest, let alone speak any of those words without my tongue falling right out of my face.

"Yeah, I didn't think so." Yolanda stepped back. "Are you lying to yourself, too, or just me?"

I shook my head briefly.

"I don't know," I admitted. "I was serious, though—it's not like that. She's not looking for a fuck buddy, and I'm not going to get involved with someone, so what difference does it make?"

"Why not?"

"Why not what?"

"Why not get involved?" Yolanda asked.

My skin went cold.

Every muscle tensed at once.

I stopped breathing.

My eyes clouded over with images of blood and meat and…

"Why not?" I repeated. A moment later I was on my feet and shoving her backwards. For once in her life, Yolanda had the good sense to back away from me as I started screaming. "Why not? *Why not?* Are you fucking kidding me? You of all people? How the fuck can you just stand there and ask me *why not?*"

"Easy, Teague," she said. Her eyes were wary, but honestly, the little explosion was already having an effect on me, calming me. She started to take a step forward, but I shook my head sharply and she stopped.

"It's ancient history," she said quietly.

"That doesn't change *anything*." My voice was hard, cold, and barely recognizable as mine. I backed up slowly, watching her stand perfectly still as I did. Once I sat back down on the bench, I let out a long breath.

She looked down at me, and her eyes changed slightly. They softened a little and looked somewhat sad. She took a step backwards as she continued to look down at me and then let out a long sigh.

"Maybe it's time for you to take a chance again," she said quietly before turning around and walking out of the showers.

I was never one to change my opinion, but Yolanda certainly gave me something to think about.

# CHAPTER TWELVE
## Admit the Reality

"You want me to go with you?" Tria asked quietly. There was hesitation in her voice, but I didn't understand why.

"Yeah, why not?" I asked. "I mean, it beats hanging out here all night, right?"

Yolanda's words had been bothering me all afternoon. It was rare for her to ever make a comment about any woman who might be in my life though the vast majority of those didn't last past round two. I had spent a lot of time trying to figure out what her angle was and why she seemed to be pushing me toward the young woman who was—in a thousand different ways—way too good to get messed up in my life.

She had promise. She had potential. She had a future.

I didn't have shit. Much more importantly, I had my demons. I glanced down and realized I was rubbing at the inside of my arm. I dropped my hand quickly and turned back to Tria.

I watched her closely as she furrowed her brow and considered whether or not she wanted to come to the crappy bar down the street and watch me beat up some random guy in a cage. It was obviously not something she had considered before, and she didn't seem to know how to answer.

"Well?" I asked as I glanced up at the clock. "I need to head over that way, and if you don't come with me, you ain't goin' at all. I don't want you walking there on your own."

"So...it's like a game, right?" Tria asked. Her tone was unsure, and her eyes watched mine carefully.

"Well, it's a 'sport,'" I said. I wasn't exactly sure what she meant by a "game."

"I've just never seen anything like that," Tria told me. "I still don't know how you can do anything inside that tiny cage-room-place."

I laughed at her description.

"Well, if you came and watched, you would know."

She hesitated and contemplated for a moment, then finally agreed to go.

"Cool!" I said with a smile. As soon as she agreed, I realized how much I wanted her to be there to see me work—see me at my best. "Let's get rockin'!"

We made it to Feet First quickly, my pace a little faster than usual as we headed down the street. I was excited to have Tria there, watching me work, and I was genuinely looking forward to the fight that hadn't even begun yet. I didn't typically get excited until right before I got into the cage.

Inside the bar, there were already people packed wall-to-wall. I didn't have a lot of time to talk to customers before I had to get ready, but I tried to chat with a few of them as I got Tria set up near the bar where she could have a good, unobstructed view of the cage. Gary was also close by, and I made sure he was going to keep an eye on her while I was fighting. The last thing she needed was some drunk asshole fucking with her while I was indisposed.

"I'm fine—really," Tria said.

I had Dordy make her one of his special froo-froo drinks. It was a daiquiri sort of thing and looked like it contained more fruit than alcohol. Hell, he might have made it a virgin drink, and she probably wouldn't have known the difference.

"Okay, well—I gotta get ready," I told her. "Just hang here. You got the best seat in the house. I'll come find you after I beat this fucker."

I grinned, but she just narrowed her eyes a little and looked at me sideways. Once I was in the locker room, I changed into my green trunks and taped up my feet. Yolanda came in and taped my wrists, but she didn't say much of anything. I knew I had strained things a bit this afternoon, but I put it out of my mind.

You can't be upset about shit you don't think about.

After she left, I stretched and waited for my cue. It came quickly, and I was pumped and ready for it.

*Hier kommt die Sonne*

My song started playing, and I moved swiftly out of the locker area, up the ramp, and into the roar of the crowd.

*Die Sonne scheint mir aus den Händenkann verbrennen, kann dich blenden*

I raised my arms up over my head and balled my hands into tight fists. I spun in a circle, flexing my back and listening to the screams from the audience. I leapt forward at the fence in front of me, snarling at the guy on the other side and pounding against the metal a few times to add to the show.

Yolanda escorted me into the cage, felt me up, and then brought in the other guy. As soon as the cage door slammed shut, he was on me. I felt a good punch that was definitely hard enough to bruise. I blocked the next two but let him come forward and get comfortable with what he thought was advantage.

He was quick and threw multiple punches at my face as I backed against the cold metal. I slammed a fist into his chest and a knee into his gut. He grunted, and in retaliation, he grabbed a handful of hair at the back of my head, yanked me forward, and then threw me back. Shouts came from all directions as he stepped back and threw a kick at me.

Big mistake.

I had a hold of his ankle, and twisted his whole leg to the side, nearly turning him completely upside down before dropping him to the mat. My body followed, landing on top of his with my knees in his gut. With the wind knocked out of him, he slowed down quite a bit, and his punches lacked the fervor that had been behind them only sixty seconds ago.

"Not ready for me, are you?" I snarled through what was probably a rather maniacal smile. I punched knuckles down into his face and watched the blood flow from his nose. His fingers reached for my shoulder, and I felt distinctive tapping against my skin.

Jumping off the mat, I waited for Yolanda to reenter the cage and raise my hand above my head, calling out my victory to all those around. With bright eyes and muscles bristling with raw energy, I searched out Tria's table.

As soon as I looked up and saw Tria sitting there at the edge of the cage, her arms wrapped around herself, I could tell right away that something was wrong. I pushed past Yolanda and headed out, beyond the fence that kept the fighters away from the customers during the battle, and over to where she sat, ignoring people's attempts to get my attention.

"What is it?" I asked over the bar sounds of music and laughter. I moved quickly to her side and looked down at her. Her eyes were red. "What's the matter?"

"I...you...oh my God," she gasped. "How badly are you hurt?"

"Me?" I questioned. I reached up and tried to find blood coming from somewhere, but I didn't think he'd drawn any. I brought my hand down and looked at my fingers just in case, but they were clean. "I'm fine."

"But he…and you…" She couldn't seem to get any words out, and I could barely hear her above the noise, so I pulled her back down to the locker room with me and shut the door to the sounds.

"Tria, I'm fine, really."

"Are you sure?" she asked.

I had to laugh.

"Positive—look." I spun around in a circle with my arms spread out. "I'm perfectly fine."

"Really?"

I shook my head a little, surprised and maybe even secretly thrilled that she was showing concern for me, and this hadn't been a bad fight at all. Little wisps of fantasy bobbed around in my head, and they included images of Tria softly kissing bruises and fussing over cuts.

"I don't have anything to hide here," I said as I glanced down my body, which was clad in only my trunks. Still high from the fight and realizing that she cared, the next words just came out with a cocky grin but without any real thought behind them. "I can show you the rest if you want to be sure."

Tria's eyes went wide, and I watched her throat bob as she swallowed. Her tongue darted out over her lips, and her cheeks flamed red as I realized what I had just said. My own tongue wet my lips, and I considered making a move, consequences be damned.

At that moment, Yolanda burst through the door. She stopped short, eyeing us both briefly before crossing her arms and glaring at me.

"There are about twenty people out there waiting to talk to you," she said, scolding me. "What's the holdup?"

She eyed Tria and then looked over to me with a roll of her eyes.

"You two going to be long? You are still working, you know."

"Yeah, yeah." I dismissed Yolanda's comment. "I'll be out in a second."

Yolanda threw one last look at Tria before she walked out.

"Look, I—"

"I don't want to hold you up," Tria said quickly. "Go on. Talk to your...um...fans or whatever."

I took a long breath in and then let it out with a huff through my nose.

"Yeah, I should," I agreed. "I need to shower first."

"Oh...um...right," Tria stammered. "I'll just go back to that table, then."

"I'll be out soon."

I watched her walk out of the locker room, then quickly dropped my trunks and showered. I was feeling unsettled, and I had to spend a minute clearing my mind before I could walk back out to meet anyone.

I was swarmed as soon as I returned to the bar, and I understood immediately why Yolanda was a little insistent on getting me out there. Feet First was more of a madhouse than usual with people from all over the place lined up to talk with me about my techniques, favorite holds, and my opinions on one martial art versus another. I chatted, smiled, and even accepted a couple of drinks before I finally managed to get back to where Tria was sitting. I nodded to Gary, who was relatively close to her and keeping most of the animals at bay, and dropped down in the seat opposite Tria.

"So, what did you think?" I asked. I was hyped up from the fight and the attention, and I knew I was beaming like the village moron, just waiting to hear her opinion.

"It's not what I thought it would be," she said quietly.

"What did you think it would be?" I asked. I leaned my elbows on the table to get a little closer so I could hear her.

"Um...more like boxing, I guess." she stated. "I thought there would be a referee or something, but there didn't seem to be any rules."

"Not many," I agreed. "That's why I like it."

"He grabbed you by the hair," she said. "Is that allowed?"

I shrugged.

"Incentive for me to get a haircut." I was still grinning, but as I watched her eyes, the smile left my face, and it was replaced with a lump in my throat and a sinking feeling in the pit of my stomach.

"It's brutal," she said as she eyed the cage.

I knew by the look in her eyes what she really meant. She didn't know what the fighting was going to be like before she saw it. She didn't know there would be bloodshed and mayhem. In her mind, this wasn't the same as watching me protect her from a group of thugs or from her asshole ex-boyfriend. This was different.

She didn't like it.

Sitting against the back of the chair, I brought my drink up to my lips and drained it. Each and every tiny option I had let creep into my mind since the conversation with Yolanda earlier in the day quickly expelled itself from any realm of possibility.

I was a fighter. It wasn't just a matter of making a living—it was a way of life for me. I loved it. I loved it, and I would never, ever consider doing anything else, and Tria would never want anything to do with it.

Her next words pretty much sealed my thoughts in granite.

"How can two people just do that to each other?" Tria asked softly. Her eyes stayed on the cage. "You don't know each other. You've never wronged each other. Why? Why would you do that for…for…for what?"

She turned to me, and we stared at one another, our gaze locked.

"Is it just for the money?" she asked.

"No." I shook my head.

"You really do like being in there, don't you?"

I could only nod.

"Doesn't it...hurt?" Her eyes became intense and filled with unshed tears, and I could sense her need to understand.

"It makes me feel," I said quietly. I nodded my head toward the chain links. "Inside there, I'm alive."

"And the rest of the time?" she whispered.

"I'm just...*existing*."

Everything I had told Yolanda ran through my mind again. There was no way I was a good match for Tria even if I was inclined to consider taking a chance on another actual relationship. She would never be all right with what I did for a living, and it was the only thing that had kept me sane for nearly a decade.

I had to forget the very notion.

I was never one to try to attain the unattainable, but I still found it hard to let go.

# CHAPTER THIRTEEN
## Set the Rhythm

Walking home was a lot quieter than our walks had been in the past. I wasn't in the mood for small talk, and Tria just seemed to be in some kind of deep thought or something. Unlike some of the times we had spent a block or two in silence as we went from home to work or work to home, this one felt very uncomfortable to me.

Tria had definitely not liked the fight. No doubt about that at all. I was pretty sure that's what she was thinking about, and I was also pretty sure I didn't want to know the details.

Back at the apartment, I opened the door and held it for Tria. She smiled up at me as she walked in, but there was no sparkle in her eyes like there usually was when she smiled at me.

Tria collected her sweats and T-shirt and headed into the bathroom to shower and change. It was freaking cold in the place, and I decided to break down and turn the heat up. In the hallway, the little thermostat read sixty-two, which I bumped up to sixty-eight and listened to the fan kick on.

Maybe it would keep me from trying to spoon my roommate

after I fell asleep.

I dropped my clothes to the floor and pulled a pair of sweats up my legs. Glancing at the floor and rolling my eyes a bit, I kicked the dirties into the pile in the corner before hauling myself out the window for a smoke.

Krazy Katie didn't look at me, and after all the bullshit she was spouting the other day, I didn't even say hello to her as I leaned against the rail and watched ash fall to the ground below me. She didn't say anything either though she kept making little huffing sounds out of her nose.

When I went back inside, Tria was done in the bathroom and sitting on the edge of the bed, wrapping her separated hair into braids.

"Hey, I was thinking," I said as I scratched at the back of my head and looked off to the side of her. "Maybe it would be better if I was on the other side of the bed. I do think I prefer it."

"Sure," Tria responded. She used a little black twisty band to hold the end of her hair in the braid and tossed it over her shoulder.

She got in on the side closer to the window, and I got in closer to the door. The whole side of the bed still smelled like her, and I was already pretty sure it was going to work out just fine. That is, until Tria asked for her pillow back, and I reluctantly handed it over and accepted my own in exchange.

It still smelled like her a bit but not as much.

Rolling to my side, I faced the door and tried to hold on to the edge of the blanket as tightly as I could. I could feel Tria right behind me, situating herself into a comfortable position and tugging slightly at the blanket as she did so, but my grip did not falter. She let out a long sigh and went still.

For the longest time, I just lay there with my eyes open, watching the partially closed door to the bedroom and wondering what the fuck I was doing.

Only a few hours after I finally dozed off, I woke up warm, content, and surrounded by that heavenly scent. I knew exactly where I was and what I was doing and didn't even to pretend to think I was dreaming.

The length of my body was lined up flush with hers, and my arm was wrapped around her waist. My fingers curled over the swell at her hip, and my thumb had found its way inside the hem of her shirt and pressed lightly into her warm skin there.

I opened my eyes, and her face was so peaceful and serene, it took my breath away. Her head was tilted slightly toward me so that her forehead was pressed into my shoulder. I had again managed to get my arm underneath her to complete the embrace and make it really damn hard to move away.

I didn't want to anyway.

For some time, I just watched her. For the most part, she was still as she lay in my arms, but sometimes her fingers would twitch a little or her eyes would move under her lids. I watched her chest rise and fall and tried not to think about how easy it would be to spread my fingers and reach up to touch her breast.

To keep myself from even considering it anymore, I pulled my hand from her side and used it to brush off of her forehead a stray piece of hair that had escaped from the braid. With a quiet sigh, I dug my arm out from under her and rolled back to my own, cold side of the bed.

An hour later, I did the whole thing again.

We fell into a routine. Tria had classes through the week and spent her evenings studying. Every morning she made breakfast though she made lighter fare than she had the first day. She told me she'd make pancakes on Sundays since I should have a couple of days to recover from all those carbs and syrup. I'd run daily, work out with Yolanda every other day, and fight Tuesdays and Fridays.

Tria didn't come back to the bar to watch me fight again, but she was also claiming it was just because she had to study for midterms. I wasn't surprised that she came up with the excuse, but I had hoped she might at least give it another try. Yolanda asked me about it, and I offered to take her into the cage to put an end to her questioning.

She glared but left me alone.

I was taking my morning run and swinging around the single tree Tria still hadn't seen in a sea of concrete when I noticed a guy hauling a bunch of shit out of one of the buildings and tossing it up into one of those large industrial dumpsters. The contents of the large cart he was pushing caught my eye.

"Hey, dude!" I called out as I altered my course and jogged easily over to him. He had graying dark hair and kept coughing into his hand.

"Damn dust," he muttered as I approached. "They don't pay me enough for all this dust. Probably asbestos in there, too."

He pointed his thumb over his shoulder toward one of the abandoned warehouses.

"You just throwing this out?" I asked him.

"Cleaning out the old ball bearings place," he said. He looked me up and down and took a step back, appearing tense. "There isn't much left in there, and they said just to haul out whatever was there. I ain't stealing anything."

"I just wondered if you were going to pitch the wood," I said. "If you are, I was going to take it."

His shoulders relaxed a little.

"It's just going in the dumpsters," he said. "Once it's in there, it's fair game, I guess."

A few minutes later, I had several pieces of plywood and a two-foot section of a two-by-four over my shoulders. I didn't head directly back to the apartment but took the alleyway over to Feet First instead.

It was way too early for the bar to be open, but I pounded on the back entrance until Stacy opened the door.

"Liam!" she scolded. "What are you doing out here?"

"Do you have a hammer and some nails around someplace?" I asked. "I want to build something."

She looked at me skeptically, shook her head slowly, and opened the door wide.

"There's a toolbox in the kitchen," she told me, "but you can't take all of that in there—there is no room for it. Take it to the locker room, and I'll bring the box."

I offered to go get the box myself, but she waved me off and muttered something about not being all *that* old. I shifted my load from one shoulder to the other and then hauled it all downstairs. I lay the pieces down on the cement floor and looked them over.

There were four decent-sized, mostly flat pieces of plywood, and the section of two-by-four was a little over two feet long. In my head, I tried to picture what a bookshelf looked like and thought about that Tangelos game my Dad used to play with me when I was a kid. You would get all these different-shaped pieces and have to fit them together into a certain arrangement, and you'd try to do it as fast as possible. Using scrap wood to make serviceable furniture wasn't too different.

Stacy brought a large toolbox down the stairs, dropped it at my feet, and asked if I wanted lunch. I declined politely before I began to rummage through the box. Hammer, nails, a hack saw, sandpaper —I didn't think I would need much more than that.

I spent the entire afternoon sawing, hammering, and sanding. I cut the two-by-four into eight small pieces to serve as feet and tops and then shaped the plywood into four similarly sized pieces. They weren't perfect, but when I started putting it all together, it worked out pretty well. It at least stood up straight without wobbling.

It was definitely useful, but it didn't look like much.

"I made you a sandwich," Stacy said as she pushed open the door and dropped a plate down in front of me. "You've been down here for hours, and I know you have to be hungry."

"Dordy'll be pissed."

"He's not in yet, and I doubt he's going to miss a couple slices of cheese and bread."

I looked up at her and gave her a smile.

"Thanks," I said. "I am kind of hungry, now that you mention it. What time is it?"

"Nearly four o'clock," she replied.

I nodded and looked at my little project a bit more closely. It needed a lot more sanding.

"Are you taking up a new hobby?" Stacy asked, snickering. "Joining a book club?"

"Nah," I said with a headshake. I was pleased that she at least recognized my creation for what it was supposed to be. "I got a roommate, and she's got a lot of books. My apartment doesn't have a bookshelf or anything, so they're still in a couple boxes. I saw this shit...um..."

I glanced up at the older woman, who had her hands on her hips as she stared down at me.

"Stuff," I said, correcting myself, "in the dumpster. I thought I could make it into a place for her books."

"Liam Teague!" Stacy exclaimed. She placed her hand over her chest. "Do you have a lady friend?"

I rolled my eyes and shook my head.

"Roommate, Stacy. That's it."

"Hmm..." she murmured as she turned around and headed back up the stairs. "I always wanted a boy who would make me bookcases."

"You asking me on a date?" I asked, snickering.

"If I was thirty years younger, you wouldn't be able to fend me off," she called as she disappeared around the corner.

I laughed and wolfed down the sandwich before I went back to sanding. Stacy came back a few minutes later to collect my plate, and as she did, she handed me a small can.

"Not sure if there will be enough," she told me as she walked back out, "but it's a pretty color blue, and we don't need the extra paint for anything."

"Thanks," I mumbled. I stared at the little can of paint in my hand before tilting it from side to side to try to determine how much was left. It was a quart can and maybe half full. I thought that would be enough to cover the bookshelf pretty nicely, but I'd definitely have to get it sanded down better first, which meant I wouldn't be able to get it done today. Tria was going to be home from school within an hour, and she told me she was going to try some new vegetarian recipe she found in a book she got at the college library.

Tria did not cook just pancakes. She could make almost anything and had been trying out various vegetable-centered dishes to cook for me though I told her she didn't have to. She continued to state that it was her part of the living arrangements, so she was going to learn to cook what I would eat.

I cleaned up the mess I had made and set the little bookshelf up in the corner farthest from the shower. I wasn't sure if humidity would do anything to it or not, but it seemed like a good idea. I made it back to the apartment with about ten minutes to spare before the Hoffman College transportation van rolled up in front of the building.

"I have to run to the grocery," Tria announced as soon as she got in the door. "I found this new cookbook at the library, and it's perfect."

She yanked the giant-ass, full-sized cookbook out of Black Hole Briefcase and flopped it down on the kitchen table. She flipped through the pages of the vegetarian cookbook and came to a recipe for Swedish Bean Balls.

"Bean balls?" I asked skeptically.

"Look at what's in it. I think it might be good."

I looked over the list of ingredients—kidney beans, rice, onions, breadcrumbs—and nothing sounded bad at all. The book said to put it all over mashed potatoes with some vegetarian gravy. I wasn't really sure what it would all taste like, but I said I would at least give it a try. Tria wrote down a list of things to buy, bitched about me giving her the cash for it, but eventually relented and took the money.

I glanced over the recipe again and was glad I didn't have to fight for a couple of days because it was going to be some heavy stuff. Yolanda would probably want to kill me if she saw me eating a big pile of mashed potatoes and gravy.

Since Tria was going to be gone for a while, I jumped on the opportunity to head into the shower and take care of business. I'd always had pretty regular daily jerk-off sessions, and having Tria living with me had certainly made that a little difficult. Waking up spooning her every night didn't help, either.

What also didn't help were the images in my mind whenever I took my dick in my hand.

It wasn't even a matter of trying to think about her; as soon as there was flesh-on-flesh, her face was in my mind. The chick from my favorite porno getting a spit roast no longer did a thing for me. I only thought of Tria's eyes, Tria's lips, and Tria's body as I ran my hand up and down my shaft.

I closed my eyes as the water poured down my shoulders and back. I curled the fingers of my right hand around the base and dragged slowly up and over the tip, while the left hand reached down to cup my balls. In my mind, I lay her down on the bed and lifted one leg up over my shoulder before slowly sliding into her. Her head was pressed against the mattress, and her back arched as she moaned my name.

"Oh yeah," I mumbled. "That's it, baby. Take it…"

My hand moved faster over my shaft, and the Tria in my head moved rhythmically with my thrusts against the sheets. I could see my hand reaching to caress her breast, stroke the nipple, and pinch it. I thrust faster. Tria cried out again, and my legs shook as the buildup exploded over my hand before being washed away by the shower stream.

"Fuck," I muttered. Even standing there in the shower, I felt like I needed a shower.

After I got myself back under control, I washed my hair, which didn't take much since it was nice and short, thanks to a coupon for a haircut Tria found for me at the grocery store. I turned around a couple of times to get all the soap off of me, then turned off the water and climbed out.

The line of little bottles Tria had on the shower ledge called to me—I really wanted to know which one made her smell so good, but I restrained myself. Something about sniffing her shower products seemed pretty creepy—tempting, but creepy.

Back in the bedroom, I poked around in the bottom dresser drawer, trying to find some clean boxers. The pile of laundry in the corner was now being shoved into a laundry bag Tria brought from her old apartment, but the clothes were starting to hang out the top. Tria had her dirty clothes in a plastic laundry basket. Since I had done a crappy job of putting shit away after the last laundry trip, I couldn't find any boxers and decided to just forget it.

I turned to grab my jeans, which were already laid out on the bed. At that exact moment, Tria turned the corner and walked into the room.

"Oh my God!" Tria screeched as she simultaneously covered her face with her hands, turned bright red, and tried to get back out of the room without seeing where she was going. She banged into the wall a bit but managed to get herself out of there.

I had to laugh, not just because the sight was pretty damn funny but also in relief. If I hadn't just jacked off, the knowledge that she was looking at my dick would have probably brought him to attention pretty quickly.

Moody little bastard.

I pulled my jeans up and buttoned them. When I walked into the living room, Tria was on the couch with her head in her hands.

"I am so sorry!" she cried without looking up. "I didn't know you were changing. I wasn't trying to...to..."

"Tria, relax," I said with another short laugh. "Fuck, Yolanda's always walking in on me, and she doesn't even have the decency to look away!"

"I just...I mean...I didn't know you were..."

I walked around her and sat down on the other side. I had spent way too much time in the cage being mostly naked to really be concerned about any chick seeing my cock, and I didn't want her to be upset about it. There was also that distinctly porn-influenced male side of me that just wanted to yank it out and let her get to know it really well so she would know for sure that being looked at didn't bother me.

That line of thinking was going to have to change pretty quickly, refractory period be damned.

"It's okay," I told her. "Really. No big deal. Shit like that is bound to happen when you live with someone, right?

"You aren't mad?" Tria asked as she peeked at me through her fingertips.

"Not at all," I said. "I would have closed the door; I just didn't realize you were back already."

"I just got here," she said, and I was relieved to hear it. Hopefully that meant she hadn't heard me in the shower with my dick in my hand. "I'm really sorry."

"It's okay," I repeated.

She dropped her hands but wouldn't look in my direction. Her shoulders moved up and down a little as she tried to get herself together again. Eventually, she sighed heavily and then stood up.

"I'm going to make dinner," she announced.

"Need any help?"

"No, I'm good."

She went into the kitchen, and I just watched her. For the most part, we seemed to be comfortable living in the same space together, but there were definitely some things that caused a bit of tension. Tria kept her clean clothes in her suitcase, refusing all my offers to empty a couple of dresser drawers for her. It bugged me, partially because she was just so damn stubborn about it, but also because it made the whole arrangement seem more transient than I wanted to believe. Even in the short amount of time she had been there, I found myself enjoying the company. I had pretty much lived on my own since I left the house where I grew up, and having someone else around was pretty nice.

Our lives just seemed to...mesh.

She was a morning shower kind of person, and she got out whatever she was going to wear and took it to the bathroom to dress. I showered after running, and I would usually just change my own clothes quickly while she was in the bathroom. She made breakfast and supper on most days but was usually either in class or studying at lunchtime. That worked fine, too, since those were my usual workout times. We both kept late hours, and though she didn't come back to watch me fight after that first night, she always waited for me to get home before she went to bed.

Every night, I woke up at least a couple of times to her warmth and scent surrounding me. Usually I would just watch her face for a while as she slept, and then I would shift back to my own side of the bed. No matter how many times I moved away, I ended up close to her again. In the morning, she was always up before I awakened and usually in the kitchen making something.

I loved watching that woman cook.

That thing I had always heard about guys looking for a woman like their own mothers is a bunch of bullshit. I was pretty sure my mother didn't even know what part of the house contained the kitchen. I kept the TV on most of the time when Tria was cooking, but I always leaned way forward so I could watch her. She put a tray of little round things in the oven, and just seeing her bending over did weird things to the pit of my stomach. Every time she pulled a spoon out of a saucepan and used her finger to get a little taste of what she was cooking, my dick got hard.

There had to be something seriously wrong with me.

"Ready to eat?" Tria called, startling me from my 1950s television show fantasies. She was smiling and wiping her hands on a towel, and I had to excuse myself to "wash my hands" before we ate.

After we were done eating Swedish Bean Balls, I still had no idea what they were, but they tasted fantastic. Conversation with Tria during dinner was also easy and flowed without effort from one topic to the next. We talked about her classes, technology, the landlord, politics, and the state of the neighborhood where we lived until the leftovers were cold, and I had managed to down about four beers. We even cleaned up in sync with one another, and by the time we finished, it was late and time for bed.

The only thing that was still weird and awkward was getting into bed together. It was likely just in my own head because all I could do was think about how I was going to wake up with her in my arms at some point. I'd watch her sleep for a while, and I was fairly certain I had her face completely memorized.

That night was no different.

I woke to my nose pressed lightly to the back of her neck and my arm wrapped around her stomach, holding her back against my chest. Somehow, my hand had actually slipped underneath her shirt, and my fingers twitched, aching to stroke softly over the bare skin of her belly.

Inhaling, I closed my eyes again, basking in the scent from her hair and skin and realizing that if I splayed out my fingers, the tips of them could touch the curved undersides of her breasts. I had to stifle a groan as I spent a moment being overwhelmed by the combination of the fragrance in my nose, the soft feeling of her skin on my fingers, and my engorged cock pressed tightly against her backside.

*Shit!*

I had to grind my teeth together to keep from screaming the word out loud as I quickly extricated myself and rolled over to the other side of the bed. My feet swung over and touched the floor, and I quietly launched myself out of the bed, out of the room, and into the bathroom.

My hand was down the front of my sweats before I could even get the lid to the toilet up. Inside my brain, the scenario from the bed continued with the added memory of feeling her skin and the pressure of her ass on my cock. My real hand gripped and pumped at my cock while the one in my imagination moved up, caressing her breasts as my lower body shifted to push inside of her from behind.

Semen coated the edge of the toilet seat and part of the underside of the lid. I braced myself against the tank for a moment as I tried to catch my breath, then wiped the junk off with a piece of toilet paper. My fingers dug into my eyes and rubbed for a moment while I realized that little bit of clean-up wasn't going to be good enough. I found a washcloth and doused it in water and soap, cleaned the toilet off more effectively, and tossed the cloth onto the corner ledge of the shower.

This was all so fucked up.

I was never one to get worked up over a particular girl, but this was getting ridiculous.

# CHAPTER FOURTEEN
## Seize the Opportunity

"The color looks perfect." Stacy made the remark as I checked to make sure the paint had dried on the bookshelf.

It ended up about three feet high, two feet wide, and a foot deep with four shelves for Tria to house her books. It wasn't pretty by anyone's standards, but the paint brightened it up, and it would at least do the job for which it was made.

"I think it turned out all right," I said, tapping the back of one of the shelves with my fingers. "It seems to be pretty much dry now, too."

"Are you going to carry it home?" she asked.

"Not much of an option there," I said with a crooked smile.

"How about you put it in the back of my car and I drive you?" the cook suggested. "I'm done here until this evening. I have the time."

"Really? That would be sweet! Thanks!"

I put some newspaper down on the back seat of Stacy's beat up old Ford and placed the bookshelf on top of it. I climbed into the passenger seat of the musty smelling car and rolled down the window.

"So tell me about this roommate," Stacy said as soon as the car started moving. "What's her name?"

"Tria," I replied.

"Is she pretty?" Stacy asked.

I rolled my eyes.

"Yeah, I suppose so."

"And do you like her?"

"For Christ's sake," I growled. "How many times do I have to tell people it's not like that?"

She glanced at me out of the corner of her eye as she pulled out into the street.

"Sorry," I mumbled. "It's just that everyone keeps assuming I'm doing her."

"I didn't assume anything," Stacy stated. "I just asked if you liked her."

I huffed out my nose.

"You did make her a bookcase," she pointed out. "You must not hate her."

"I like her fine," I replied.

"Well, tell me about her, then."

I reached up and scratched the back of my neck.

"She's smart," I said. "She's studying economics."

When I didn't say anything else, Stacy prompted me for more.

"She's a great cook. You'd like that," I told her.

"You don't eat my cooking so much anymore. I noticed that."

I laughed.

"That would make living with someone easier," she said with a nod. She turned the wheel and headed down the street and around the block. "Have you ever had a roommate before?"

"Not really," I replied with a shrug. "I mean, I lived with Yolanda for a couple weeks when I was kicked out of my apartment, but that was temporary, ya know?"

"That's when you first started working for Dordy, right? When you first started fighting?"

"Yeah." I nodded. "Well, getting paid for it, anyway. Yolanda got me the job. I don't think it would have occurred to me that I could beat people up for a living."

"You were living on the streets for a while there, weren't you?"

"For a bit," I said with another shrug. I swallowed hard and stared out the window.

"It's nothing to be ashamed of," Stacy said. "I spent quite a bit of time living out of my car back in the day."

"Oh yeah?"

"When my husband walked out, I didn't have a job. No education, no experience—I thought I would always be a housewife. I couldn't pay for the house anymore, and he was just gone, so I took the kids to live with my parents in the country while I looked for work here. It was a while before I found something that would let me actually pay for a place. Dordy took a chance on me, just like he did with you."

"Whatever pays the rent, huh?"

"Oh, I like what I do well enough," she said. "My kids are all grown and moved off now, but you lot make good substitutes. My kids stayed with my parents for some time while I was working things out. They deserved better than I could give them then."

I nodded, and Stacy turned the last corner and parked in front of the apartment building. I jumped out and lifted the bookcase from the back seat.

"Pie in the sky blue! Sky blue!" Krazy Katie started screaming from the fire escape.

I rolled my eyes and shook my head.

"Ignore her," I said to Stacy. "She's a nut."

I gently placed the bookshelf down on the walkway and turned to thank Stacy for the ride.

"Don't you worry about it," she said. "It was my pleasure."

"It made the trek home a lot easier," I said with a smile. "I'll see ya tomorrow night."

I turned to pick up the bookcase and drag it up the stairs, but she stopped me.

"Oh, and Liam, dear?" Stacy reached her arm out the window as she called back to me. I walked back to the car and leaned against the roof with one hand. "You deserve better, too, you know."

She patted my arm and then drove away with me standing there in the street and watching her go. I let out another big sigh, picked up the bookcase, and headed inside.

I had to move the stand that held the television over a bit to make room for the bookcase along the wall. Once it was situated, I opened up the first box of books and tried to arrange them in some kind of order on the shelves. Most of the books were fiction—a few classics, a couple of romance novels, Terry Pratchett, and some Stephen King. It was kind of a weird combination, but none of it really looked like crap.

Well, except for the romances.

There was some non-fiction mixed in—all stuff for her classes or whatever. I put those on the bottom shelf since they were bigger books and the bottom shelf was a little taller than the other two. For the most part, I just arranged them by size.

I sat back when they were all on there and admired my work. With the books on it, it really didn't look too bad. The paint made all the difference, and I was going to have to thank Stacy for it again.

I was just standing up and dusting off the top of the shelf when I heard the door open and Tria come in. She noticed the bookshelf immediately, and her eyes widened in surprise.

"Where did you get that?" she asked.

"Around," I said with a shrug. I couldn't help but smile as she walked over and inspected it. "It's not very pretty or anything, but at least you don't have to dig around in those boxes anymore."

"It's perfect, Liam!" she exclaimed.

Before I knew what was happening, she had turned and thrown her arms around my neck. A moment later, I felt the light press of her lips against my cheek, and I was relatively sure all the organs in my body had turned to liquid and congregated in my feet.

"Thank you so much," she said softly as she pulled away. Her cheeks had flushed, and I found myself clenching my fists to stop myself from jumping her right there and fucking her on the floor. My tongue felt thick, and it was hard to take in a breath. I could still feel the coolness of the moisture her mouth had left against my skin.

"No problem," I finally managed to say after swallowing a few times.

Tria smiled, then turned and knelt down in front of the small shelf. She started poking around at the books and talking about how much easier it would be to find what she was looking for, but I didn't hear a word of it. I just stepped away until I felt the back of my knees hit the couch, and then I sat down heavily. As soon as my head stopped spinning, I went outside for a smoke so I could get myself back together again.

I lit the cigarette and rubbed my eyes. Krazy Katie was up above me, hollering out across the street at the guy who was waiting at the bus stop. Apparently, she was pretty sure he was her mother because she kept talking about being inside of his womb.

Fucking nutcase.

Then again, who was I to judge? Considering how nutty Tria was making me, I might have been about ready to join Krazy Katie and start screaming at the neighbors.

I was fucked.

Deep water kind of warmth and heaviness covered me as I slowly regained consciousness without actually opening my eyes. The feeling was familiar but in a way I found slightly disturbing, like I was doing something horribly wrong. My backside was chilled, and I was pretty sure Tria had rolled over on the blanket again. The front of me was nice and warm though, so I knew I was pressed up against her body in a totally inappropriate, inexcusable, and completely delectable way.

I didn't want to wake up and roll away from her, especially considering there was no way I would be able to get the blanket back from her again. Once she got a grip on it, it was a death grip, and I would sooner go into her purse looking for Tic Tacs than try to get it away from her. Besides, both my arms were around her again, and it was damn hard to get the right one out from under her when she was asleep. I had no idea how I managed to get it there in the first place, but about half the time I woke up, that's where my arm would be.

I took a deep breath and tilted my head up a bit, skimming the tip of my nose over her temple and into her hair. If I lived with her for the rest of my life, I probably still wouldn't understand how she could smell so good. My breath rushed out my nose, and I pulled back a little so I would be able to look at her face at least once before moving to my own side of the bed. I opened my eyes, and I found myself staring into the bright brown irises of the woman in my arms.

Even the warm parts of my body chilled.

For a long moment, all I could do was look at her and try to comprehend. I knew something was very, very out of place, and I knew I had ultimately been caught with my hand in the cookie jar, so to speak, but I didn't really know what I was supposed to do about it now.

Oh yeah—apologize and make it look like an accident.

"Oh…shit," I mumbled sleepily. "I'm sorry, I…"

I started to pull my arm out from around her waist but paused when I saw Tria smile and felt her grip my forearm. In the moonlight from the window, I was pretty sure I could see the flesh around her cheekbones darken, and the sight halted the beating of my heart.

"It's okay."

"I didn't mean to...um..." I started pulling my arm back, and my fingers grazed over her stomach, but I stopped again when I felt Tria tighten her hold on my arm and shake her head in quiet laughter. My eyes drifted down to where her fingers coiled around my arm and then back up to her face.

"Liam, you do this every night," she stated.

Tensing again, I tried to determine what the best course of action would be at this point. I wasn't awake enough to be thinking clearly at all, and I wasn't coming up with any kind of grand plan, that was for sure. What I did manage to get through my thick skull was that she did not seem to be upset at all.

"I do?" I responded softly.

"Yes, you do."

"Shit," I muttered. I didn't know if I should confess at this point or not. "I wasn't trying...I mean, I didn't mean to—"

Tria shook her head slowly before turning her eyes back to me. She looked at me through her long lashes, and her cheeks tinged with her blush.

"I don't mind," she said.

"You don't?" God, I sounded like an idiot. I wondered if I had completely lost the ability to form a coherent sentence. I hoped she would realize I wasn't normally a brain dead moron in bed.

God, I wanted to show her what I could be like in bed.

I looked back at her face, and what I saw there stopped all such thoughts. Her eyes were tight, her jaw clenched, and I could feel her hand trembling slightly against the skin of my arm.

"When I first moved here," Tria said in a whisper, "I couldn't sleep at all."

Her fingers gripped my arm a little tighter, and her eyes moved to the window for a moment before she turned back toward me and seemed to focus on the top of my arm.

"The noises outside—the car alarms, and the sirens, and the… the…"

She took in a sharp breath and shifted forward a little, pressing against me more.

"The *shots*."

I glanced at her, and my brow furrowed at her expression until I realized what she meant.

There were a ton of gangs only a handful of blocks away, and they were always going at each other. Sometimes they had all out fucking wars, but a lot of the time, they just took potshots at each other, usually around four in the morning. When I first moved to this apartment, the gunshots would wake me up as well. After so many years, they only woke me up now if there was a shooting in the building, and that hadn't happened in a while.

Tria took several more breaths, and I felt her fingers relax. She glanced at me, but then quickly looked away again.

"Since the very first night I moved here, I hadn't been able to sleep," Tria continued. "I probably didn't sleep more than half an hour the first night I lived in this neighborhood and probably never slept more than three hours total any of the other nights. I just couldn't."

Her eyes still didn't move back to me but remained trained on my upper arm. Her fingers moved over the edge of the muscle there.

"It was even worse after that night we met," she said. "I don't think I closed my eyes for days. I kept seeing them closing in on me."

She finally looked back into my eyes.

"I was too scared to sleep," she admitted quietly. "But with you…with you holding me, I feel safe."

Without hesitation, my arm wrapped back around her, and my fingers took their place against her side. The arm underneath her lifted slightly so I could pull her a little closer against my chest. Her hand slid farther up my arm and held tight to my bicep.

"You *are* safe," I stated simply.

I was never one to cuddle, but I wasn't about to let go of her now.

# CHAPTER FIFTEEN

## Toe the Line

The shit just got weird after that.

During the day, things went on just as they had been. Tria cooked and went to school. I ate and worked out. The nights when I wasn't working, Tria usually made dinner, and she would study while I pretended to watch television but really watched her.

Then we'd go to bed.

Things would start feeling really tense right before our usual bedtime. Tria would gather up her homework or books or whatever and shove them into Chewbacca's Carry-on so they'd be ready to go the next day. I'd go out on the fire escape for a smoke and then sit around on the couch and act like I had something to do. Eventually we'd look at each other, and one of us would mumble something about it being time to go to bed.

Tria would take her sweats and a T-shirt into the bathroom while I'd change in the bedroom, then we'd be all awkward and tense as we'd get into our respective sides of the bed. She'd usually smooth the blankets evenly across the bed—as if I were ever going to touch them again. I would turn off the light, and we'd both lay back on the pillows for a minute.

As the darkness would creep around us, we'd move to the center of the bed.

I would usually raise my arm up and over her shoulders, and she would settle against me with one hand on my chest. My other arm would wrap around her middle, and I would pull her closer to me. At that point, I could feel her relax into me as I eased against her. Our eyes would close, and we'd both be asleep moments later.

As weird as it would start out, it was still the best part of the whole day.

It was even better than breakfast pancakes.

It was like a little soft cloud of utopia. I didn't wake up any more at night, which I guess I had been doing because I was feeling guilty about touching my "little sister" who was now my roommate. I was getting the best sleep I could remember getting in years, and Tria seemed pretty happy about the whole arrangement, too. As long as I could keep the morning wood away from her ass, everything was good.

If she ever noticed, she didn't let on.

Not that everything was absolutely perfect. There were certainly a few points of contention. I was really bad about closing doors. I think I just lived alone for so long, it didn't occur to me a lot of the time. I left the bathroom door open when I was in a hurry to pee, and I left the bedroom door open when I changed clothes. Tria didn't walk in on me too many times because she developed the habit of just yelling at me from another room instead, just in case.

She wasn't completely peaches and cream, either. I found out on several evenings that Tria did indeed have a bit of a temper, which I had suspected. There was something about her getting all riled up about various issues that I have to admit turned me on. Typically it had to do with some injustice she learned about in her classes or over someone being rude to her in one way or another or something just unexpected happening that didn't fall into her plans.

On the Wednesday before Thanksgiving, she was already bellyaching before she was even inside the door after returning from school. I could hear her stomping in the hallway before she had her key in the lock.

"It's supposed to be the damn Thanksgiving holiday!" She was grumbling to herself as the door opened. "How can someone do that? I mean, really!"

"Something wrong?" I asked, like a complete and total fool. I knew it would get her going, and I was counting on it. Sometimes her tirades were better than porn.

"Something wrong? *Something wrong?*" she bellowed. "Yes, there is something wrong, as a matter of fact. My English professor, Dr. Kapple, is a total fucking asshole, and I hate him!"

I managed to keep my balls by *not* making meowing sounds right at that moment. I knew this particular kitten had all her claws.

"What'd he do?" I asked. I rubbed my hand across my face to hide any signs of amusement.

"He assigned a paper due right after the Thanksgiving holiday," she told me. "I'll have to spend the entire weekend writing it!"

"Total dick," I managed to say without laughing.

"He is!" she agreed. She tossed Colossus' Rucksack on the kitchen table and started digging through it. I leaned forward from my position on the couch so I could see what she pulled out. I still didn't trust that thing and had even had a couple of nightmares about it. I'd probably seen too many horror movies about serial killers who kept body parts in big trunks or bags or refrigerators and shit. Not that I thought Tria was capable of something like that, but the bag was big enough and full of enough shit that I was quite convinced anything could be in there.

"Well, at least you don't have to go to campus for a few days," I reminded her. Her shoulders slumped a little, and she pulled out a couple of books, a notepad, and some pens from the bag on the table. She turned around, and her expression had changed.

"I was all caught up," Tria said with a big sigh. Her anger dissipated, and for a moment she just looked tired and sad. She dropped down on the couch and seemed to deflate. "I needed some time off. Midterms just about killed me, and I still don't know what to even cook for dinner tomorrow."

"Don't bother," I said. "I don't eat most of what's on the typical Thanksgiving menu anyway. Last year I got takeout Chinese."

"Seriously?" Tria asked with a raised eyebrow. "That is *not* a Thanksgiving dinner. I found some recipes; it's just…not very cheap."

"So we'll make something else," I suggested. "I'll even help, if that doesn't scare you too much."

Tria snickered.

"It does, actually."

"Well, you could still make something easy," I said. "Sandwiches and chips are perfectly fine with me."

"I can probably make apple pie at least."

My mouth started to water at the thought of apple pie, which led me to think of another Thanksgiving dinner and how the menu pretty much fit in exactly with my level of culinary skills.

"You make apple pie," I said, "and I'll make all the rest."

She eyed me for a minute.

"You're serious?"

"Serious." I leaned back against the couch and put my arms up over the top of the cushions. My arm wasn't quite around her, but it was kind of close. "I'll take care of dinner. You do dessert and get that paper done so you can relax the rest of the weekend."

She still seemed pretty skeptical, which was probably warranted, but she agreed to the plan.

The smell of apple pie permeated the whole apartment by midmorning. In the kitchen, the scent was even stronger, and trying to gather up all the stuff I had bought at the grocery for our special Thanksgiving dinner while being tempted by the pie was not easy.

I wanted to shove my whole face in it.

"Hey, Tria?" I called out.

"Can I come back in there yet?" she asked.

"No!" I replied. "No entrance until I'm ready! I was just wondering if you could get the blanket from the bed. We're going to need it."

"The blanket?" she repeated. "Did I hear you right?"

"Yes, the blanket!"

"Why?"

"No questions!" I dropped my voice low. "Just do as I demand!"

I could hear her chuckling as she went into the bedroom, and I put the last of the stuff into a paper sack before rolling the top edge up a bit. I didn't want Tria to see what was in there before we got to where I wanted to take her.

"Got the blanket?" I yelled into the other room.

"I have one," she replied.

"Cool!" I said. "Grab the pie and let's go!"

"Go?" Tria asked. She came around the corner with the blanket from the bed rolled up under her arm. "Where are we going?"

"To have Thanksgiving dinner!" I told her. I gave her a big, goofy smile. "Duh!"

"Am I supposed to follow you blindly," she asked, "or do I get to know where we are going first?"

"I was thinking I would show you where that tree is," I said.

"What tree?" she asked.

"You know...you said once that you missed trees and shit," I replied with a shrug. "I told you there was one in the neighborhood."

"*Trees and shit?*" Tria giggled.

"You know—green shit." I shrugged again.

Tria pressed her lips together, but the edges still curled up.

"So, there really is a tree?" Tria asked with a laugh. "I thought you just made it up!"

"There really is one," I assured her. "It's not that far."

"How far?" She narrowed her eyes at me suspiciously.

"Well...um...close enough to take our Thanksgiving picnic there."

"Thanksgiving picnic?" Tria looked down to the sack in my hands and then moved her eyes back up to mine before smiling broadly. "I think that sounds pretty nice."

We gathered everything up and started the walk to the tree along my running path. It took a while to get there, but when we did arrive, I knew it was worth it.

The tree wasn't very green anymore and had about half of its golden-yellow leaves still on its branches while the other half lay all around the little patch of dirt and weeds surrounding the trunk. I had no idea what kind of tree it was, only that it was thin and usually not something you would consider pretty at all. But with the yellow leaves all around it, the scene didn't look too bad.

The main thing was, I could see Tria smiling.

"It ain't much," I admitted.

"It's perfect," she told me. She spread out the blanket, and we both sat down on it. I pulled over the paper sack and held it close to me so she couldn't see inside. First I took out two heavy paper plates, which I swiped from Feet First, and a couple of napkins. I handed them to Tria, and she laid them out in front of us. Then I started bringing out the actual food.

Buttered toast. Pretzels. Jelly beans. Popcorn.

Tria busted out laughing.

"Oh my God, Liam!" she said through snickers. "Did you make a Charlie Brown Thanksgiving dinner?"

"Yep," I replied. I was grinning like a nut and glad my idea had worked. It's not like I could have really cooked anything, but it still counted as tradition in a warped and cartoonish kind of way, and she didn't have to worry about going to any trouble.

"The tree is the perfect match for this," Tria said. "When we first walked up here, I thought it kind of looked like the tree from *A Charlie Brown Christmas*!"

"Maybe in a couple weeks, we can come up here and decorate it," I suggested.

We laughed, ate our feast, and talked about all of our favorite *Peanuts* characters until it got dark. With the exception of Tria's pie plate and the blanket, the rest of the stuff was trash and went into the nearby dumpster at the abandoned warehouse.

"This dumpster is pretty handy," I remarked offhandedly. "Got me wood for your bookcase, and now I don't have to carry all this shit back to the apartment."

"Wood for the bookcase?" Tria tilted her head to one side to look at me. "What do you mean?"

"Oh…um…" I hadn't really paid any attention to what I was saying. I never said where the bookcase came from because I didn't know what she would think of her bookcase being made from a bunch of trash. She seemed to like it, and I hoped this wouldn't taint her view. "Yeah, I um…I found the wood here. There was this old dude cleaning out one of the factories, and he was just throwing the wood and shit away, ya know? He said I could have it."

"You...you made the bookcase?" Tria said quietly.

"Yeah," I said with a shrug. "Stacy at Feet First gave me the paint."

"Stacy?"

"She cooks there," I said. "She likes to think she's everyone's mom. She's been working there since the day Dordy bought the place."

I stopped rambling and glanced over to see her wipe her eye with the back of her hand.

"What's wrong?" I asked. Fuck, she didn't like shit that was made from trash. I should have kept my fucking mouth shut.

"I had no idea," she said as she quietly interrupted my thoughts. "I didn't know you *made* it; I thought you just found it."

She stopped in her tracks, and I did the same. Once again, I felt her arms around my neck and her lips pressed against my cheek.

"Thank you, Liam," she whispered close to my ear. "I had no idea...none."

She sniffed and wiped at her eyes again.

"You are so incredibly sweet," she told me, and I had to snicker a little.

"Tell that to the guys I work with, will ya?"

"No, they scare me."

"Scare you?" I questioned. "Why would those guys scare you? I wouldn't let them touch you."

"I'm not scared for *me*." She corrected herself and continued. "I'm scared they are going to hurt *you*."

I pondered that thought the rest of the way home.

The very best days were Sundays because I didn't work or work out and Tria usually had all her schoolwork done on Saturday. She would just read, or we would watch a movie on the borrowed cable. In the afternoon, she did grocery shopping with whatever money I had for that and did a much better job than I ever did of coming up with meals on a budget. Her cooking was awesome, and Yolanda was starting to give me shit about hovering too close to my maximum weight. I'd gone over twice in the past couple of weeks, and it was pissing her off.

Being Yolanda, she had to choose a Sunday to cross the line about it.

Tria had made some kind of casserole dish with rice and broccoli in it. I ate about four servings and then lay on the couch holding my stomach, thinking I was probably going to die and deciding it was all worth it. Tria just snickered and told me she'd take care of the dishes, too, since I was barely able to move.

I probably would have fallen asleep if it hadn't been for the pounding at the door.

"Uggghhh…" I groaned as I hauled myself off the couch to see who was there. I opened the door to Yolanda's sour face, which immediately soured my mood. "What do you want?"

"Checking in on you," she replied as she walked past me. "You did say if I didn't think you were eating right, I should just come by and check."

Fuck! I did kind of remember saying that. Now she had totally called my bluff.

"You could have called first," I grumbled before I sat down. Once I was back on the couch, I couldn't stop the additional groan from slipping out of my mouth.

"What the hell did you eat?"

"I have no idea," I admitted. "It was fucking awesome, though."

"Dammit, Liam!"

"Come on, Yolanda," I moaned. "I don't fight for two more days. Nothing but fucking whey and iceberg between now and then."

At the moment, the thought of a salad sounded pretty awful. Even a glass of water wasn't appealing.

"Tria!" Yolanda shouted as she headed toward the kitchen. If I could have moved, I would have gone after her. "You have to stop feeding him all this crap!"

"Leave her alone," I muttered, but if someone were to ask, I would have to admit it was halfhearted. For starters, I was too stuffed to move or do anything else about the inevitable confrontation. There was also the demented guy part of me that kind of wanted to see what would happen between the two of them if left on their own to duke it out, so to speak. Not that I thought Yolanda would hit Tria—I knew she wouldn't—but a verbal battle could be just as entertaining.

Tria seemed a little taken aback at first and just looked at Yolanda with wide eyes.

"Don't you know how to make a fucking salad?" Yolanda asked her.

I hated salads, and Yolanda knew it. She was always trying to force me to eat that shit anyway. I was a vegetarian, not a fucking rabbit.

I watched Tria's eyes narrow, and I was glad I wasn't wearing something confining like my tight jeans. If I was going to be honest, I hadn't worn those jeans recently because they were a little tighter these days than they used to be. Anyway, Tria's hands balled into little fists as she stuck them on her hips and took a step forward. Watching her do that made my cock strain to get out of my sweats, and I could feel my mouth turn up into a smile as I watched her move up to the woman who had just invaded her kitchen and practically insulted her cooking.

This was going to be interesting.

"Excuse me?" Tria's voice was succinct and breezy, like it was traveling on a puff of air. I was pretty sure that in a minute the puff of air was going to feel like it just escaped from a furnace.

"I said, 'Stop feeding him all this shit!'" Yolanda roared as she waved her hands around in the general direction of the kitchen table.

Tria's eyes narrowed further, and I held my breath as she took another step closer to my trainer, a woman who easily had twenty pounds of muscle over her. Tria had to tilt her head up to look Yolanda in the eye, but the difference in size wasn't stopping her.

"I'm sorry. I know you are Liam's friend," Tria said, "but frankly, you can just go ahead and yell at him if you want to, not me! I just cook it; he's the one who eats it!"

"Oh, yes!" Yolanda snorted. "We'll just leave it up to 'Mister Self Control' over here, shall we?"

"Fuck you," I growled.

"Does the term *enabling* mean anything to you?" Yolanda asked as she narrowed her eyes into slits.

"I don't even know what the hell you are talking about!" Tria yelled.

"I don't want him making himself sick again, or fucking *worse*, for the sake of his goddamned weight class!" Yolanda screeched. She pointed a finger at Tria's chest. "You are doing that to him!"

"I most certainly am not! And if you want to point fingers, there's someone over there on the couch who happens to be a grown man!"

"Grown man, my ass."

"Yolanda, for fuck's sake!" I finally shoved myself off the couch and moved over to where the two of them were toe to toe.

"You have any idea what he does to lose weight fast?" Yolanda was saying.

"No, I do not," Tria said. As Yolanda's words registered, all the ire was suddenly directed at me. "What does she mean, 'sick again'?"

"Ah, fuck!" I turned around and headed back to the couch.

"Want to know?" Yolanda asked, sneering at Tria.

"Shut the fuck up!" I yelled at her. I'd had enough, not only of her assumptions but also having her bring up ancient history nobody needed to know anything about. "And while you're at it, get the fuck out!"

"Do you want to go back to that again?" Yolanda asked with her arms crossed over her chest. The pose emphasized her biceps. "Because if you do, I'm not dragging you back. I'll tell Dordy to fire your ass."

I glanced at Tria, saw the confusion in her eyes, and knew there was nothing good in the slightest coming of this. What was an amusing little catfight had turned into something that I found extraordinarily uncomfortable.

"Get out," I said again. My voice was no longer raised, just blunt. "It's been four years, and that's not happening again, you hear me?"

"I've heard that particular song from you too many times," Yolanda responded.

"Go." I spoke again as I pointed at the door.

"Weigh in tomorrow," she said, and her tone didn't leave any room for argument. "I'm going to start watching for change, not just going over two-oh-five. You start fluctuating a lot, and I'll fuck you up. Then I'll bench you until you get your shit together."

"Whatever," I mumbled. "Get out."

The nonchalance was a total act. I definitely could not let Yolanda push me out of the cage—I needed the money now more than ever. I was actually thinking about seeing if she could find me another fight sometime during the week because the cost of two really was quite a bit more than one. Food was about the same because Tria was better at budgeting that, but the water bill had doubled, and the electricity was a little higher, too. I had also helped Tria cover the last couple of books she needed though she swore she was going to pay me back. It all equated to my being broke. The few hundred dollars I normally kept for emergencies was down to about twenty bucks.

"We're not done here," Yolanda said with a shake of her finger—pointed in my direction this time. "Don't you dare be late tomorrow, either!"

She left without another word, and my ass found its way back to the couch.

"What did she mean about you making yourself sick?" Tria asked as soon as the door closed.

"Nothing," I said. "She just exaggerates."

"That didn't sound like exaggerating," Tria said. "She's really pissed off."

"It's nothing," I repeated. I tried to lie back down on the couch, but she wasn't letting this go.

"Liam, don't bullshit me." Tria came over and sat down on the couch, pushing my knees a bit so there was room for her. "What did she mean by all of that?"

As I looked up at her, for the very briefest of moments, I considered telling her the truth.

Then I thought better of it.

"Nothing you haven't heard before," I said. "I told you what I used to do—fasting, running until I puked, laxatives—all that shit. It makes you sick if you do it too much. Yolanda always gets pissed off if she thinks I'm doing that. She just worries too much. That's all."

Tria looked at me with narrowed eyes, and I did my best to hold my gaze steady. She seemed about to start questioning me again, so I quickly piped up.

"If she had actually walked in when I was shoving my face full of that stuff, she probably would have broken the dish over my head! It still would have been worth it because your cooking is awesome."

Her lips smashed together, and she held in a laugh as she stood up and headed back to the kitchen to finish up the dishes. Feeling guilty about the out-and-out lie I had just told her, I forced myself to my feet so I could help. She didn't mention Yolanda or what she said again, and I relaxed as we cleaned up and watched a bunch of shit on TV before we got ready for bed.

Awkward time again.

I straddled the windowsill to smoke. It was cold outside, and I was only in my sweats and a light T-shirt. Even Krazy Katie had brought out a sleeping bag for warmth. She was sitting with it all wrapped up around her, a stack of cigarette butts in front of her, and the soft lyrics of "Kumbaya" coming out of her mouth.

I kept quiet, hoping she wouldn't decide to sing any louder. Her singing voice was fucking awful. One night last spring, she decided to sing the entire first Wham! album in the middle of the night, and I almost called the cops myself.

Tria came out of the bathroom just as I was finishing up and climbing back in the window. She wrapped her arms around herself and shivered a bit.

"Sorry," I said. "I probably should have just walked outside—I wasn't thinking."

"No, no. I don't want you changing how you do things just because I'm here. I'm in the way enough as it is."

"You aren't in the way," I told her, dismissing the comment.

She huffed out her nose but didn't respond to my remark. We both climbed into bed in silence without looking at each other at all. We always started out on our backs though neither of us ever fell asleep that way. I fluffed up my pillow and leaned against it. After a few deep breaths, I reached my arm up and across the top of her pillow, and Tria moved over to rest her head on my shoulder.

"There is a job that just opened up at the library on campus,"

Tria said as she settled against me.

"Oh yeah?" I replied. She hadn't mentioned looking for jobs while she studied her ass off for her midterms, but I figured she would start looking before too long. It was going to be a lot easier with both of us bringing in money even if she only worked a few hours.

"I was thinking I would apply for it," she said. I felt her shoulders rise into a shrug. "It seems to pay all right, and if I can get enough hours, I wouldn't be in your hair anymore."

"What the fuck does that mean?" I asked.

"If I can get enough hours, I can get my own apartment again, and I wouldn't have to keep mooching off of you."

"You aren't," I told her *again*. "You do all kinds of shit around here to earn your keep."

I snickered a little.

"I cost you money," she stated.

"Not much." I shrugged. "And you do a lot for me."

"It's not money, though."

"I don't need it," I lied. "It's all good."

"I can't be in your way forever!" She was insistent.

"You aren't in the way," I insisted right back at her.

"I have to be able to support myself," she said.

"Says who?" I asked. "I bet if you checked some stats on it, you would find most college students are not living on their own."

"Most college students have Mom and Dad paying for the dorm."

"Yeah, okay," I agreed, "but those who aren't on campus are living with roommates, and even those in the dorms are usually sharing a room."

My logic appeared to be working.

"I don't want to be a burden," she said softly.

"You aren't," I told her.

"You said you had always lived on your own though," she reminded me. "I have to be…cramping your style."

I laughed.

"Using that phrase is so unstylish, it can't cramp anything."

"That made no sense at all!" Tria laughed. "Maybe you need to do a little studying with me. At least read some of my English books."

"Nah," I said. "I rarely have to rely on loquaciousness in the cage."

Tria lifted her head to look me in the eye with raised brows.

"You dropped out of high school?" she asked for clarification.

"Being a dropout doesn't mean I'm stupid," I said.

"Obviously."

She put her head back down on my chest, and I pulled her in a little closer before speaking again.

"Get the job if you want," I said, "but you don't have to move out. It will be easier for both of us if you stay, with or without a job. Besides, I…"

My voice trailed off. I wasn't sure what I wanted to say that wasn't going to equate to wanting to get between her legs, even though that wasn't the real reason. Well, not all of it anyway.

"You what?" she asked quietly when I didn't continue.

"I'm used to you being here now," I admitted. "It's nice to have someone to talk to and someone to watch movies with me. I don't want you to leave."

Well, that remark put it all out there.

"Okay," she finally whispered. "If that's what you really want, I'll stay."

I hoped my relief wasn't too obvious.

"I also don't want to go back to subsisting on cheese sandwiches and breakfast cereal."

Tria laughed and playfully smacked my chest.

"Ow!" I cried as I grabbed her hand and held it flat against my skin. I could feel my heart pounding through both of our hands. "No beating the pillow."

"You make a good pillow," she said.

I had no idea how to respond to that, and Tria didn't seem to be inclined to say anything else, so we dropped into silence. Mostly I was just glad she didn't seem to be planning on leaving quite so soon anymore. Maybe now she would actually unpack something.

I was never one for sharing my life with anyone else, but thinking about Tria leaving hurt my chest.

# CHAPTER SIXTEEN
## Fear the Worst

A damn good left hook sent me to the floor on my back.

A second later, there was a big black guy with a long, dreaded goatee on top of me, slamming punch after punch into my face. I kneed him, kidney punched him, and tried to get a leg wrapped around him so I could flip us over, but most of my efforts were concentrated on protecting my head.

The guy was an animal.

Screaming from the crowd filled my ears, and with a final shove I managed to flip us over. Where my arm had been defensively protecting my face, it was now in the perfect position to move over his throat and cut off his airway. He kept punching feebly until he passed out, and I got up off the floor.

Yolanda's hand was wrapped around my wrist and holding my arm up high as she announced my victory and pulled me back to the locker room.

"You need stitches." She made the decision as soon as the door was closed. "It's more than I can do here. I need to take you to the

ER."

"Fuck that," I muttered, but then I realized the gauze she had given me only seconds before was already soaked through, and there was a decent trickle of blood running from my temple down the side of my face and down to my shoulder.

"You are bleeding a lot," she said. "You are going to the hospital."

It didn't happen often, but I knew once those words were out of her mouth, I wasn't going to have much of a choice. She helped me get my clothes on and dragged me out the back door to her car.

"I don't have the money," I informed her.

"I got it," she said. "This one's on me."

Friday night, and the hospital was a fucking zoo. We waited for about two hours before anyone was available to look at me, and then they decided I wasn't bad off, and I could wait longer. I borrowed some change from Yolanda and tried to call Tria a couple of times, but oddly enough, the phone rang busy. Neither of us had cell phones, and the landline was unreliable.

By the time my temple was stitched and Yolanda dropped me off at home, it was almost six in the morning. I was pretty much the walking dead at that point, and my head pounded despite the maximum dose of ibuprofen the nurse had given me.

Yolanda wouldn't let her give me anything stronger.

The key didn't seem to want to go into the lock, but I figured the fatigue-blurred vision was mainly to blame. Before I managed to get it in, I heard Tria's voice on the other side.

"Liam? Is that you?"

"Yeah, it's me," I called through the door. "I tried to call—"

The door opened, and Tria's eyes scanned me, and she reached out to pull me inside by my hands. She led me over to the couch, where she sat me down and turned the side lamp a bit so she could see me better.

"Oh my God," she mumbled. "Can this day get any worse?"

"I'm all good," I assured her. "Just needed some stitches, and the emergency room was packed."

"You have blood all over you," she informed me. "Give me your shirt, or it won't come out."

I unbuttoned my shirt and pulled my arms out of the sleeves. I winced a bit and looked down at my shoulder where there was a pretty good-sized bruise forming.

"You lost, didn't you?" Tria assumed from my appearance there could be no other conclusion.

"Nope," I replied. "I told you—I always win."

I grinned at her, but she didn't return the smile.

"Your T-shirt, too," Tria said. "It's got blood on it as well. My God, how many stitches did you need?"

"Only seven," I said. "It really isn't that bad. Head cuts bleed a lot."

I pulled off the white T-shirt I had under the other one, and Tria collected them both from me. She took them into the kitchen where I could hear her running water over them. I leaned over the arm of the couch and closed my eyes.

I don't know how long I remained passed out on the couch, only that I awoke to Tria's voice and figured out pretty quickly that she must be talking on the phone. It was odd because I didn't recall her ever getting any phone calls before.

"I know what you are saying... just...just let me talk to her, okay?"

I tried to open my eyes, but the bright light coming in through the window was blinding and made my head pound. I closed them again immediately.

"Five minutes, that's it...fine..."

There was a longer pause, and then a change in Tria's tone.

"You don't have to do this," she said quickly. "I'll find a way to come and get you...but...I know that, but...if you stay...yes... yes..."

She sighed heavily.

"Your grades didn't suck that bad...I know, but I can't help but try to find a way...are you sure?"

I heard her sit down heavily on one of the kitchen chairs. Even though I didn't really understand what she was talking about, there was something about her tone I didn't like at all. Partially covering my eyes with my hands, I sat up and looked through the cracks in my fingers until my eyes got used to the sunlight.

"If you are sure," Tria was saying. "No...no way. I wouldn't dream of it. I'll be there....not sure yet, but I'll figure it out...love you, too...No, I don't want to talk to him again. I'll find you when I get there. Bye for now."

I rubbed at my eye and accidentally rubbed against the bandage over the stitches. I winced and hissed through my teeth.

"How are you feeling?" Tria asked as she hung up the phone in the kitchen and came over to sit on the edge of the couch.

"I'm good," I replied. I wasn't sure if I believed it myself, but it seemed like the best response to give. "Had a lot worse, that's for sure."

"Well, you look terrible," Tria said.

"Thanks," I said with a wry grin. "What time is it?"

"Just past noon," she told me.

"Still Saturday?"

"Yes." Tria shook her head at me.

"Hey, you never know!" I would have laughed, but I was afraid it would hurt my head if I tried.

"You sure you are all right?" she asked again, her voice full of concern.

"I'm fine," I said. "Really."

She looked me over, and I could see her gaze fluctuating between my eyes. I wasn't sure what she was looking to find, but apparently she found it. She gave me a quick nod and then tried to kill me with her next sentence.

"Good," she stated, "because I have to go home."

I knew the whole "life passing before your eyes" was only supposed to happen when you were faced with death, but that didn't stop the last few weeks from running through my head in a matter of seconds. Everything from when I saw her surrounded by those animals in the street, to feeling her hand press against my chest when I confronted her douchebag ex, to wrapping her up in my arms the previous night, flashed in my brain as I considered what she was saying.

She was leaving.

Going home.

"What the fuck?" I yelled, which made my head pound more and made Tria startle. "What the fuck are you talking about? Going home? What are you doing, dropping out of school?"

As much as I wanted to think school was the main concern, what I really wanted to know was why she was leaving me. Had I done something to piss her off? I didn't think so, but I'd pissed people off before without realizing it, so anything was possible. Maybe it was the fighting. Maybe she was realizing with the way I looked, the other guy must look a lot worse.

*Maybe she found some of that shit I still have shoved into the back of that dresser drawer.*

More than anything, I didn't want her to go. I was just starting to think that maybe, just maybe, we could be more. Maybe Yolanda was right, and it was time for me to take a chance again.

I hadn't even tried to kiss her.

"No, no," Tria said with a shake of her head. "Nothing like that —just for a few days."

Well, at least my heart was pumping blood again, but that just fueled my anger.

"Did Douchebag call and tell you to come back? And you're listening to him? You said before he was going to try to come up with a reason for you to go back there so he could keep you from leaving again, and now you are going to let him?"

"It's not him." Tria shook her head back and forth. "It's Nikki."

"Who the hell is Nikki?" I asked. I was suddenly annoyed that we did very little talking to each other about our lives.

"She's my best friend," Tria said softly. "She was there for me when I needed her. I can't turn my back on her. Without her, I wouldn't even be here."

I stared at her for a moment, watching the wetness coating her cheeks as it glistened in the light from the lamp.

"She got you out of there," I said. It wasn't a question.

Tria nodded.

"I knew I couldn't leave without a big confrontation. Keith had already told me that he wasn't going to put up with my moving away. He even tore up the acceptance letter from Hoffman when he found it. I had been so happy when I got it, and he just tore it up!"

Tria leaned forward and put her face in her hands.

"He wasn't going to let go," she said, "even though I told him I wasn't seeing him anymore. Even though I told him I wanted to go to school, he wouldn't drop it. I shoved all my stuff in my dad's old suitcases and ran to Nikki. She took me up near the Canadian border where her cousin lives. They were all on some extended fishing trip up to New Brunswick, so she hid me there until I could arrange to come down here."

"I had a little bit of money after Dad died," Tria continued. "I had been working at one of the local stores after high school and saved a bunch of that as well. I used it for the deposit on the apartment and the bus ticket. Nikki kept lying to Keith and Leo until I could move here, saying she didn't know where I was. Her husband, Brandon, is one of Keith's buddies. He was harassing her, too, but she still wouldn't tell anyone."

She raised her head and looked at me.

"I can't just abandon her," she stated definitively. "I can't, not when they're going to…"

"Going to what?" I asked when she didn't go on.

"I'm not supposed to tell anyone," she said. Her voice was reserved, but I wasn't going to give in that easily.

"What the fuck?" I snarled. "You can't say something like that and then not finish."

"I know," she responded quietly. "But I think I heard it about five thousand times when I was growing up. No one outside the community was ever supposed to hear about the legends and rituals of the area."

"About *what*?" Nothing she was saying made any sense.

"Well, she and Brandon have been married almost two years," Tria said. "They'd been trying to have a baby, but nothing has happened."

"Okay." I frowned. I understood why that might be upsetting for a couple, but that shit happened all the time. Usually it wasn't anything serious.

"The doctor doesn't think there is anything wrong with her, so they checked Brandon out. He has low sperm count or something. He isn't going to be able to father any children."

"Well, there are other options, right?" I had the sinking feeling I was missing a major point.

"I told you," Tria said, "the community is shrinking. She has to have a baby from the Beals community."

"So, who is going to father the kid?"

"All of them." Tria's eyes met mine, and she nodded to me slowly as I comprehended what she was saying. "They'll just keep going until she's pregnant."

The implications of her words slammed into me, and images from a website Wade had found once rocketed around in my brain. It featured this chick lying back in a chair while a line of guys waited to fuck her. What I had considered kind of interesting at the time now seemed thoroughly sickening.

I was never one to bash another culture, but this was just fucked up.

# CHAPTER SEVENTEEN
## Kiss the Girl

For the next hour, Tria explained how the Beals council had determined the best way to make sure their culture and way of life continued, which was to make sure every couple had many children. There was a minimum of three required because you couldn't just replace yourselves. You had to add to the population. Since then, any couple who didn't have the allotted number of kids was "helped out" by the rest of the community—either by making a surrogate mother available to carry a child for a woman who wasn't fertile or by making sure any fertile woman was impregnated by some man from Beals.

Husband or not.

Apparently they had been doing it for generations, which meant more and more often, the children they did have were more closely related to each other than the generation before, and their numbers were beginning to dwindle again. Cousins marrying cousins was common enough, but they were starting to have other relations intermingle as well.

"Brandon is technically Nikki's uncle," Tria told me. She sat down opposite me on the couch and handed me a refilled glass of apple juice. "They aren't so far apart in age—her grandmother had him just a few years before Nikki's mother gave birth to her. She says she loves him, but there is part of me that thinks it's just because she was brought up there."

"You were brought up there, too. So why aren't you doing the same thing?"

"I certainly heard it enough," Tria said. "But things were always different for me."

"Because you weren't born there?" I asked.

"Well…partially," she said as she cringed. "I mean, I obviously didn't fit in with everyone else. I was…*accepted*…but with reluctance, you know?"

I didn't, but I nodded anyway.

"Leo is the leader of the council, so whatever he says goes. He said I was his daughter, so everyone kind of had to accept me. Still, I knew I was different, and even though I was young when it happened, I still remembered living outside of Beals with my mom and then in foster care. Even my dad was more a fringe member of the community."

"What would your dad have thought of all this?" I wondered aloud.

"I don't think he would have approved," Tria said as she shook her head. "I know there were a lot of things he and Leo disagreed about, and sometimes they even argued. I don't think Dad knew about a lot of the things the council decided. It doesn't matter now, though. I have to go back."

Tria had to physically stop me from grabbing my jacket and heading out the door.

"What are you doing?" she cried.

"I'm going to find that fuckhead Harrison and do what I told him I'd do—shove his severed dick down his throat!"

"Liam! You don't even know where he is!"

"I know how to read a fucking map!" I shook my arm to get her hand off me.

"You can't just drive up there and beat him up!"

"Why not?"

"Well," Tria said as she tilted her head to the side, "you don't own a car for starters."

Ok, I had to give her that point. I ran my hand through my hair and huffed out a breath. I let her take hold of my arm again and lead me back to the couch.

"I can take care of it," Tria said.

"How exactly are you going to do that—blunt object or firearm?"

"Keith doesn't matter." She shook her head and looked down at her hands in her lap. "This is about Nikki. I have to go back. I need to be there for her."

"No, you don't," I said. I placed my glass on the coffee table and sat on the edge of the couch cushion. I turned myself sideways to face her. "Don't go back."

"I can't just ignore what's going on with her," she told me. "Nikki is going to go through with this, and she wants me there."

It all sounded like a bunch of bullshit to me.

"It's just that douchebag's way to get you back there so he can keep you from returning."

"I wouldn't put it past him," she agreed. "I'm sure he knows I would do anything for Nikki. Still, it's not like he can keep me from leaving."

I raised an eyebrow at her. She didn't believe a word she was saying, and it showed.

"I have to go," she whispered. "Nikki risked everything for me. I owe her."

I stood up.

"I'm going with you." I felt myself stand just a little taller, the decision solidifying my resolve. There was no way I was going to have her go halfway across the country on her own. There was no way I was going to let her be that far away from me with that asshole in the vicinity.

"Don't be ridiculous," Tria muttered as she shook her head.

"Don't fucking say that!" I exploded. "I fucking hate it when you say that! I'm going with you!"

"You most certainly are not!" she yelled right back at me. She stood up and placed her fists on her hips. "I'm not going to go there to help Nikki just to end up having to play interference between you and Keith the whole time!"

"I won't start anything," I promised. I might not start anything, but I'd end it, and "starting" was kind of a subjective thing. If he happened to look at me wrong, well, that would be like him starting something.

"My ass," Tria replied. She grabbed both empty glasses and headed into the kitchen.

I followed her and watched her carefully wash each of the glasses before she grabbed a towel to dry them inside and out. She seemed to be taking extra care to get every single drop of water off of them before putting them in the cabinet. When she turned to me and glared with her arms crossed, her breath came out in a huff that moved her hair around.

"I'm going," I repeated.

"No."

"Not up for debate," I told her. I crossed my arms over my chest to show her I could be just as damn stubborn as she was. "I swear, I'll be something that vaguely resembles a gentleman up until he starts acting like a douchebag."

I hoped and prayed that he would act up because even the smallest excuse would allow me to beat the ever-loving shit out of him. That thought put a genuine smile on my face.

"I can already see you plotting inside that head of yours," she told me. "Absolutely not."

"Why not? Give me one decent reason that isn't outweighed by the dozen I can come up with that will tell you not to go by yourself."

"Liam!" Tria threw her hands up in the air and turned around to walk back into the living room. She stopped at the juncture between the two rooms and leaned against the wall there with her arms still crossed. "What am I supposed to say? My roommate followed me across the country to pay his respects to someone he never met?"

I hadn't really considered what they might think of the whole thing because I didn't give a flying fuck. Tria, of course, was concerned. Her concern was going to be enough to convince her I shouldn't go. If she wouldn't let me go with her, and she ended up back there alone, I wouldn't be able to get a hold of her. She might be brainwashed into staying with them, marrying Douchebag, and having his demon spawn.

Fuck no.

"So, tell them something else," I heard myself say.

"Like what?" She snorted. "That you just stopped by to pick up some fresh lobster?"

While I was ignoring the obvious sarcasm, my mouth took off without consulting me first.

"Tell them I'm your boyfriend."

Holy shit.

From top to bottom, my body stilled completely.

"Don't be ri—"

I tilted my head to one side and glared at her, halting the rest of that hated phrase. Tria bit down on her lower lip like she was trying to hold in whatever she wanted to say next by sheer force of her teeth. When she did speak again, I could barely hear her.

"I can't just...just..."

"Just what?" I asked. I managed to remember my feet were mobile, and I took a step toward her. As I moved forward, Tria took a step backward until she was pressed firmly against the wall.

"I can't just lie to them!" She looked distressed at the very idea.

"Besides being a shitty liar, I can't act to save my life. I can't pretend we're in a relationship when we're not!"

I moved forward again, and she tried to move back but had nowhere to go. Her heels were pressed against the baseboards, and her fingers touched the pale drywall behind her. In the back of my mind, I realized even when I made the suggestion that she wouldn't be able to do it. I knew she couldn't lie. You couldn't live with someone for a month and not figure that out.

"So don't lie."

My skin tingled as if I were on the edge of a storm front. Hell, maybe I was. I could have been standing at the top of a fjord or the edge of the Grand Canyon. I could have been stepping from Apollo 11 onto the surface of the moon.

She didn't move but stared at me with her eyes widening as I moved closer. Slowly, I placed my hands against the wall on either side of her head. My body angled over the top of hers, and I bent my elbows to bring myself closer to her face.

"What do you mean?" she asked in a choked whisper.

"Don't lie," I repeated.

I leaned in closer to her. My gaze drifted from her eyes to her mouth and then back again. I waited for her lips to part to tell me to stop, but all she did was moisten them quickly with her tongue. I brought my head close to hers—almost touching—and paused again. She lowered her eyes to my mouth, her lips parted slightly, and I could see her chest moving faster with her rapid breathing. I didn't need any further prompting.

I pressed my lips to hers, and everything else in the world ceased to exist.

There was no kitchen or living room in a crappy little apartment on the shit side of town. There were no roommates for the sake of financial security or convenience. I wasn't a fighter ignoring life around him, and she wasn't a college student trying to make the world a better place. There was no sordid background, no fucked up customs, no douchebag ex-boyfriends.

There was me, and there was her, and there was us.

Her mouth was warm, soft, and far more enticing than my fantasies had ever been. I felt her hand against my chest and feared she would push me away, but she didn't. Her hand moved up slowly over the fabric of my T-shirt and rested against my shoulder as I tilted my head and kissed her again.

Gently.

Slowly.

Even with the unhurried pace, I broke away breathless with my head spinning. My eyes met hers, and I was sure she felt what I was feeling. Without any more pause, I brought our lips together again eagerly and opened my mouth to find her tongue with mine. I moved my hand from the wall to the side of her face, and I tilted her head to kiss her more deeply. She moaned into my mouth, and her taste was nothing short of divine. Finally I slowed, savoring the flavor of her mouth before stopping a moment. I didn't open my eyes but leaned my body into her.

"Don't lie," I whispered against her lips.

"I won't," she responded, and her hand moved up higher to pull tightly against the back of my head as she brought us together again.

I reached down and lifted her up by her thighs so I was holding her against the wall where I could reach her better. She wrapped her legs around my waist, and I moved against her—no longer trying to hide the desire I felt for her as my cock grew and pressed between her legs. Her fingers gripped the back of my head as she turned to meet my lips from another angle.

Hoisting her up a little more, I leaned back and carried her out of the living room, into the hall, and through the bedroom door. In a single motion, I laid her down on the bed and covered her body with mine, never allowing our lips to part in the process. It was like curling up beside her while she slept, only better.

With her supported by the bed, my hands could occupy themselves with something other than holding her up. I slid them up her thighs and over her hips, and I realized just how long it had been since I had felt the smooth curves of a woman's body in my hands. I felt the warmth of bare skin with my fingers as they reached the top of her jeans, and I slid my hand inside.

Tria moaned into my mouth, and her hands moved to my shoulders. She gripped me for a moment before her fingers moved down to my chest. I braced myself against the bed with one hand while the other moved up her side, feeling the soft flesh underneath her shirt and searching for more. I shifted my hips against hers in an instinctive rhythm.

She pressed her hands more firmly against my chest, and I moved to suck at the skin of her neck as my hand reached for her breast. I felt her breath against the side of my head as her fingers dug into my skin, pushing harder now.

"Liam, stop!"

I froze, and my blood pooled in my feet as I came to the understanding of where I was, what I was doing, and with whom.

*She's a virgin.*

I had to lock every muscle to keep my body from continuing down the sordid path it wanted to take on its way to fulfill every shower-dream I had experienced since I met her. I squeezed my eyes shut and forced my hands flat against the mattress before I shoved up and away from her body.

"I'm sorry," she whispered.

"Don't be," I said. "Just, um…give me a minute."

When I pushed myself up and off of her, I rolled over to my back as she sat up and wrapped her arms around her shoulders. I could feel her looking down at me but didn't meet her gaze. I willed my cock to stop throbbing both painfully and obviously in my pants, but the moody little bastard wasn't listening. My heart was beating too fast in my chest, and my hands were aching to run over her skin, but I knew I couldn't do that—I *still* couldn't do that.

The thought was more than I could take.

"Going outside," I said as I shoved myself off the bed.

I glanced at her long enough to see her nod her head before I left the room. I walked out into the living room and grabbed my smokes out of my jacket pocket before running out the door and down the stairs. I lit the cigarette before I ever got outside and then leaned against the edge of the fire escape as I blew the smoke up into the overcast sky.

I closed my eyes and tried to figure out how I had gone and managed to do exactly what I told myself I wasn't going to do. I wasn't going to put her in this position. I wasn't going to get in the way of her life. I wasn't going to make a move on her and fuck up this little arrangement we had.

I tried not to feel as if what she had done and said was a rejection, but the thought bounced around in my head anyway.

I tossed the butt into the street and started to run. As I ran, the skies went from overcast to raining down on me. First, there was just a sprinkle and then a downpour before I made it to the tree. Circling the tree made me think of Thanksgiving dinner, and that just pissed me off some more.

I'd fucked up royally.

Taking back what I had done was impossible. I kissed her. I didn't just kiss her but hauled her into bed and would certainly be fucking her right now if she hadn't pushed me away. This was everything I said I wasn't going to do, and now it was too late to take it back. I couldn't just pretend I didn't want in her panties because I wasn't much better at lying than she was.

Picking up speed, I turned the corner around an old steel plant and saw our building. The rain ceased as quickly as it had started, leaving nothing but cold mist in the air. The back of my thigh was cramping up, and I was breathing too hard. Smoking before running, combined with the lack of warming up, was not a great idea. I slowed before I got to the grate that marked three miles and coasted to a stop right in front of the building. I leaned over with my hands on my knees and coughed a couple of times before reaching behind my leg and rubbing at the cramped muscle.

"Fucking hell," I muttered. I stood up straight, reached my hands up over my head, and then leaned against the broken security door so I could stretch the muscle. A crow landed above me on the ineffective streetlamp outside the building, tilted its head, and cawed at me.

"Fuck you," I snapped at the nasty black bird. It squawked again and apparently captured the attention of Krazy Katie.

"The birds of leaving call to us," she sang down at me. "Yet here we stand endowed with a fear of flight."

I glared up at her.

"Shut up, you crazy bitch."

She just laughed in response and then continued with her babble.

"The winds of change consume the land, while we remain in the shadow of summers now past."

Raising both hands, I flipped both her and the bird "the bird" before stomping back into the apartment building. I got up to my front door and hesitated, realizing immediately that this was exactly what I didn't want to have happen.

I was hesitating because she was in there, and I didn't know if I should go in or not. I wasn't sure just how pissed off at me she was going to be, and rightly so. I mean, I yelled at her, kissed her, dry humped her, and then ran out on her.

She probably already had her bags packed.

She wouldn't want to have anything to do with me traveling

with her. She would end up going back to Douchebag, and she wouldn't finish school. If that were the case, it meant I had pretty much fucked up her entire life because I was horny.

What an asshole.

I leaned against the wall just beside the door and held my face in my hands. My head was getting a little swimmy, and I realized my impromptu run had also left me dehydrated. Growling at myself, I straightened up and turned to open the door.

It was quiet inside.

It only took a second to see she wasn't in either the kitchen or the living room, which didn't leave me many more options. Though I would rather have hidden behind a beer at the kitchen table, I had to fix this.

How?

Convince her it was a joke? A mistake? I didn't mean it?

I wasn't completely sure I was going to be able to do that and decided maybe a bit of a stall tactic was warranted—at least long enough to grab a glass of water. Once in the kitchen, I downed it quickly, half hoping she would just appear behind me so I didn't have to walk back into the bedroom.

*Maybe she left while I was out.*

I glanced over at the suitcase that still sat, partially open, at the end of the couch, and found myself annoyed she still hadn't bothered to put anything into the dresser drawer I cleared out for her.

*Because she knew she wasn't going to stay long.*

I wanted to slam my head against the wall a few times but figured if she was still here—and she probably was—the noise would just scare her. I took a long breath to prepare myself and pushed forward. I turned the corner slowly and found Tria sitting at the edge of the bed. She looked up as soon as I came into view, and I could see redness around her eyes.

*I'm such a fucking asshole.*

"I'm sorry," I said quietly.

Tria looked away, wiped at her eyes, and then looked back at me with a fierce glare that almost sent me stumbling backward.

"For what?" she demanded. "What exactly are you sorry for?"

"For…um…for the uh…"

"For what?" she yelled louder. She stood up and walked toward me. "Tell me right now, Liam Teague! What exactly are you apologizing for because I need to figure out whether or not I'm going to slap you!"

I gulped but couldn't come up with what I should say next.

"Is that all you want, huh?" she asked as she took another step closer. She came right up to me and shoved me in the center of my chest. "Are you just hoping the convenient roommate and cook would become a convenient fuck, too? Is that it?"

I had to take a step back from the words she was hurling at me. Of all the reactions I was expecting, this wasn't even on the list.

"What…um…no!"

"So then what is it, Teague?" she said, her voice sounding like a snarl. "What are you sorry about?"

"Because of…of what I did?" I didn't mean it to sound like a question, but I wasn't really sure myself.

"Tell me!" she screeched, shoving me again. She didn't actually move me back, but I could tell she was trying to put some force into it. "Are you sorry you kissed me or sorry you ran out on me afterwards?"

Tears began to stream down her face.

I didn't know what else to do, so I told her the truth.

"I don't want to fuck up your life," I said. "I don't want you to leave because I'm an ass."

She looked up at me, and her expressive brown eyes seemed to be searching right through me and into my soul. Something told me she was going to find more there than she ever wanted to see.

"So what is it, then?" she said. Her voice was still strained but had lost its venom. "What are you so sorry about?"

"I'm not sorry I kissed you," I admitted. "I just didn't mean to —"

I couldn't finish the sentence because her arms wrapped around my neck and she pulled my mouth to hers.

I was lost.

Completely and totally lost within her.

I was fucked.

I wrapped my arms around her waist, holding her to me as she pulled my head down toward her roughly. She pushed her tongue into my mouth, and I welcomed it. She moved one of her hands from my shoulder to the top part of my arm, and then to my chest. She grabbed at the material of my shirt as she pressed her mouth against mine again.

There were so many unfamiliar emotions going through me, I didn't know what to do to comprehend them all. There was lust and desire—without a doubt—but that was expected…normal… welcomed. It was the other shit I didn't know how to process.

The fear.

Her grip on me relaxed slightly, and I held her close as my mouth moved across her jaw and down her neck. Her breath came in short gasps as her fingers tried to latch onto my hair.

"I don't do this," I whispered against her ear. "I'll just screw it up, Tria. I don't want you hurt because of me. I'm not worth taking the chance."

"Why don't you let me decide that?" she replied, and her mouth was on mine again.

I have no idea how long we stayed there, standing in the doorway, making out between the hall and the bedroom, but we were both out of breath by the time we stopped. Tria pulled away first, because I might never have, and then she looked at me for a long moment.

I couldn't decide if her gaze made me feel uncomfortable or not. Eventually she sighed and then placed her cheek against my chest, leaning against me.

"I had given up, you know," she said.

"On what?"

"I didn't think you…you know…"

Pulling back a little, I looked down at her.

"I didn't what?"

"That you just weren't interested," she said with a shrug.

I let out a short, humorless laugh.

"I just didn't want to be a dick," I told her.

She tilted her head up and pressed her lips softly to the base of my throat.

"Don't run out on me like that again," she said into my neck.

"Okay," I said.

"Promise."

"I promise." My arms went around her back, and I pulled her closer against my chest. "I thought you were pissed."

"I wasn't *pissed*," she told me. "I just…wasn't ready for *that*. I can't go from roommate to lover in thirty seconds."

"Oh…um…." My voice trailed off with no direction or purpose.

"Are you going to be okay with that?" Tria asked in a small voice.

"With what?"

She let out an exaggerated sigh before looking up into my face.

"I'm not ready to have sex with you."

"Oh! That."

"Yeah, *that*."

I trailed my fingers down the side of her face.

"Whenever you're ready," I said, and I hoped I wasn't lying to her. "I'm not in any hurry."

She raised an eyebrow at me, and I shrugged in response.

"How long do you need?" I asked. "Ten minutes?"

She laughed and leaned against me. I held her tightly and rested my cheek on the top of her head, wishing I had been joking so we could both laugh. There was no doubt that I would wait, but I didn't have to like it.

"I can keep kissing you, right?" I asked for clarification.

"That sounds like a good plan," she said with a nod. "I just don't want to…"

"What?" I asked when she didn't continue.

"I know you've…been around."

I had to laugh at that one.

"Have I?"

"Well, um…I think so." She looked up at me with her eyes full of concern. "I mean, you're just so…so…"

I had to prompt her to continue.

"You're about the best looking, most built guy I have ever seen in my life!" she finally blurted out. "You have to have had hundreds of girlfriends! You could have anyone!"

More laughter. I took her hand and brought her back into the living room, figuring the bed wasn't the best place to have this sort of conversation. We sat next to each other on the couch, and I reached over to put my arm around her and bring her back to me.

Now that I had her close to me during the daylight hours, I didn't want to let her go again.

"I have only ever been in one relationship," I told her, "and that was years ago. I just…don't really do well with them. Yes, I've had hookups but no girlfriends. Not in ages."

"Why not?"

All of Yolanda's words flooded back through my head.

"Yolanda said I didn't give anyone a chance," I finally said. "I don't know if that's true or not. I just…fuck."

I unwrapped my arm from her and stood up again.

"I can't do this, Tria…I just…I'm not cut out for this!"

"For what?" she asked, and the innocent and understanding look on her face was enough to bring me down.

"I fucked up once," I said quietly. "This is where it got me. I don't give a shit about anyone or anything. I'm just…*here*, Tria. What can you possibly see in that?"

"Why?"

Even if she could have convinced me she would listen without judgment, I couldn't have told her.

"I'm not going to tell you," I said bluntly. "That's part of the shit you'd have to deal with."

She stared at me for a good long time, then reached out and pulled me back to the couch beside her. She slid her hand up my arm and reached out to touch my face.

"You don't see yourself very clearly, Liam," she told me, "but it doesn't matter, not right now, at least."

"What does that mean?"

"You tell me," she said. She focused on my eyes and didn't waver. "Do you want to try to do this?"

"What if I fuck it up?" I asked.

"How about we deal with the present first and worry about shit that might happen later?"

I licked my lips and tasted her on them.

"I guess so," I said.

"Very convincing."

"I told you I don't know how to do this shit."

"I'm not so sure I know how to do 'this shit,' either," Tria said, "but I'm willing to try. Are you?"

I nodded.

"And as much as I would like to spend the next few days figuring it out with you, I have to figure out how to get home. Nikki needs me there."

"First things first, huh?"

"Something like that."

"So, when is all this shit supposed to go down?" I asked.

"The day after tomorrow," she said. "Actually…um…there is a bit of a problem."

"What? Just one?" I said with a halfhearted laugh.

"Well, one big one," she said. "The bus fare."

"What about it?"

"Um…I don't have it," she replied quietly.

"Oh…um…shit." I lay back on the couch cushions.

"I've got about four dollars at the moment," Tria clarified.

"I don't have much more than that," I admitted. "I had to get an advance from Dordy yesterday to cover rent. I ended up bringing in about fifty bucks last night."

"Shit."

"Yeah."

"The ticket to get here was a hundred and seventy-five dollars."

"Now we need two," I reminded her.

"You don't have to—"

"Shut it!" I rolled myself closer to her and covered her mouth with my hand. "I'm going. We'll figure it out."

She mumbled against my fingers until I moved my hand.

"How?" she asked.

"I'll ask around," I said. "I know a few people who have cars. Maybe I can find one who would let me borrow theirs for a few days."

"That's a big favor," Tria remarked.

"I've got a few people who owe me."

"I owe you," she said quietly. She kept her gaze on mine as she reached up and touched the edge of my jaw. I could see the beginning of a tear in the corner of her eye, and I leaned down to kiss it away.

"You cry too much," I told her.

"I can't help it," she said with a shrug.

The salty liquid on my lips was quickly covered by her mouth. She gripped my shoulders, and I ran my hand up her side. I felt her shiver under my touch and wondered if this could be enough for me.

I was never one to take it slow, but Tria might be worth the restraint.

# CHAPTER EIGHTEEN
## Take the Trip

I dropped the phone back down and sighed.

"Any luck?"

I glanced up at Tria, paused for a second, and then shook my head.

"People who say they owe you one later are full of shit," I told her. "I got three flat out no ways, two offering to let me borrow a car next week, and one who just laughed. The best I got was from Dordy himself, who has an old motorcycle he said I could use."

"Well, let's do that!" Tria said.

I huffed out a breath.

"To be completely honest, I have never ridden one—not even on the back. I haven't even been on a bicycle since I was a kid. I don't think I've got time to figure it out before we have to leave, and I don't want to splatter us both all over the highway."

It was a little embarrassing to admit it, but it was better than a remake of *Blood Runs Red on the Highway*.

"Oh!" Tria said with widened eyes. "That's okay—I can ride."

A deeper glow of sex appeal surrounded her as those words left her mouth.

"You can?" My arms and legs tensed, and for a moment I knew exactly what it felt like to be a cat ready to pounce on its prey.

"Yes, I can," she said, and her cheeks reddened as she looked away. "I had a motorcycle back in Maine. A snowmobile, too. In the winter, it's the only way to get around."

Between her words, the blush, and the sheer amount of testosterone coursing through my system, I couldn't take any more. I lowered my eyes as I moved across the room toward her. Tria glanced back at me and took a slight step backwards as I approached. She opened her mouth slightly as I grabbed her, lifted her up, and pressed her against the wall. I crushed my lips to hers.

"You have any idea how hot that is?" I asked against her mouth.

"Do you have a thing for this wall?" She giggled.

"Maybe," I shrugged. "I didn't before, but it's definitely growing on me."

Tria chuckled against me, causing her to shake a little in my arms. She reached around my neck and used her index finger to brush the hair on the back of my head up in a little line. She tilted her head to see her fingers better as she repeated the motion, causing the short hairs to fan out backwards. I raised an eyebrow at her.

"I've wanted to do that since you got your hair cut," she said with a blush.

"Why?" I gave her a look.

"I don't know," she said. "It just looked like it would feel cool."

"Does it?"

"Yes," she said with a wide grin, "it does."

After we collected the bike from Dordy, we decided on an early morning start. As if going to sleep with her hadn't already been awkward enough, the tension was about ten times greater as we climbed into the bed, facing a completely new situation.

I just wanted to fuck her hard and fast and then roll up against her and go to sleep, and I was pretty sure that wasn't what she had in mind.

Like we did on most nights, we came together in the center of the bed and I wrapped an arm around her shoulders. After that, it was like we didn't know what to do next. A few hours ago, I had her pinned down against the very same mattress and was seriously considering popping her cherry.

Fuck! There had to be something wrong with me.

The problem was, I wasn't sure if there was something wrong with me because of what I had done or what I hadn't done. In all actuality, I had completely forgotten her lack of experience. I hadn't been with a virgin since I was one myself, and I knew I couldn't push her too hard or too fast. I was going to have to let her set the pace.

"Tria?" I said softly into the darkness.

"Hmm?"

"I...um...shit," I muttered. "I don't know how to say this."

"Just say it."

"Okay." I huffed through my nose. "I want you. I want you *now*."

I felt her stiffen a little.

"I know you're not ready for all that," I added quickly. "I just want to be clear. I'll wait. I'll wait as long as you want, but unless you set the ground rules, I'm going to fuck up because I...well...I want you as soon as you're ready for it. Shit, this isn't coming out right."

"I think I know what you mean."

"So...ground rules?"

"In the morning," she replied with a yawn. "I have to sleep on it."

I wanted to *sleep on it*. Or in it.

Instead, I just nodded. Eventually, I closed my eyes, and before

I even realized I was asleep, the alarm was going off, and Tria was jumping out of the bed to shower and make breakfast. I had to jerk off quickly and quietly while she was in the bathroom because the very thought of her naked body so close to me, combined with the remembered taste of her mouth, drove me up the fucking wall.

After I dressed, we made quick work of breakfast, and before I knew it, I had my arms wrapped around Tria's waist and my head tucked against her shoulder as we flew down the highway at seventy miles an hour. At first, I loved the way she looked on the bike, and I loved having her nestled between my legs with my arms wrapped around her middle, but the novelty wore off quickly. I knew a lot of people who really liked motorcycles, but I also knew within the first two hours that I wasn't one of them. I tried not to think about the other seventeen hours of travel that Tria seemed to think we could do in one day, arriving in Beals in the wee hours of Monday morning.

My ass did not agree.

We stopped every couple of hours so we could both stretch and get something to eat or drink. Unlike being in a car, we couldn't really talk to each other to help pass the time. The helmets we wore were basic ones and definitely not tricked out with two-way radios or anything like that. Tria was very determined to get there as quickly as possible, so we mostly stopped at rest stops along the highway just to keep the momentum going.

Tria had just come back from using the facilities right off the highway while I hung out and smoked near the motorcycle. We both got on the bike—her in front, me in the back—and I was finishing up my smoke before putting the helmet back on. There were three guys getting off their own bikes next to us, and one of them looked over in our direction.

"What kind of man lets the chick drive the bike?" The dude sneered.

I tensed, and Tria followed suit, knowing I wasn't going to just let it go.

"Liam..." she said softly.

"Hush," I responded. I took a last drag off my cigarette, flicked the butt across the parking lot, and got off the bike. I walked over to the asshole slowly and with purpose—my eyes right on his. Once I was chest-to-chest with him, I tilted my head slightly to one side and spoke.

"A pretty fucking confident one," I told him.

He took a slight step back and glanced at his buddies, who seemed to be letting him deal with his own issues, sans backup. Didn't matter to me—none of the three looked like they could take a real punch. I flinched forward slightly, balling my fists and moving like I was going to strike. He managed to fall down as he jumped back.

His buddies laughed as I got back on the bike behind Tria. Even she was snickering slightly as we placed our helmets on our heads and headed back down the highway. Moments later, my ass was numb from the vibrations again, and I was bored out of my fucking mind.

The only thing that was even remotely interesting about the ride was Tria's position between my legs. Unfortunately, I couldn't even enjoy that with the constant rumble of the bike, the swift wind around us, and the general uncomfortable nature of the whole thing.

About a thousand years later, we reached Portland and fueled up with what little cash we had scraped together. I honestly wasn't sure how we were going to find the gas money to get home, but I was also a lot more interested in hitchhiking than I was in riding the bike at that point. My ass felt as if it had just gone ten rounds with a heavyweight, and Tria didn't even seem like she was still awake as she replaced the gas nozzle on the pump.

"We need to find a place to sleep," I told her.

"I'm good," she mumbled. "It's only about five more hours."

"Bullshit," I growled. "You don't even look like you can walk any more, and my thighs feel like I've had a large vibrating vehicle between them for the past ten hours. I'm pretty sure my ass is going to fall right off if we go another hour."

Tria reluctantly agreed, and we checked out a few of the standard motels right off the highway, but we couldn't afford any of them. I finally had to start trying the less recognizable names in hopes that they would give me a discount, considering the lateness of the hour.

After another hour of searching, Tria wasn't just looking like she was going to fall off the bike; she was actually starting to doze right there in the seat. There was only one last place to check at the final exit north of Portland before we were going to be out of options.

The dude at the creepy, dirty motel was less than helpful.

"We ain't that kind of place." He sneered at me as he spoke.

"Come on, dude," I begged. Yes, I had gotten to that stage. None of my threats were working. "Twenty bucks for four hours—I know you aren't full, and it's after midnight. It's practically free money."

"I told ya, we don't do that shit! Fuck the hooker behind the dumpsters at the Holiday Inn or something."

"She ain't a fucking hooker!" I yelled.

"Whatever."

I stomped out, and Tria glanced up at me, eyes drooping as I returned to the side of the bike. She must have been able to tell I had struck out again.

"It's okay," she said. "I can keep going."

"No," I said, "you can't. I didn't come out here with you just to have you fall asleep and kill us both on the fucking road."

"We're kind of out of options," she said.

"There has to be a park around here," I said. "You could at least get a couple hours while I looked after you."

"Hmm..." she mumbled. She didn't even have the alertness to

argue with me anymore.

I really needed to get her into a bed, but I was completely out of ideas. Growling at myself, I looked up into the sky and wondered if whatever deity was up there hated me. Without any obvious answer, I dropped my eyes again, and I saw a very familiar logo.

Fuck no.

Could I stoop that low?

High up in the sky, on what could have been the spike for the king's banner on top of a castle, there was a huge, neon sign. On the left side sparkled a pair of silver circles as they twisted and turned within each other, creating a spinning vortex of marketing overachievement.

It sickened me.

As I glanced over at Tria, I wondered if she could even make it the few blocks up the street to get there. She wasn't following my gaze but staring blankly at the center of one of the motorcycle's gauges. I definitely had to get her into a bed soon. She wasn't going to last a few more minutes.

Yes. For her, I could stoop that low.

"Come on," I told her. "I have a plan—just a little ways up the street, if you can still make it."

Tria nodded dumbly as I got back on the bike, which I was quite sure I hated now. We drove up a long hill, and I motioned for Tria to pull into a large parking lot and stop the bike near the front. Right between the entrance and exit drives was the tall pole with the spinning silver circles at the top.

She pulled off her helmet and looked at me out of the corner of her eye.

"If you think you are going to rob this place, I would much rather deal with a park bench than a jail cell."

"No worries," I told her. "Come on. Get that...that *thing*."

Tria pulled the Great Bag of China out of one of the

motorcycle's packs and followed me into the posh lobby of a five-star hotel. I walked straight up to the front desk and asked for the night manager. She eyed me with contempt, and I just ignored it.

With a giant, pride-swallowing sigh, I reached into my back pocket. I grabbed my wallet, pulled out a black plastic card with a pair of silver loops and a number on it, and handed it to the woman. She took it with trepidation and a scowl.

"Call your corporate office," I told her as I pointed at the card. "Then dial that extension."

She eyed me, and for a moment I thought she might just call security and have us both thrown out, but then she picked up the phone and started dialing. I could feel Tria's gaze on the back of my neck, but I didn't look in her direction. I knew I was going to be pummeled with a bunch of questions as soon as the next opportunity presented itself, and I hoped to keep just a little bit of peace for a few more minutes. With any luck, she would be too tired to harass me and would just fall asleep.

"This is who?" The lady behind the desk was speaking into the phone. "You...you mean *Michael Teague*? I mean *Mister* Teague? Oh!"

She looked back at me with astonishment.

"I'm terribly sorry, sir," she continued. "Yes, I know it's late, but...but I'm the night manager at location oh-seven-four in Portland, Maine, and there is a...um...gentleman here who handed me a card with...sir? Um..."

She leaned over to her right to look at me more closely, and I turned to show her the left side of my head. I reached up with one finger and tapped the two silver earrings hanging there.

"Yes, sir, he does. Um...tattoos?"

I sighed dramatically and turned around, then lifted my shirt to show her my back.

"Yes, sir."

I watched her eyes get wider as she listened to the voice on the other end and stared unabashedly at me. Finally, she stopped and held the receiver in my direction.

"He'd like to talk to you…"

"No," I responded as I looked back to her. "Just give me a fucking room."

She licked her lips nervously before relaying my message into the phone.

"The presidential suite? Um…of course, sir. I'll take care of it… anything he wants…of course…thank you, sir. It was a pleasure to"— she pulled the phone away from her ear and scowled at it—"speak with you," she finished. She hung up the phone and looked at us again. "I'll have you all checked in momentarily, sir."

It was pretty impressive that Tria managed to remain silent as we were handed key cards and given directions to the executive elevator of the Silver Springs Hotel. She didn't say anything as we got inside, and I pressed the button for the eighteenth floor. She managed to stay quiet all the way down the hall and to the door to the room.

Once I opened the door, she was too distracted by the room to ask any questions.

I had to admit, it was a pretty damn fine suite, all leather and cherry with a large screen television, a computer set up on the desk, and plenty of room for your own laptop if you brought one, too. There was a small hallway with doors to a closet and bathroom. There was a dining area, a living room, and large double doors that opened up to the bedroom and master bathroom. It was probably about double the square footage of our apartment.

Tria halted in the doorway for a moment and then made her way slowly inside the room. She took it all in with a couple of big sweeps of her head to the left and the right.

"Are you going to explain all this to me?" she finally asked without turning around.

"Do I have a choice?" I walked over to the refrigerator and pulled out a bottle of orange juice and a tiny bottle of vodka. I took two big swigs out of the orange juice, added the vodka to it, twisted the lid back on, and shook it up.

Tria moved to sit on the plush couch and continued to look at me pointedly.

I dropped down onto the couch next to her and took a large gulp of my screwdriver.

"Can we just make out instead?" I asked.

"Not a single lip until you tell me," she responded bluntly.

Well, damn.

"My uncle owns Silver Springs Hotels," I finally said.

"The entire chain?" Tria asked with surprise. "They're all over the place."

"A hundred and fifty or so in the States, yes," I told her. "There are a couple dozen outside the US, too."

"So, he's rich."

"Without a doubt."

"What's with the earrings?" she asked. "I thought you just wore them to look cool."

"Are you saying they don't look cool?" I smirked at her, and she blushed. "I bet they make you hot, don't they?"

"I'm not going to dignify that with an answer," Tria said all haughty.

"You don't have to," I responded, "I can just tell."

She snickered and then pondered for a minute.

"Wouldn't he…you know…give you a job? I mean, if he'll give you a suite for the night, he'd give you a job, too, wouldn't he?"

"Yeah." I shrugged and downed the rest of the bottle. I dropped it on the dark-stained coffee table, careful to avoid the coaster because I felt like being an asshole. "He's offered."

"Liam!" she exclaimed. "Don't you realize what that means?

You wouldn't have to live like that anymore!"

"Like what?" I asked, knowing full well what she meant. I was baiting her, and I didn't care. It was better she understood this now.

For a moment, she just stared at me.

"Like in that horrible neighborhood," she finally said. Her face was tight, and her eyes narrowed at me. "You wouldn't have to let people beat you up for cash."

"They don't beat me up."

She reached over and touched the spot over my eye that still held stitches.

"Really?"

"It's nothing," I responded. I pulled back a little.

"You could live better," she emphasized.

"I don't care about any of that, Tria," I informed her. "I've been there and done that, and I can tell you right now, it doesn't mean shit."

There was a long pause as I stared out the window and wondered who would be the most pissed off if I smoked in the room. There was a nice, big balcony—maybe I'd just go out there.

"What happened to you?" Tria asked quietly.

"Nothing," I said automatically.

"Bullshit."

"That's my line."

Another long pause. Just when I thought maybe she would give up, she spoke again.

"I want to know you," she told me.

"Not much to know," I replied with a little grin, which she did not return. I sighed, and then I was dumb enough to make eye contact with her. "I'm just me, Tria. I fight. I work out. I hang out with friends sometimes. That's it. I don't have anything else to give you."

"Give me your past," she whispered. "Tell me why."

I watched her look carefully at me, searching my face for answers. I felt my resolve crumble around me. I couldn't even identify the feeling; I just knew that there was a part of me that wanted her to know—to understand. There was a part of me that wanted to tell her everything.

I was never one to open up, but I could not deny those eyes.

# CHAPTER NINETEEN
## Tell the Tale

"My family has a lot of money," I told her as she moved around the suite to get ready for bed. Even though we only had the bare necessities, Tria seemed insistent on putting everything in dresser drawers and out on the bathroom counter, which I thought was pointless, at the very least. I sat on the couch, drank another screwdriver, and tried to deflect her every question.

"Not just your uncle?" Tria asked for clarification.

"No," I said, "pretty much everyone."

"How much is a lot?" she asked.

"Only my father's accountant knows," I said with fake humor.

Tria stopped placing clean clothes into the dresser long enough to stare at me. I pretended to be very interested in the condensation of the orange juice bottle.

"Are you going to elaborate?" she eventually asked.

"I wasn't planning on it," I replied. I tilted the bottle up to my lips before looking at her again. "It's really late, and you need to sleep. All this shit is way too long a story for now."

"You are just blowing me off," Tria said, the accusation hanging between us.

I couldn't really deny it because it was absolutely true. She still needed sleep, though.

"We stopped here because you were about to fall right off the bike," I reminded her. "You need to go to bed."

As long as she was moving around, she was awake, but I was pretty sure as soon as she lay down, she would doze off, and I would be saved. She crossed her arms and raised her brows at me.

"You're exhausted," I told her. "You need sleep."

"Then tell me in bed."

I rolled my eyes and got up off the couch. Tria finally relented and agreed to get herself ready for bed. I let her take the shower first while I smoked on the balcony, hung out, and flipped through the crappy cable channels offered by the hotel. I was mildly annoyed by the realization that I could rack up a huge bill on the porn pay-per-view for Michael to sort out later, but having Tria there with me made that a lot less feasible. I decided to order almost one of everything for breakfast from room service to make up for it.

Once we were both ready for bed, Tria climbed onto the plush mattress and sighed deeply. I smiled, finding the decision to come here was a good one after all. At least she was warm, safe, and comfortable. I was almost glad the other motels and shit around the city wouldn't take us because they would have been nasty. If nothing else, Michael made sure his hotels were the very definition of posh.

I climbed into bed and got into the usual position with her coiled up next to me. The bed was incredibly luxurious. The pillows were stuffed with something that felt like feathers but didn't make my nose tickle. The sheets were obviously high quality, and I felt like I was merging with a pile of clouds or some such shit. It was good, that was for sure.

It was so good, I had to lean over and kiss Tria. She responded, and she brought her hand around my head, rubbing her fingers through my hair backwards again. I trailed my hand up her side, then back down again, moving a little lower to grip her hip. I started to move around to her backside, but she stopped me.

"You never gave me ground rules," I reminded her.

"I know."

I was pretty sure I could see her cheeks darken in the subdued light. I reached out and touched the side of her face. She turned toward me, and her throat bobbed as she swallowed.

"I'm not sure what they should be," she said.

"Oh." I had to think for a minute before I responded to that. "Um...well, the kissing is okay, right?"

A little smile crossed her face, and she nodded a couple of times.

"And this is okay?" I ran my hand over the side of her face, down to her neck, and then over her arm. I took her hand and brought it up to my lips for a moment.

"Yes," she said.

I let go of her hand, and she returned it to the back of my head where she once again played with the short hairs, stroking upward, against the grain. I worked my mouth against hers, and I gently ran the tip of my tongue across her lips before reaching inside. As we kissed, I slowly caressed her side and moved over her hip. As I started to reach around to her backside, her hand left my head and reached around again to stop me.

For a moment we stopped kissing, and Tria looked to the side, not meeting my gaze. I moved my hand back to her side and tickled the soft skin right below her T-shirt. She smiled again, and I touched my lips against hers briefly. When I pulled away, her eyes remained closed.

"You need to sleep."

"You haven't told me anything." She pouted as she spoke.

"In the morning," I suggested.

"No," she said. "You're just delaying."

"How about I tell you, and in return, you let me grab your ass when I kiss you." I was joking, but it was the only way I could see myself getting out of this.

"Deal!" she responded immediately.

I eyed her for a minute and knew she was completely serious.

"I don't..." I started, then closed my eyes and took a deep breath before continuing. "I don't talk about my history. It doesn't matter anymore."

Tria's chest rose and fell with a deep breath. She shook her head slightly and then rolled over to face away from me.

"Don't do that," I said.

She turned her head to look over her shoulder.

"You said you'd try this," she reminded me. "What exactly do you think is involved in a relationship?"

"I also told you I wasn't going to tell you shit and that I was going to fuck it up. Do you believe me now?"

"That was yesterday," she said. "You made a deal with me just now. Are you going back on it?"

I glared at her for a moment, but this time there was no wavering in her determination to get something out of me. It was too late to start this shit, but I knew I was going to have to give her something.

Besides, her ass was calling to me.

I sighed, knowing that I couldn't deny what she was saying, either. I didn't know a lot about being in a relationship, but I knew enough to understand there was give and take; there was compromise. If I give a little, it sounded like she was willing to give a little, too.

Maybe a short and quick version would be enough.

"My dad kicked me out when I was seventeen," I told her in a rush. "I haven't spoken to him since. My uncle, Michael, tries to get us back together every once in a while, which is why he offers me jobs. I don't want them. I don't want anything to do with them."

Tria rolled back over to face me and propped herself up on her elbow as we talked.

"Your father owns the hotels, too?"

"My father is the owner and CEO of Teague Silver," I told her. "It's a conglomerate of companies that started with a bunch of silver mines. Originally, it was a chunk of the Comstock Load, if you remember anything about US history, but now there are mines in Mexico, Peru, Chile, Argentina—all over the place. That expanded into smelting ore and mining copper. Now there are jewelry stores and a bunch of other related shit, too."

"That's why the earrings are significant," Tria said with a nod.

"Yeah—everyone in the family has them," I told her. "They're engraved on the inside, too. You have to look closely, though."

Tria's face scrunched up a bit.

"How does that fit into hotels?"

"Michael wanted to expand and diversify the company," I explained. "When I was a kid, he ended up buying this failing hotel chain and turning it into Silver Springs. He's got a few other things like that—casinos in Vegas and some riverboat casinos in the Midwest, too. I think the last thing he started up was partial ownership in some computer hardware company."

"So your family owns all of that?"

"Yep," I replied. "The silver goes back generations."

"Wow."

"Like I said, I've been there and done the rich thing. It isn't what it's cracked up to be."

"But still," Tria said with a shake of her head, "you walked away from all of that? Why?"

No fucking way.

"Enough for one night," I said. "Go to sleep. We still have a ways to go tomorrow."

Tria growled at me a bit, but I wasn't going to budge, and she didn't really have the energy to argue with me about it anymore. I moved my fingers up her arm and to her cheek, which I stroked softly. Tria's eyes drifted closed for a moment, and I took the opportunity to press my lips against hers. She responded, her hand gripping the back of my neck again.

As our tongues touched, I let my hand drop back down her arm, over her elbow, down to her waist, and then to her hip. I paused for a moment before reaching around, going slowly just in case she hadn't really meant what she said or had changed her mind.

She didn't move to stop me.

With my fingers spread out, I cupped one ass cheek and pulled her lower body closer to mine. I groaned into her mouth, unable to help myself as her grip tightened on my neck. Our mouths moved together, and I held her firmly against my body as we kissed and touched.

We broke apart, breathless.

Relaxing my grip, I let go of her ass and my fingers drifted back up her body until they reached her cheek again. I leaned forward, touched her lips softly, and then backed away.

"Now go to sleep," I commanded.

With an exaggerated sigh, Tria settled against me with her head on my shoulder and was asleep in seconds. I joined her quickly afterwards.

I woke hugging the pillow Tria had slept on.

It still smelled like her, and I found myself gripping it tighter and inhaling the scent before I even bothered to open my eyes. The bedroom was empty, and the door to the bathroom was open and the light was off, so I figured she must have been up for a while. I dragged myself from the Egyptian linen sheets to take a piss.

In the outer room, Tria was on the computer, intently staring at whatever was on the screen. For a long moment, I just watched her face as she sat there, and I wondered if that's what she looked like when she was in class, listening to a lecture. She glanced up at me when I shuffled to one side, and her eyes narrowed into a glare immediately.

"I haven't been awake long enough for you to be pissed at me," I stated.

Tria tilted her head to one side and turned the monitor so I could see it.

It was fucking Wikipedia.

"When were you going to tell me?" Tria asked. "Ever?"

I briefly scanned the webpage with the heading "Teague Silver" and the section Tria was reading, detailing the marriage of Douglass Teague, the monarch of the silver industry, and Julianne Hoffman, the sole heiress to Hoffman College.

"These are your parents, aren't they?"

"Yeah," I muttered. I reached back and scratched at my head nervously.

"Your mother owns the school I'm going to?"

"Yeah," I repeated, not really sure if she was asking a question or not. From what she had up on the screen, it was pretty obvious my family was connected to almost every legal business venture in the world.

"So were you ever going to share that information?"

"Probably not," I admitted.

"Liam!" She swiveled in the desk chair until she was facing away from both me and the computer. She leaned over and dropped her forehead to her fingers.

"What?" I snapped at her. I was still tired and had never been accused of being a morning person anyway. The sudden attack just as

I was waking up was pissing me off. "After a forty-eight hour relationship, I should have given you a copy of the family tree? You want a list of birthmarks? If I withhold the name of my favorite teddy bear from when I was five, will that piss you off, too?"

Tria looked up at me, her eyes still dark.

"Like all the other shit I told you last night, none of it matters."

"You knew I was going to Hoffman since the night we met," she said. "It never occurred to you to mention your mom runs the place?"

"She doesn't *run* it. She *owns* it. She shows up for gala events in a dress that costs as much as a year's tuition, cuts ribbons, opens champagne bottles, and throws money at people to make her feel like she's helping the 'less fortunate.' That's what she does."

"I'm trying to do this...this *relationship,* and I don't even know who you are!"

"I'm the same guy you've been living with," I told her. "There's nothing different about me because I have some blood ties to a bunch of people who mean nothing to me. I haven't seen them in nearly ten years, and as far as I'm concerned, I'm never going to see them again. I'm not a part of that family you see on the screen. My name probably isn't even mentioned. I'm no more a part of the family there than you are of that fucked up douchebag. If they mean nothing to me, I don't know why they should suddenly be so fucking important to you!"

"Because you could have everything!" she yelled at me. She tightened her hands into fists, and she held them against her thighs. "Why do you do this to yourself? Why?"

"Well, currently it's pissing you off, and that's good enough for me!"

"You don't make any sense at all!" She slammed her palms down on the desk.

I couldn't really argue that with her, either, because I knew I wasn't making sense. I didn't want to make sense; I just didn't want to talk about this shit at all.

Apparently, she wasn't ready to give up.

"I wasn't even around then!" she shouted. "So how could it possibly have been to piss me off?"

"I'm psychic."

"You're an idiot!" she screamed back at me.

Her eyes blazed at me now, and the heat from the pointless argument flowed around in my veins and warmed my skin. I could see the slight outline of her breasts through her T-shirt as she breathed heavily.

"You're fucking hot when you're pissed," I told her.

Tria's eyes widened, and her toes pushed against the plush carpet at her feet. The chair moved back slightly, but I was faster. With three steps I was across the room with my hands on her, lifting her up and out of the chair. I shoved the PC off the desk and onto the floor before I dropped her ass down where the computer sat moments before. My hands moved up her body and grasped the sides of her head.

I didn't know what she was trying to say as I covered her mouth with mine. At that point, I didn't care. I just knew I wanted to touch her—to be close to her—and I was too far away. I wanted to be closer.

I *needed* to be closer.

Inside of her.

"You drive me crazy," I mumbled into her ear. I moved down her neck, snarling at her as my mouth moved across her skin. "I want you so fucking bad. Fucking undefined ground rules."

I slid my hands down her back and grabbed her ass as I captured her lips again. I pulled her right to the edge of the desk and lodged myself between her legs, making it very obvious how much of an effect she had on me. She tensed under my touch, and I suddenly felt like an asshole, but I didn't move away. I just started kissing her jaw and then her neck instead, so her mouth was free to tell me to fuck off if she wanted to.

She didn't.

She wrapped her arms around my head and shoulders, and her fingers brushed backwards over my hair. I didn't grind my hips into her like I wanted to, but instead, I kept still between her legs. I could feel the warmth of her body against my crotch, and that was enough for right now. I still wanted a bit more, though, so I moved my hands up her sides, pushing her shirt up a little as I went.

"Liam." Tria chastised me as she reached her limit.

"You didn't give me any rules yet," I reminded her. I didn't move my hands up any farther, but I kept them on the bare skin of her sides as I kissed down her neck. The backs of my fingers tickled her sides. "Besides, you've seen me without a shirt. It's only fair."

"I didn't even think you owned a shirt for the longest time." She giggled as she tilted her head back so I could kiss up the front of her throat.

"You liked me that way, too, didn't you?" My words were a challenge.

"I don't have to say," she replied with a shrug.

"You wanted to run your hands all over this, didn't you?" I said as I grabbed her wrists and placed her hands on my stomach. I moved them up slowly until I reached the top of my chest, where I let her go. I angled my body forward so more of it was touching her, and her hands pressed on my shoulders as she laughed again.

"I'm sure I just wanted to feel your hair!"

"It wasn't this short then."

"Oh yeah." More giggles.

"You are a terrible liar," I said. "Besides, I know what you really want. You want your hand on my cock."

I pressed against her a little more.

"You can, you know," I whispered. "Any time you want—it's just waiting for you."

Before she had a chance to shove me away or just tell me to shut up, a knock at the door made her jump. I growled under my breath.

"Did you order breakfast?" I asked.

"No," Tria said. "I wasn't sure if I should."

"Fucking housekeeping." I grumbled as I released Tria and stomped toward the door.

The latches were far more complicated than they needed to be, and I was already pissed off before I got them unlocked. I flung the door open, prepared to tell some bitch in an apron to go fuck off. Instead, I was met with Michael standing on the other side.

"What the fuck?"

"Well, I figured something interesting must be happening," Michael said with a shrug. "For all these years, you've never accepted any kind of handout. I had to come see for myself."

Michael stepped around me and entered the suite just as Tria was straightening her shirt. She was still sitting on the desk, and her cheeks flushed bright red as he took in the sight.

"Seriously, Liam?" he said as he turned back to me. "All this just for a hooker? I thought something horrible must have—"

Without any consideration at all, I hauled back my right hand and slammed my fist into his jaw. Michael spun to one side before he dropped to the floor beside me, half in and half out of the room. He glanced up at me and rubbed his chin.

"Liam, no!" Tria cried from across the room. She jumped off the desk and headed toward us.

"Don't you *ever* fucking talk about her like that!" I screamed at him.

"Holy shit," Michael muttered. "I wasn't expecting that."

He looked up at me as he got himself back to a sitting position and then used the doorjamb to help right himself. He stood and dusted off his Dockers.

"Say another fucking word about her, and you'll get more," I promised.

"Is that so?" He looked from me to Tria and then back to me again. "Well, I guess this is more interesting than I originally assumed. Do I get an introduction?"

"No," I said flatly.

"Liam…" Tria reached my side and took hold of my arm before she turned to Michael. "Are you all right?"

"I'm fine, dear," he responded with a crooked half smile, "though it is the first time I've ever been on the receiving end of one of those. You are pretty impressive with the fists, Liam. I have to admit, I didn't completely understand that by just watching you hit other people."

Tria gripped my hand and looked at me pointedly.

I rolled my eyes at them both.

"Tria, this is my uncle, Michael. He's the one who thinks one night in a hotel at his expense warrants a plane trip, apparently. Michael, this is Tria…my, um…"

I stopped and glanced down at her for a second.

"My girlfriend," I finally added.

Michael's eyes went wide as he reached out and shook Tria's hand briefly.

"A pleasure," he said. "Unexpected, to be sure, but definitely a pleasure."

"Fuck off. What are you doing here?"

"I came to see what was wrong," he replied. "I figured you were in some kind of trouble, not on a date."

"It's not a fucking date."

"Well, whatever it is," he said, "I'm starving. Have you had breakfast? I understand the crepes are excellent here, and I'm sure the chef would do you a veggie version."

I was never one to give into Michael's schemes, but I was hungry.

# CHAPTER TWENTY
## Reach the Destination

Room service arrived with a variety of breakfast dishes, which they set out on the table with linen napkins, mimosas, and polished flair. Tria sat next to me with Michael on the other side. He couldn't seem to keep his eyes off of her, which was pissing me off. I was inclined to hit him again, but I didn't.

"I must say"—he turned to Tria—"you are most surprising."

"How so?" she asked.

"Just your being here with my nephew," he answered. "Apparently, any sort of insult toward you warrants quite a nasty right hook. I didn't realize Liam had someone else in his life. This is fairly recent, I take it?"

"Cut the shit," I said. "Do you want something, or did you just come all the way out here to annoy me?"

Michael stopped talking and smiling. He glanced down at the table for a second before pushing his chair back and standing up.

"I thought you might be in trouble," he said. "I just wanted to make sure you were all right."

"I'm fine." Once again, I found myself snapping at him.

"Liam!" Tria clenched her teeth as she said my name. She grabbed onto my arm again, like that was going to change what I was doing or saying.

"I'll just go then." Michael grabbed his jacket, tossed it over his arm, and headed toward the door.

Tria stood up as well, but when she tried to haul me up with her, I shook my arm free of her grasp. She glared at me as she followed Michael to the door. "I'm sorry. I don't know why..."

Michael chuckled, but there was no happiness in the sound.

"It's not the first time," he told her. "This has certainly been an enlightening little encounter though. Full of other firsts."

Michael reached up and rubbed his chin.

"He's not usually like this," Tria said quietly.

"Do you think I can't hear you?" I asked. I reached forward and grabbed my glass of plain orange juice, wishing it was the one from last night with the vodka additive. I hated mimosas.

"Well," Michael said, "I'm glad to hear that since this is all I ever see."

"Fuck off," I muttered under my breath.

"Liam! What is wrong with you?"

Michael huffed another laugh through his nose.

"I'd invite you over for Christmas," Michael said as he opened the door to the suite and headed out into the hallway, "but I already know your answer."

"Bye!" I called with fake enthusiasm. I wriggled my fingers sarcastically.

Yeah—sarcastic fingers.

"What is wrong with you?" Tria said as she came back and sat down across from me.

"Nothing," I said. I stood and grabbed the last muffin off the tray. I shoved the whole thing into my mouth at once and then answered all her questions with incomprehensible mumbles for the next three minutes while I threw all our shit back into the bag.

"Liam," Tria continued as she carefully placed the last of her toiletries in the Dragon's Duffle, "he came all the way out here just to make sure you were—"

"You got everything?" I interrupted her to prevent her from making the comment that was surely coming. "We need to get going."

With the last of our personal belongings accounted for and a couple of bagels stashed in Tria's purse for later, I announced that we were leaving. I stood at the door waiting for her, ignoring her protests about how we still needed to talk.

What the fuck was it with women always wanting to talk about shit that no one else thought was important?

"What's this?" Tria said, and the tone of her voice caught my attention.

I looked over to where she stood by the table where we had eaten breakfast and watched her raise her hand. Gripped in her fist was a handful of cash.

"Fucker," I muttered. "How much did he leave?"

"Three hundred," Tria said in a hushed whisper as she thumbed through it.

"Leave it," I said.

"What?" Tria's head snapped back to meet my gaze.

"I don't fucking want it."

"Liam, we don't even have enough money for gas on the way home."

I closed my eyes and rubbed the back of my neck.

"Fine," I growled. "You keep it. Let's go."

I didn't even bother to stop at the front desk to tell them we were checking out. I figured they would notice soon enough. Tria said nothing else as she stashed Thor's Tote and lifted her leg to straddle the motorcycle. I climbed on behind her, extremely conscious of how close my ass was to the purse that could potentially suck me inside of it, never to be seen again. I shuddered as I wrapped my arms around Tria's waist.

We took off north of the city, and before too long, I felt like we were right in the middle of the fucking jungle. Even as a kid, I had always lived in the city, and the only vegetation around was what you planted yourself. This was completely different.

I had never seen so many trees in my life, and they were all huge. Even though there was snow on the ground, the trees were still green. As we flew past them, I decided I didn't like trees—not one bit. Part of it was just because there were too damn many of them, but mostly because I couldn't see anything around them. Unlike buildings in the middle of a city block, no one could sneak out from behind one except if there were a corner or a door—places easily defended.

The forest made me feel exposed and vulnerable.

I tightened my grip around Tria's waist and leaned the front of my helmet against the back of hers. I didn't know what she must have thought about the gesture, but she released one of the handlebars and reached behind her head to touch the edge of my jaw just below the rim of the helmet.

The remainder of the trip to Tria's hometown was pretty uneventful. We only stopped a couple of times and didn't talk much when we did. There was definitely still tension between us, and I felt it the most when Tria brought out the cash left by my uncle and used it to fill up the gas tank of the motorcycle.

I was still pissed at that asshole for showing up there.

We drew close to the edge of a small town, and I noticed the little sign near the edge of the road pointing the way to the island town of Beals. We crossed a long bridge from Jonesport, which was cleverly named Bridge Street, over the water, and to the island. We cruised around the island, staying near the water at the edge of town.

At one point, we passed the local high school and a place called Barney's Cove Lobster, but Tria didn't stop until we got farther out.

She pulled off the road near a small house with a big tree in the back. The place looked like it had been abandoned for a long time. I didn't see any cars or anything parked outside. There was a shed near the back of the property but no signs of life.

Tria reached up and pulled off her helmet, so I followed suit. She stared up at the house for a few minutes before she glanced over her shoulder to look at me.

"This is the house where I lived with my dad," she told me.

Now it made sense. With a tug, I pulled her back against me a little, and she didn't resist. I kept both my feet on the road to balance the bike as she leaned back and continued to stare at the house. There was a good-sized back yard that butted up against the beach. The sound of the waves crashing against the rocky shore was constant and made me want to take a nap.

"You were, um…really young when he died, right?" I asked when I couldn't stand any more silence.

"Six," she confirmed.

"He was in the army?"

"He was a mechanic in the army, yes," she said. "He was considered a hero here because no one else in the area had ever served overseas before. Everyone looked up to him, not just me. He always said that he never wanted to live in a big city and that anyone with any sense would choose a small town."

I snickered.

"Well, maybe college will teach you some sense," I said. "Maybe you'll come back here when you graduate."

I definitely didn't like the idea, but I really didn't know what else to say. Living in a Podunk town like this would drive me up the wall. I doubted this place even had a decent bar.

"I don't know," she replied with a shrug that sent her hair up my nose. "I think I kind of like living in the city."

Thank God.

"I'd suggest trying to live in another area of the city. Where we are is pretty crappy."

"Well, yes," she agreed. "I don't think I want to live right where we are forever, but there are some nice places around Hoffman College campus."

She looked over her shoulder again and narrowed her eyes.

"I'm sure you know all about that, though."

I sighed dramatically, and Tria went back to watching the house. I could feel the tension again, and I didn't like it.

A breeze came by and brought with it the scent of brine and fallen leaves. I blinked, and in my mind I saw the lush green lawns and tall red brick buildings of the college that had been in my mother's family for three generations. I remembered holding her hand as we walked down the long sidewalk from the dormitories to the student center where I would be able to watch the swim meets and wrestling matches.

I shook my head slightly, forcing the thoughts away. I leaned forward on the bike and pulled Tria closer to me.

"I was supposed to go to Hoffman College," I said quietly into Tria's ear. "I was supposed to study business there so I could become a big shot executive and take over Dad's companies when he retired. Mom always said I had choices. I could become the president of the college instead, but I knew that was bullshit even as a kid. I'm pretty sure I was supposed to be the CFO of Teague Silver by now."

Tria tried to turn her head to look at me, but I held her a little tighter to my chest and kept her still.

"When I left home, I realized that dream was gone. I didn't know what I was going to do, and I knew the one place I was guaranteed acceptance into a college program was Hoffman, but there was no way I could set foot in there again."

My chest rose and fell with a deep breath.

"I was driving past the campus when all of that hit me," I told her. "Everything about my life was going to be completely different, and you know what?"

"What?" Tria asked softly.

"I was happy about it."

Tria wriggled enough to turn in the seat and reach her hands up to my face. She looked into my eyes as she moved closer and eventually brought her lips to mine.

"We should get going," Tria said as we broke apart. "Nikki's probably wondering where I am by now, and explaining you isn't going to be easy."

"Sure it is," I said. "I'm the boyfriend, remember?"

To get to the home of Tria's friend, we had to drive a little farther down the coast and around one of the jutting peninsulas of the island. Considering what Tria was apparently used to living around, I suddenly realized why the condition of the buildings in our neighborhood hadn't really fazed her.

The first few structures we passed were nothing more than shacks made out of plywood and a few nails. There was an old guy sitting out front of one of them, cooking fish on a charcoal grill. There were broken bicycles, part of a car, and a ton of other junk all over the yard around the shack. Weeds growing about waist height surrounded the whole place. It was a stark contrast to the area Tria's father's house had been on the other side of the island.

As we traveled farther down the road, Tria slowed to take a sharp turn. There was a line of RVs stacked up next to each other, overlooking the water. They were actually more run-down than the shabby shelters we had just passed. Farther from the water, there were half a dozen small houses, which weren't in too bad a shape, though there was a still a decent amount of junk lying around them. Most of them needed a good paint job and new gutters, too.

We stopped at the last RV site in the row. The structure itself was about the strangest I had ever seen. It was actually two RVs set up right next to each other and apparently fused together. A wooden porch had been attached to the front of it. There were a few pots, which looked like they probably had some flowers in them in the warmer months, on the slanted stairs.

Tria and I got off the bike, and Tria pushed it a little closer to the porch as the front door flew open, and a tall, lanky woman with short, stringy black hair rushed out.

"Demmy!" she cried as she jumped over the two steps of the porch and ran over to Tria. They hugged immediately as I stood there awkwardly. "I'm so glad you're here."

"I'm glad I'm here, too," Tria said with a pinched smile. "It feels like it has been forever. Please call me Tria, though."

"Sorry. I forgot." Tria's friend looked over at me. "Who's this?"

Tria looked quickly between us before making introductions.

"Liam, this is Nikki," she said. "She's my best friend ever. Nikki, this is Liam. My…um…my boyfriend."

Nikki's eyes widened as she looked up at me and slowly reached out her hand. I returned the gesture and shook her hand quickly.

"You didn't mention him on the phone," Nikki said.

"Well, Keith was there with you," Tria said with a shrug. I glared over at her because she hadn't mentioned him being on the phone at all. "He and Liam don't exactly get along."

I barked out a laugh.

"So Keith was right." A deep voice came from the porch. "You have shacked up with some musclehead. I really thought you were better than that, Demmy."

I immediately moved toward the guy leaning against the doorframe. He was a good five inches shorter than me, with black hair hanging in his dark eyes. Tria stepped up and blocked my way with her hand on my chest, the same way she had months ago when Keith had come to her apartment.

"Don't even think about it," she said. Her voice was full of warning. "You told me you weren't going to do this!"

"I told you I wasn't going to *start* anything. *He's* starting it."

"No!"

"He insulted you," I said under my breath. I balled my hands into fists.

"I will handle Brandon," Tria said in a lowered voice, "and you will wait for me to get this shit under control, and you will not hit anyone! As a matter of fact, you aren't even going to say a word until I tell you to! Now shut up, and I'll let you touch my boobs tonight."

My mouth dropped open for a moment, but I quickly closed it again. I swallowed hard as I gazed at her and realized she was completely serious. I gripped my hands into fists a couple more times and then released them as I swallowed a second time.

Tria raised an eyebrow at me pointedly.

I was never one to stay quiet, but after that look from Tria, I shut my mouth.

# CHAPTER TWENTY-ONE
## Challenge the Beliefs

Tria turned back to the couple and quickly introduced us.

"This is Nikki," she said, "and her husband, Brandon."

I huffed a short breath out my nose and gave them both a slight nod.

"Brandon and Nikki, this is my boyfriend, Liam. He came with me."

"What the hell are you doing, Demmy?" Brandon asked with wide eyes. "He can't stay here!"

"Brandon!" Nikki said as she turned quickly to him. "I asked her to come here and help with the arrangements. It's not like Liam's going to be fucking me tomorrow, so what difference does it make? And call her Tria!"

"You agreed to do it," Brandon said. "You agreed to all of it."

"Did I say I was backing out?"

The look on Brandon's face made me wonder if he didn't hope she would do just that.

"Maybe we should take this inside," Tria suggested, and after a bit more grumbling, I followed the rest of them up rickety wooden steps to the front door.

The configuration inside the double-RV was odd to say the least. The back part had been cut away to connect with the door of the second RV. The first part had been gutted to be one room housing a kitchen area and a living space. It was cluttered inside but not dirty. The furniture was worn but not quite falling apart. There were pictures of lighthouses on the walls. Lobster knickknacks adorned most of the flat surfaces, and there were piles of homemade candles on every unoccupied square inch. There were stacks of *National Fisherman* magazines next to a plastic folding chair that faced the couch and a cardboard box filled with mason jars sat near the door.

Under the kitchen table, there were stacks of canned goods, boxes of saltine crackers, and various other bought-in-bulk items. Nikki brought out iced tea in plastic cups that looked like they were collected from some sporting event, but whatever logo had once graced the side was too worn to be discernible. There was a huge pile of them on the counter by the refrigerator.

I felt like I was in some twenty-first century version of *Sanford and Son*, and I wondered at what point an old guy was going to escape from a back RV and clutch at his heart.

"You have no idea how much this means to me," Nikki was saying to Tria.

"You would have done the same for me," Tria replied.

I cringed and glanced over to her, wondering if she realized what she was saying. I could tell by her expression she hadn't really considered how the words could be taken.

"I mean," Tria went on, "if I needed you…for anything…"

"I know." Nikki smiled slightly.

There was a pause in the talking, which became way too long for my liking. I tried sipping the tea, but it was unsweetened, and the bitter taste hung around in the back of my throat.

"So, when's the party?"

"Liam." Tria chastised me with her tone and widened eyes.

"What?" I said. "You want to just pretend we're here for something other than a warped fuck-fest?"

"Liam!" Tria's eyes widened again, and she mouthed *shut up* at me.

"It's okay, Tria." Nikki spoke up. "What is it that midwesterners say about elephants hanging out at the table or something like that?"

"It's just an elephant in the room," Brandon corrected.

"Right." Nikki agreed with a nod. "Brandon went to the high school in Jonesport. He knows a lot more about life outside."

"How'd you manage that?" I asked, genuinely curious. "I thought you guys were all pretty much isolated here."

"We do tend to keep to ourselves," Brandon said as he eyed me coolly. "But the exile is self-imposed. We stay here because we choose to. I volunteered to go outside for schooling to bring knowledge back to the community."

His eyes shifted to Tria.

"Which is what Tria *should* be doing."

"Brandon." Nikki sighed as she looked at him.

"Tria's not coming back, you hear me?" I yelled. "So just get over it."

"Liam!"

"*Tria!*" I mocked her tone. "This whole 'use the guy's name as a form of punishment' thing is getting old."

Brandon snickered under his breath.

"Brandon!" Nikki scolded him again.

"What did I do?"

"Just stop it!"

More silence as everyone shuffled their feet and pretended to be interested in their drinks.

"Well?" I wasn't going to let this go. "Is anyone going to answer my question?"

"It's tomorrow," Nikki said. "As soon as the moon rises."

I couldn't help it—I rolled my eyes.

"Does the moon fuck you, too, or just watch?"

"Liam!"

"Is boiling lobster part of it?" I asked.

"All right, Liam!" Tria suddenly shouted as she stood up. "You are either going to stop with the crass remarks, or you are going to shut the fuck up. Do you hear me?"

God, I loved her temper.

Raising an eyebrow at her, I leaned back on the couch and crossed my arms over my chest without a word. She seemed to understand my answer, so she sat back down and turned to Nikki.

"I have to admit this isn't a ritual I know a lot about," Tria said.

I had to squeeze my lips together to keep quiet.

"It takes place up on the hill near the clearing in the trees," Nikki said. "You remember the one?"

"Yes, I know it," Tria said. She glanced at me sideways but quickly looked away again. "There are a lot of ceremonies held there."

"I'll be in the center," Nikki continued, "and all the women of the community will stand around me in a circle with their husbands behind them. The single men stand farther behind, either near their mothers, or sisters, or some other woman who is there to represent them."

Nikki paused for a moment to collect herself.

"Leo will start the ceremony with an offering, and then...and then Brandon goes first."

"Ultimately, it will still be my child," Brandon said. "So it starts with me."

This time I had to ball my hands into fists and only barely resisted the urge to muffle myself with a hand in my mouth.

"If Brandon had any male relatives, they would go next," Nikki explained. "Since he doesn't, it will go by the men who have already fathered the most children, and then by age—oldest to youngest—of the men without children."

Tria looked down at her hands and nodded.

"And you're really going to do this?"

"It's our way, Tria," Brandon said in a cold voice. "Maybe you should remember that."

"Careful." I growled under my breath.

Brandon glanced at me before looking back to Tria.

"We have to do it for the tribe," he said. "We don't have to like it, but it's our decision."

"Nikki?" Tria turned to her friend.

"Well, the good news is," Nikki said with a half smile, "that I'll be fairly drugged up the whole time. Makes everything a little easier on me."

Tria's eyes met my questioning ones.

"Peyote," she said simply. "It's used in a lot of the rituals."

"You ever do it?" I asked. My hands were starting to shake, but I locked them into fists to keep them still.

"Yes," she replied but didn't elaborate.

Nikki told us about a few more details of the ceremony and how Tria was mostly to be there for her afterwards. She didn't go into the details about what they were going to do, only that I wasn't invited.

"Can he stay here?" Tria asked. "I mean—while you and I get the arrangements made?"

Nikki looked quickly to Brandon, who just scowled at her.

"They came all this way," she said to him.

He turned to glare at me for a minute, then got up off his chair and headed for the kitchen.

"Fine." He grumbled as he walked away. "But he's bringing beer."

"I'll buy it," Tria said as she looked over to me. I knew what she was saying—that Michael would be buying it. I just shrugged.

The two women continued talking, the conversation turning to people they knew in town and what Tria was going to wear to the ceremony. I took the opportunity to sneak outside for a smoke. I stood on the little porch and leaned on the slightly slanted railing, lit a cigarette, and blew smoke into the misty air. As I stood there, the mist turned to steady rain, so I took a step back to make sure I was completely covered by the roof of the porch.

I heard a sound to my left and glanced over to watch Brandon open and close the front door quietly. I looked back out into the dirt driveway and watched the potholes fill with water from the rain.

"Could I have one of those?" he asked.

I looked at him out of the corner of my eye, trying to figure out just what the hell he was doing, but the request at least seemed genuine. I grabbed the pack out of my back pocket and pulled one out. I handed it and the lighter to him, and Brandon lit up. He coughed a couple of times, which made me smirk.

"I don't really smoke anymore," he said.

As if I couldn't tell.

He took a couple more puffs to get used to it and then tried inhaling again. He handed the lighter back to me with a quick thanks and stared out into the rain.

"So, how does this work?" I asked, partially because I was curious but also because I felt like being an asshole. "You stand outside in the rain and watch guys fuck your wife or what?"

He tensed, and I felt my body react the same way in a natural, defensive gesture.

"No," he said through clenched teeth. "It's a sacred ceremony."

I tried to keep myself from snorting out loud, but I failed.

"Never heard a gang bang called *sacred* before."

"You know," he said as he turned toward me, "I wouldn't expect you to understand."

"Well, you are right there," I agreed. "I wouldn't let anyone lay a hand on Tria—not for any reason."

"It's not the same at all," he said. "It's not like we're…fuck it. You don't get it, so there's no point in talking about it."

"So why don't you enlighten me?" I suggested as I tried to hold my sarcasm at bay. "Go ahead and justify this shit, if you can."

Brandon sighed and took a drag on the cigarette. He seemed to be getting the hang of it.

"We're dying," he said quietly as smoke curled around his long hair, "in a very literal way. Every year we lose more people to death than we gain from births. If we don't do something about it, we will cease to be. Beals and our way of life would be no more."

"It's because of the fucking inbreeding, you know."

"I know enough," he said with a nod. "It was one of the reasons I went to school in Jonesport. They were offering a course in genetics. We do look outside the community to strengthen the gene pool, but it's not that simple. There are very few people who aren't born to this life that want to embrace it. We're simple."

"You mean you're poor," I corrected.

"That, too." Brandon moved a couple of steps away, which allowed me to relax a little. "That's why people like Tria are so important to us. She may not have been born here, but she grew up here. She understands us better than other outsiders."

"That's a crock of bullshit," I said.

He stared at me through narrowed eyes but did not reply.

"Did you entice all the lovely ladies with promises of orgies?" My sarcasm came out again at full throttle.

"This isn't what I want, you know!" he shouted back. "If there was another option, don't you think I'd take it? Do you think I want her to have to go through this?"

"I dunno. Maybe you get off on it."

"Fuck you! Like you're any better than us."

"Maybe not," I said. "But I wouldn't put up with this shit."

"I suppose I should be impressed that you hit people for a living." Brandon sneered. "Like hanging out in some crappy bar pummeling people is something you can consider a long-term goal. You gonna support a wife on that? You gonna tell your kids 'It's okay, it's the good sort of beating people up—and they're asking for it'?"

"Kiss my ass! You don't know a fucking thing about what you are saying, so shut your goddamn mouth."

He laughed.

"Yeah, that's what I figured," he said. "You don't know anything about us, but you think you can stand there and judge me.

I don't know why I should be shocked that doing the same to you pisses you off."

There was something deeply flawed in his logic, I was sure, but I couldn't come up with exactly what it was. It did make me wonder what it was like to be in his shoes. I was certainly familiar enough with the idea of family expectations weighing on your conscience. The main difference was that when push came to shove—I got the fuck out. He was going to stay here and put up with it.

"If you don't like this shit, why do you stay?" I asked.

"A lot of reasons," Brandon replied. "My family has been here for generations, just like almost everyone else around here. We've been brought up to listen to the council leader and do as he says."

"Who's that?"

"Leo Harrison," Brandon said. "He's Keith's father. Keith will take over for him when he retires."

"Oh, that will make thing so much better!" I didn't try to hide the sarcasm.

"If you think Keith is fucked up, wait until you meet his father."

"Will I want to hit him?"

"Maybe." Brandon laughed. "He's only got one leg though, so it wouldn't go over well."

"What happened to the other one?"

"Fishing accident," Brandon said with a shrug. He didn't give me any more details. "He pretty much runs this community with an iron crutch."

He finished the last of the cigarette, stubbed it out on the bottom of his shoe, and tossed it into a metal bucket at the edge of the porch. There were a couple of cigar nubs in there, too. I did the same with mine and then followed him back inside the house.

Tria looked at us as soon as we walked in together. She took one glance at me and then quickly appraised Brandon's condition, likely looking for bruises or busted lips. I gave her a look, and she blushed as she looked away.

Apparently, I wasn't the only one who was ready to call it a day. Nikki excused herself to go collect blankets, and Brandon poked around in the kitchen, claiming he had something to do. As far as I could tell, he was rearranging the silverware drawer.

I might have felt bad for them both if it wasn't for...

Nah—I did feel bad for them.

Nikki brought over some blankets and pillows and then danced back and forth on her feet before speaking.

"I'm sorry," she said, "but I wasn't expecting two. Even if I was, I'm not sure where I'd put you."

"I'm fine on the floor." Before Tria could protest, I placed a couple fingers over her lips. "Don't argue; just take the couch."

She nodded. I removed my fingers, and Nikki placed worn sheets, blankets, and pillows on the couch for Tria. She gave me a thick blanket for more padding, and I arranged it on the floor next to the couch. Nikki and Tria said their goodnights, and the couple headed to the second RV and what I assumed to be their bedroom.

There was a nosy little part of me that wondered if they were going to have sex tonight. Maybe that "one last hurrah" before she gets passed around.

I shuddered.

"So, you didn't talk her out of it?" I asked.

"No," Tria said. "She doesn't want to be talked out of it. She wants a baby. This is the way she plans to get it, and I have to respect that."

"Respect the unrespectable?"

Tria dropped down onto the floor near the edge of the couch and crossed her legs.

"It's no different than if she were doing the opposite."

"I have no idea what that means."

"I mean," Tria continued, "if she wanted to *not* have a baby instead of wanting to *have* one. I don't approve of abortion, but if my friend decided she needed one…well, I would help however I could. It wouldn't be something I would choose for myself, but it's her decision. I have to honor what she chooses to do. That's what friends are for."

"Fucked up," I muttered for the hundredth time.

I moved the plastic chair, newspapers, and various other crap on the floor and sat down next to Tria with my back leaning against the edge of the couch. My ass hit the floor with a bit of a twinge, and I was reminded again of how uncomfortable I had been on the motorcycle. I stretched my legs out and flexed my ankles until my backside loosened up a little.

"Did you and Brandon have a nice talk?" Tria asked. There was a little table next to the couch that must have been intended as a nightstand because there were two good-sized drawers in it. Tria was taking stuff out of the bag and putting it in the drawers. "You were out there a long time with him."

"What the fuck are you doing?" I asked, ignoring her question. I pointed my finger back and forth between the bag and the nightstand drawer.

"Putting things away," she said with a shrug.

"You've been in the apartment for a month, and you've kept most of your shit in your suitcase," I told her. "But here you put everything away. You did that in the hotel, too."

She wouldn't meet my eyes and just shrugged again, which pissed me off.

"You go on about how I won't say anything," I grumbled. "Maybe it's time for you to talk."

"What is that supposed to mean?" she asked. She looked at me out of the corner of her eye but didn't stop taking things out of the Gorgon's Gunnysack and placing them in the drawer.

"You don't think that's a little incongruous?"

"I think you using the word *incongruous* is incongruous."

"Nice." I reached up and scratched at the back of my head.

"How about me using the word *double standard*?"

"That's two words."

"Well, at least my math sucks, huh? Does that fit better with your impression of me?"

She stopped shoving things into the drawer and seemed to slump a bit.

"I know this is temporary," Tria said. She waved her hand in the direction of the open drawer. "I'll put these things in here, and then in a couple of days or so, I'll take them back out and go home. Same thing with the hotel."

She paused and fiddled with the strap on the bag. She took a deep breath, licked her lips, and then continued.

"But at the apartment..." She paused again to consider her words. "Everything is different there. I don't even know what to call it—*your* apartment, *my* apartment, *our* apartment—nothing seems right, so it's just *the* apartment. You call it that, too."

"I do?"

"Yes."

"Oh."

"Right now it just feels surreal," she continued. "Like I'm going to wake up at some point and figure out that leaving Beals was all a dream."

"More like a nightmare," I retorted. "I mean, where you left was the nightmare. Whatever. That didn't come out right."

"It wasn't," she said. "I know you've mostly heard the bad stuff, but there are good people here. They're all kind of like a big family. They take care of each other, and they took care of me. I miss it."

That comment sent a chill over my skin.

"You're making a new home," I told her. "Isn't that what you want?"

I hoped it was.

"Yes," she said. "And I don't want to come back, but I still miss parts of it. Nikki especially. She always makes me feel welcome here."

"And I don't," I said.

"I didn't say that."

I reached over and placed my hand on the side of her face. I circled the edge of her jaw with my fingers. I had no idea what the right things to say were—I just knew I didn't want her to feel like she wasn't welcome where we lived now.

"Unpack your things," I whispered. "I want you to stay there."

Her teeth worried her lip, and she continued to look off to the side. I moved my head over until I was in her line of sight.

"I want you to stay there," I repeated.

"Even if I don't have sex with you?" she asked.

"Why do you keep harping on that?"

"Because it's what you want," she replied. She moved her head away, effectively pulling out of my grasp. "You said it yourself—you don't do relationships. You're in it for the sex, and you aren't getting any."

If she had yelled it at me, I would have found it hot, but the way she said it—so quiet, and tired, and defeated—it just made my chest clench instead.

I was never one to pry into someone else's psyche, but I needed to understand.

# CHAPTER TWENTY-TWO
## Reveal the Past

"Why are you doing this?" I asked her. "Didn't we talk about this before?"

"Yes," she admitted. "But when Michael said...when he just assumed I was bought and paid for...it just made me realize the people who have known you the longest probably know better than I do."

"Fucker," I snarled. "I should have kicked him while he was down for saying that shit to you."

"It's true though, isn't it?" She turned her eyes to me, and my chest tightened up again.

"No," I said, "it isn't. And beyond that, Michael *doesn't* know me. None of them do."

"Well, I don't know you either," Tria said. The venom had crept back into her voice. "You don't tell me anything about yourself."

"You know everything important." I shrugged. I reached over

275

to try to take her hand, but she pulled away again.

"How you got to where you are," Tria said, "is important. I want to know, Liam. I want to know what happened to you and why you are the way you are."

"How am I, exactly?"

"Cold," she said without hesitation.

"That's not what you say at night," I replied as I wiggled my eyebrows.

"You see?" Tria jumped right back into it. "It's shit like that. I say something that you should consider insulting, and you respond with a half-assed joke instead of being pissed about it, or upset, or whatever. You're indifferent to everything around you, and I want to know why."

"Why?"

"Why what?"

"Why does it matter?"

Tria's chest rose and fell with her breaths as she tilted her head to look at me.

"I need to know how I can fit into this," she said. "I can't figure that out if you don't tell me anything. If I can't figure it out, well..."

She let her voice trail off as she shrugged and looked away from me.

"Well, what?" I tried to keep my voice down so the couple in the other room wouldn't hear us. "Well, then you'll just say *fuck it* and move on? Is that what you mean? Are you *threatening* me?"

"No," she said quickly. "I'm not. I don't mean to be, anyway. It's just...I have to have more, Liam."

"More?"

"I want to know more about you. More about your past."

"You don't want to know," I told her, hoping it was true, or that I could at least convince her it was. I shifted uneasily on the floor.

"You have a habit of telling me what I want," Tria replied.

"Maybe you could let me decide that once in a while."

I ignored her sarcasm.

"Can't we just make out instead?"

She immediately moved away from me and looked at me pointedly. There was just no winning with her and her stubbornness. My best bet was to just get her to sleep, so I went with that angle. After all, it had worked pretty well the night before.

"You need to sleep," I said.

"So tell me a bedtime story."

"That shit isn't going to help you sleep."

She ran her hand down the side of my face and rested it lightly on my shoulder. Her eyes were drooping, and I was hoping she would just crawl onto the couch and drop off into slumber.

"Tell me the real reason Yolanda was mad about what you were eating."

No such luck.

I turned my head to stare at the curtains covering the window, hoping she would get the hint and let it go but also knowing she wasn't going to.

"Liam." Tria sighed and reached up with her finger to run it over my jaw as she turned my head to face her more. Like a total idiot, I looked into her eyes again. Even in the subdued light, they were bright and shining. "I want to know. Please tell me."

All my resolve crumbled.

"What do you want to know?" I asked with an exaggerated groan.

"Tell me about Yolanda," Tria said. "Tell me how you met."

The very idea made my skin crawl. There was definitely a significant part of me that couldn't believe I was considering doing the one and only thing I always swore to myself I wouldn't do—think about any of my history. How was I supposed to talk about it without thinking about it? Images I didn't want to see were already flashing through my head.

Glancing at her, I met her eyes again. I didn't know what her look meant—if she needed to know more about the man she was with before making any real decisions, if she wanted to get under my skin, or if she was just curious. Whatever it was, I wanted to give it to her, and the thought scared me.

"Fine," I said, "but I'm smoking while we talk."

"Deal!" she said with a genuine smile that loosened the tightness still hovering in the center of my chest.

We stepped quietly through the front door, and Tria made herself comfortable on the top of the wooden steps while I lit up. She just sat there without saying a word until I got the idea and started talking.

"Yolanda...found me," I told her. I took a big breath and leaned my head against a four-by-four that held up part of the porch roof. I looked down, no longer meeting her eyes. "I was...not doing well. I needed money...and she found me. She recognized me and took me back to her place. She got me to straighten up, got me back in shape, and has kind of been some combination of trainer and mother ever since then."

"She recognized you?" Tria asked.

"Yeah," I said with a nod, secretly glad she chose that portion to focus on. "Yolanda was a trainer then, too, but she had a side job. She used to go around to high school competitions, scouting talent for some agent on the side. She was at a wrestling competition I won the year before."

I laughed humorlessly.

"She only barely recognized me. I'd lost about forty pounds since leaving."

"Leaving where?"

I glanced at her for a moment.

"My parents threw me out," I said. She knew this, but I was

stalling. "I, um...I had some money in the beginning, but it doesn't last as long as you think it will, ya know?"

"Yes, I do."

"I was kicked out of where I had been living," I told her. "Well...sort of."

"What do you mean?"

"I didn't just...get kicked out of the place," I finally said. I glanced at Tria and saw her sitting there, patient as ever.

"Why won't you just tell me?" she asked quietly.

"Because what I have now isn't worth shit. If you knew how bad I was...fuck, you'd probably never want to even look at me." I stared at the ground, refusing to look up at her as I chewed at the pad of my thumb.

"Do you really think I would turn away from you because you went through a rough patch?" Tria asked. "You think I don't know something bad happened to you? Do you think I can't see that? Do you think I'm that blind?"

I looked into her eyes and forced myself to stay focused on her even though it hurt.

"I wasn't kicked out because I couldn't pay rent," I told her. "I was squatting there."

"Squatting?" Tria asked through narrowed eyes.

"Yeah. You know, just hanging out there. I didn't have a lease or anything; I just broke in and stayed there. It was me and a couple other guys and one chick. We were all just living there."

"And you got caught," Tria said, surmising correctly.

"Yeah, I'd been homeless for a while before then, but that's the point when I was really living on the streets. Before I had a car I was sleeping in."

"How old were you?" she asked.

"Eighteen," I told her. "What's funny is I had quite a bit of money then."

"If you had money, why didn't you just rent the place?"

This was it. This was going to be the point of no return. This was very likely the thing that was going to make her turn and run for the hills. Unfortunately, it wasn't the only confession in a long list of sins.

"Because…because…" I took a long, deep breath, closed my eyes, and blurted out the rest. "Because I was a junkie. I didn't want to use the money for rent because then there wouldn't be enough for heroin. I had a nice car when I left my parents' house, and I sold it so I could buy more smack and needles and shit to get high. I was a strung-out junkie when Yolanda found me near the gym where she worked."

I kept my eyes closed, half waiting for her to run off into the rain. My hands were shaking, and even holding them in fists against my thighs wasn't working to still them. After a minute or two, when I knew she was still there beside me, I looked at her again.

"How long?" she asked. "How long have you been off it? I mean—you *are* off it, right? I would have noticed if you were doing something like that—"

"Years," I said, wanting to get the words out fast enough to stop her train of thought. My voice managed to contain a hint of desperation. "Ever since the last time—the time Yolanda was going on about when I gained too much and got the shit kicked out of me. That was the only relapse I ever had. I swear—I'm totally clean now. Over four years—I swear!"

"I believe you," Tria said simply. She stood up, stood beside me, and laid her hand on my cheek.

"You do?" I asked quietly.

"Of course," she replied. "Why wouldn't I?"

"There's more," I said. I had to swallow hard, but I kept talking. "I did shit—a lot of shit I'm absolutely not going to talk about—but it was bad. I would have done anything for the drugs."

"Did you kill anyone?"

I felt a lump lodged in my throat.

"No," I whispered, wishing I could believe I wasn't responsible for it myself. "But I've seen a lot of death."

"Do you still struggle with it?" Tria asked quietly. "I mean, with wanting to...to do that?"

"Wanting to do heroin? Yeah. All the time. Not every day anymore, but yeah, I struggle."

She traced over the edge of my jaw with her fingers, scratching at the scruff that had formed during our trip.

"Thank you," she said softly.

"For what?"

"Giving me some of you," she replied. She stood up on her toes and pressed her lips to mine.

"Will you unpack when we get home?" I asked. "In *our* apartment?"

She chuckled.

"If you really want me to."

"I really do."

She rose up on her toes again and ran the fingers of both hands on either side of my jaw and up into my hair. Her head came forward slowly, and she brought our lips together again.

"I hope you mean that," she said quietly.

"I do mean it," I told her. I pressed my lips back to hers as I wrapped one arm around her back to bring her a little closer to me. We kissed softly for a minute, and then Tria pulled away reluctantly.

"We need some sleep," she said. "Tomorrow is going to be insane."

"Well, I can't argue with the second part of that," I said.

We went back inside, and I settled myself on the floor. Tria climbed over me and onto the couch, and I lay down on my back below her. I knew right away that I wasn't going to be able to sleep where I was. Despite the extra padding, the floor was pretty damn uncomfortable. That didn't bother me so much—I'd slept in much worse places—but listening to Tria breathe and not being able to touch her was driving me batty.

I closed my eyes and just lay there for a while. After the first few minutes, I felt something against my arm and moved the opposite hand to grasp Tria's fingers. She sighed but didn't say anything. The physical touch helped, but it wasn't quite enough to let me doze off.

Several minutes later, I heard her soft voice.

"Liam?" she whispered. "Are you awake?"

"Yeah," I mumbled. I opened my eyes but couldn't really see much other than dark blobby shapes that were either slightly darker or slightly lighter than the other dark blobby shapes around them.

"I can't sleep."

"Me either," I said.

"I think I'm used to soft beds," she said with a quiet giggle.

The slight laughter ended quickly, and I felt her fingers tighten around mine. I took in a deep breath and then sat up straight.

"Scoot up," I said.

"Scoot up?"

"Yeah—move so you're at the edge of the couch."

"Liam, we are not both going to fit on here."

"Just do it."

Tria shifted, and I climbed over the top of her and wedged myself in between the back of the couch and the back of Tria. I wrapped one arm securely around her waist and slid the other in the crack of the cushion so I could reach around her head and bring it to my shoulder.

"Is this your way of getting to touch my boobs?"

"No," I told her. "When I do that, I want to have time to enjoy them. Maybe we'll stay at one of my uncle's hotels on the way back."

"Hmm…that might be nice."

"You'd like that?"

"Yeah, I would," she said. "I'd never been to a hotel like that before."

"Well, maybe we'll get one of the regular rooms and use the leftover money to pay for it. I don't need him showing up at the crack of dawn and interrupting my fun again."

"Maybe." Tria shifted around a little bit to get comfortable. "But that suite was amazing."

It was entirely possible that I was going to have to do a little more pride swallowing. Tria shifted again.

"I'm going to fall off," she said.

"I'm not going to let you fall," I told her. I tucked my face into her hair and inhaled before touching my lips to the edge of her ear. "Go to sleep."

Her body rose and fell with a deep breath, but she settled against me, and soon I could hear the regulated breathing of sleep. I tightened my grip a little and lay my head next to hers, trying to expel thoughts of the past from my mind.

I fell asleep with a vague memory of the smell of sweat and a bitter taste in the back of my throat.

I woke to soft, female voices.

"I can't believe you're sleeping like that."

Tria shook with quiet laughter.

"He gets kind of a death-grip," she said. "He's like this every night."

"So you *are* living with him?" Nikki asked for confirmation.

"Yes. It wasn't really planned; it just sort of happened."

"I had it all planned from the beginning," I mumbled with my eyes closed. "Welcome to my parlor and all that shit."

Tria laughed aloud as she turned slightly to smack my arm.

"You did not!"

She wriggled, and I abruptly released her from my grasp, leaving her to fall to the floor with a thump. Nikki laughed and walked away from us and into the kitchen. I rolled over and peered over the edge of the couch. Tria lay on her back with a surprised look on her face. Her hair was all over the place—and from the position on her back, it framed her face in a wild tangle of frizzy strands.

"Your hair makes you look like one of those chicks from an eighties rock video," I told her.

"Thanks a lot!"

I gave her a half smile.

"You're beautiful," I told her as she sat up and tried to calm the mass of hair.

"I'm surprised I have any hair left," she mused, "the way you are always trying to use your nose to build a nest in it!"

I laughed.

"You smell good," I said with another smile. "If I could figure out what you were putting on your hair that smelled like that, I'd probably just bathe in it."

"You are *not* right!" Her information wasn't news to me.

"Anyone want breakfast?" Nikki stood near the wall by the kitchen and held up a tray of what appeared to be gigantic muffins.

Tria quickly fumbled around inside her purse and without too much trouble came up with a hair band. I was always surprised at how quickly she managed to find shit in there. I peered over the edge of the Purse of Doom—feeling brave—and glimpsed inside as she wrapped her hair in a bun at the top of her head. I couldn't figure out what any of the shit in there was, and I quickly retreated until I was a safe distance from the potential event horizon of the thing.

After breakfast—which was awesome though I wouldn't eat more than one of the huge things—Tria pulled me to the side.

"Well, she still intends to go through with it," Tria informed me. "I'm going to stick with her today and help her get ready."

"What am I supposed to do?" I asked, trying not to sound petulant.

"Can you keep Brandon company?"

"Seriously?"

"He's nervous and freaking out," Tria whispered as she glanced over her shoulder. "I don't know what you said to him last night, but he keeps asking her if she's sure she wants to do it. She does—I can see that now—but he's not so sure anymore, and that's got her all upset. He needs to be there for her as much as I do."

"This is too fucked up," I mumbled under my breath.

"Please, Liam," Tria implored, and I couldn't bring myself to say no.

So as the women-folk locked themselves in the bedroom, I was stuck trying to entertain myself all day with a guy who I really didn't want to be anywhere near. Lucky for me, he didn't seem to be in much of a talking mood. For the most part, we smoked cigarettes and drank beer in silence on the porch.

As the afternoon dragged on, Brandon was getting more and more tense. I was trying to make sure he paced himself and ate something throughout the day so he wasn't totally shit-faced by the time we were supposed to go to whatever fucked up little magical altar in the woods where this was all going to take place. I glanced over at Brandon's empty bottle between his hands, noticed the condition of my own, and figured it was time for another.

"Want me to grab you one?" I asked as I stood up.

Brandon just nodded, so I headed inside to the fridge. Through the window, I stared at the water pouring from the sky and wondered if it was ever going to fucking stop. How was it that the whole town didn't just float into the sea? I also wondered if my jacket was going to be enough to keep me from being absolutely soaked before the whole thing was done.

I couldn't believe I was actually going to hang out and watch a public train.

Before I got back to the front door, I heard an unfortunately familiar voice.

"Where'd the bike come from?"

"Demmy," Brandon replied.

With determination—but for what, I wasn't sure—I opened the door and stepped back out onto the porch. Douchebag looked up immediately.

"You have to be fucking kidding me." Keith glared at me with flared nostrils.

I was never one to turn down boobs, but punching this asshole in the face just might be worth the loss.

# CHAPTER TWENTY-THREE
## Take the Plunge

There was a part of me that was highly amused by the whole thing. I could tell by the wide-eyed look Douchebag flickered between me and Brandon that he had no idea I was here. I could also tell by Brandon's nonchalant attitude that he didn't mind me being here anymore, and he also didn't give a shit that Keith was pissed off about it.

"What the hell is he doing here?" Keith yelled at Brandon. "Do you know who this asshole is?"

"He came with Demmy...er...*Tria*," Brandon replied.

"He's the one I warned you about!"

I walked casually over to Brandon and handed him his beer. I turned to Keith and kept looking at him as I tilted my own beer to my lips just as casually, then pulled out a smoke and lit it.

"You want one?" I asked Brandon.

"Yeah," he replied.

Holding in the smirk was impossible as I handed Brandon a

cigarette, then held out my lighter, flicked it, and lit the smoke for him.  I knew how friendly and natural the whole action would look from Keith's point of view, and the only thing that might have amused me more would be his arrival while I was squeezing Tria's ass with my tongue down her throat.

Yeah, I could be a dick when I wanted to be.

"You don't smoke!" Keith shouted.

Brandon just shrugged as he inhaled.  He had definitely gotten the hang of it over the past day, and he blew the smoke out in a long cloud.  Keith just looked back and forth between us for a minute, and I tried to hold in the smirk and look like I was more interested in my beer than anything else going on around me.  Finally, he glared at me again.

"You are not welcome here," the douchebag said to me.

"I'm just hanging out," I said.  "You know—supporting my girlfriend while she supports his wife."

I gestured toward Brandon with my thumb a couple of times as I let the word *girlfriend* slip out just as casually as I had lit Brandon's cigarette.  Keith's face darkened, but his back straightened up as he seemed to get control over himself.  He stood taller as he turned to Brandon.

"This area is reserved for people in our community," Keith said.

Brandon stood on the top step of the porch.  I leaned against a post behind him, which I hoped would continue to hold the roof up even with the extra force of my shoulder against it.  Keith went on.

"You know how outsiders can affect us, and you were already warned about this one and how he has influenced one of our own.  How can you let him stand there?"

Brandon glanced over his shoulder and up at me.  The doubt in his eyes was obvious along with the same sorrow and confusion that had been there all day.  The tension around his eyes lessened as he looked at me, and he gave me a bit of a grin.  Keith's little speech might have been pretty once, but it wasn't hitting home for Brandon any more—I could see that and assumed Keith could, too.

"He seems okay," Brandon said with a shrug. "He's definitely no worse than that asshole Eric you hung out with from school. Besides, he's with Tria, and you were always going on about how Tria was one of us, no matter what."

More smirking because I was pretty sure those same words had once been used by Keith, against Brandon. From Keith's narrowed eyes, I knew I was right. Brandon leaned back a little and sipped his beer, and Keith must have decided to ignore him.

"I said you aren't welcome here," he told me again.

"And I pretty much ignored you," I replied. "You wanna go for round two?"

"Always about the fighting, isn't it?" he said. "Always about the violence. Have you hit her yet?"

"Fuck you," I said with a glare.

"You don't belong here!" he bellowed.

"Well, you got that right," I replied as I waved my hand toward Brandon and then back behind me and toward the house. "I wouldn't stand for this shit."

"What have you told him?" Keith asked Brandon in disbelief. "You shouldn't be talking to him at all!"

"What does it matter?"

"Dammit, Brandon!" Keith yelled. "I told you about him and how he's screwing around with her! You really want her involved with someone like that?"

Brandon looked over to me, and his shoulders rose and fell again.

"I dunno," he replied quietly. "I mean, he seems okay, and Tria really seems to like him. I mean—it's not like what he's doing is illegal or whatever."

"He fights in a fucking bar for cash." Keith snarled and it was obvious he was losing the cool façade he had been trying to keep up. It was funny, and I gave him a big smile as I took another sip of beer.

"Yeah, and you do what?" Brandon's words were sharp. "Wait around for your dad to retire or die so you can get his disability checks? It's not like you're doing anything all that noteworthy. When was the last time you even went fishing?"

"What the hell?" Keith threw his hands up in the air. "This guy is around for a couple hours and has you poisoned against your own people?"

"I'm not poisoned!" Brandon said. He pushed himself off the steps and stumbled a little. "Everything I'm doing today is about my family, and we are a part of this community! You think I want this? You think I want to watch you lose your virginity with my wife?"

It just figured.

Keith's hands clenched into fists, and he looked away from us with a tensed jaw. I was pretty sure his dark complexion was the only thing hiding his embarrassment.

I couldn't help myself; I snorted out a laugh.

"Well, at least you don't have to worry about getting her actually turned on or anything," I said with a nasty, cocky smile. "By the time you get to her, she'll be so full of cum you ought to be able to slide in pretty easi—"

The punch to my face wasn't from the direction I expected it, and it caught me off guard. I spun to my right, caught my balance before I fell over, and then looked to Brandon as I righted myself. He was standing with his legs spread slightly and knees bent. His hands were still in fists like he was ready to take me on fully, but I just held my palm out to him as I stood up straight.

"You're such a tough guy," Keith said with a sneer still plastered across his face and his own embarrassment forgotten for the moment. "You don't even defend yourself?"

"No reason to," I replied as I rubbed my chin. It was a pretty good hit for a guy without much muscle. "I deserved that one."

"Yes, you fucking did," Brandon growled.

"I know, dude. Sorry. My mouth is on its own sometimes."

Brandon narrowed his eyes for a second and then nodded briefly as his hands relaxed again at his sides. He bent over and picked up his dropped cigarette and spilled beer.

"You just don't get it," Brandon said quietly. "Nikki wants a baby, and I haven't been able to give her one. What am I going to do? We don't have health insurance, and there's no way we could afford going through a doctor to have it done."

"You're doing it for your people," Keith said. He smiled down at Brandon as he nodded.

"I'd do anything for her," Brandon said. He got this faraway, dazed look in his eye, and I figured I shouldn't have given him another beer.

"Yeah, we had that discussion," I reminded him. I rubbed at my chin a bit more, and it was pretty achy.

"You have got to be kidding me," Keith grumbled as he looked between Brandon and me. "What's next? He going to join in the ceremony?"

"Hell, no," I replied.

"He's going to be there," Brandon said.

"I am?" I responded. I was definitely going to need more beer. I wondered if the peyote would be in a little bowl next to the chips and dip.

Brandon shrugged.

"You're with Tria," he said simply. "You should be there with her."

"Until she comes to her senses," Keith said. "Now that she's back home, she'll remember where her place is!"

"Tria has a home," I said as I narrowed my eyes at him. "With me."

"Come on, Keith," Brandon moaned. "This shit is hard enough

as it is. Can you just lay off for tonight?"

"I can't believe you are taking his side over—"

The front door opened then, and Keith halted his little rant as Tria came outside. She had changed her clothes and wore a fitted shirt and long skirt that looked like it was made of soft, tan leather. There were green beads down the arms and sides, creating a line all the way to the bottom of the skirt.

Tria looked at Keith and then quickly looked over to me. I could see her checking out the side of my face, and I wondered how much of a mark there might be.

"You're fighting already?" She glared at me.

"I'm just taking the hits here, baby," I said with a smile. "No blood, no foul."

Tria looked at Brandon then, who nodded and confirmed my story.

"It's true," he said. "I hit him, and we're all good."

"You're what?" Tria's eyes darted between us in disbelief, and I would have been lying if I said it didn't amuse the hell out of me.

"It's all good, babe—really." I raised up my bottle, and Brandon did the same before draining the rest of it.

"Babe?" she repeated with an eye roll. "Seriously?"

"You prefer *sugar*? Pumpkin? Muffin?"

Tria groaned.

"I told you to stay away from him," Keith said. His voice was dark as he pointed a finger at her.

Tria didn't look at him or respond. Instead, she turned to Brandon.

"We're set for tonight," she said. "Nikki wasn't sure who was driving us up there. We can't take everyone in that car."

"Well," Brandon answered as he glanced from me to the douchebag, "Keith said before that he would take me and the guys— Luke, Devin, and Conner. Sue was going to pick you and Nikki up. Um…Liam could ride with us…?"

His voice trailed off, and he looked over at Keith as he spoke the half-question. Keith rolled his eyes and looked away. I considered punching him just for being rude, but Tria turned sideways right at the same time, and I got a good look at boob profile. Reminded of my goal, I took a long breath to calm down.

"He is not going," Keith said with certainty.

"Keith," Tria said quietly, "I want him there."

"Doesn't matter what any of you want," I said. "If Tria goes, I go. End of discussion."

"You don't have any rights here," Keith informed me. "You don't get a say in this."

Brandon suddenly spoke up.

"Community and tradition first. Right, Keith?"

"Always."

"Above our own wants and desires."

"Exactly."

"So, Nikki chose Tria to be with her—as per our tradition," Brandon surmised. "And as a member of our community—like you always say she is—Tria can bring her significant other with her, even if he's not from Beals."

Keith's eyes darkened.

"So he rides with us," Brandon proclaimed with a smile.

"Okay with me," I shrugged.

The anger behind Keith's eyes was undeniable, but there was also resignation. Brandon had fought him at his own game and won.

"Who knows?" Brandon said as he raised his hands up with the palms toward the sky. "Maybe he'll see how awesome we are and decide to move back here with Tria after college."

"Over my dead body," Keith mumbled under his breath.

"Arrangeable," I replied with a raised eyebrow.

He was about to say something, but a noise from behind me caught the attention of all of us. Nikki stepped through the doorway in the strangest dress I had even seen. It was mostly earth tones but with some orange and blue worked into it with beads—hundreds and hundreds of beads. They made geometric patterns all across the top half of the body of it and around most of the sleeves as well. It was high necked, long sleeved, and covered her completely. As I looked closely, I thought the image in the center of the dress—over her stomach—was maybe supposed to look like a lobster.

It was...*interesting*. I suppose it was beautiful if you like that kind of thing, but it wasn't the least bit sexy, which I guess is what I thought it would have looked like, given the circumstances.

"You're beautiful," Brandon said with a wide, genuine smile. "My mother's dress fits you perfectly."

"Thank you," Nikki said simply.

"Your mother's?" I heard myself ask.

"She wore it a long time ago," Brandon said.

"Brandon was conceived in a ritual like this one," Tria informed me quietly.

I just shook my head slowly, not really knowing which parts of all of this were the most disturbing. I turned to Tria, and she reached out and pulled me by the arm until we were a few feet away from the rest of the group. Keith and Brandon went back to talking to each other, and Nikki stood on the porch and watched the road.

"You sure you don't want to just go to that shit-hole diner in town for a cup of coffee instead of this party thing?" I suggested, even though I knew it wasn't in the cards. I couldn't have been less interested than if someone told me we were going to watch gay porn all night.

With a coy smile, Tria looked up at me through her lashes.

"Liam Teague!" she exclaimed. "Are you asking me out on a date?"

The tension that had been building in me dissipated as the corners of her mouth turned up.

"I've never taken you on a date," I said. I was a little startled by the sudden realization.

"No, you have not," she said. "Actually, I've never really been on a date. I mean, Keith and I sort of went to prom, but since we didn't have money for the tickets or suitable clothing, we just went to a party out on the beach and called it prom. I don't know if that counts or not."

"It doesn't." I decided it wouldn't count—not because I didn't think it *should* count, but because I didn't want it to.

"Well then, I've never been on a date at all."

"I guess I ought to fix that," I told her.

"When we get home, I'm going to hold you to that," Tria said.

"Deal," I replied. "And I want to point out that through exercising restraint to rival that of Atlas himself, I haven't punched anyone yet."

"Yet?" Tria took a slight step back and crossed her arms.

"Hey, the night ain't over."

She turned her head to look at where Keith and Brandon were still talking softly to each other, then to Nikki, and then back to me.

"I didn't know he was going to show up here," she said. "I didn't think we'd see him until the ceremony. Sorry about that—I should have warned you or something."

"You can't warn me about something you don't know is going to happen," I said. "Besides, I don't need a warning about Douchebag. He's too weak and too stupid to worry me."

"Be careful," she said. "Keith has a lot of support here."

"It's all good," I said, trying to reassure her. "Just keep your distance from him, okay? I don't want you around him unless I'm there."

"He's not going to do anything to me," Tria said, but her eyes betrayed her words.

"Shitty liar," I reminded her. "You had to hide out to get away from him before."

"Well, I don't think he'll do anything with you here," she clarified.

"Yeah, me either, but I want you to stay close anyway."

I slipped my arm around her waist, pulled her body close to mine, and then pressed my lips to the top of her head. Keith looked over at us then, and I made a point of sliding my hand lower to rest on her ass. He glared, and I raised an eyebrow at him as I gave her a little squeeze.

"You're doing that on purpose, aren't you?" Tria asked.

"Yep," I replied. "Fucker needs to keep his eyes to himself."

Before Tria could make any further comment or admonishments, the sound of rubber wheels on asphalt came from down the road. A rusty old Gremlin pulled up and parked. Inside were a woman and a young man. Nikki introduced them as her mother, Patricia, and brother, Steven.

We went through the whole "Why is he here?" thing again. I bit my tongue a lot, trying to understand why my being here was such a big deal when Nikki was about to get banged by a whole group of guys right in front of her own family members.

The whole thing was just sick. This was fuckupedness to end all fuckupedness.

"It's time," Nikki said from the top step of the porch.

Everyone starting piling into vehicles, and I headed toward Keith's truck with Brandon. Tria glanced at me nervously, and I rolled my eyes. Keeping my mouth shut and my fists to myself was going to be a herculean task over the next few hours.

I was never one to back away from a challenge, but I had the feeling this night was going to be a disaster.

# END OF PART ONE

# AUTHOR'S NOTES

Do not despair!

I know it's a cliffhanger ending. It's not my usual style, but I swear you do not have long to wait! *Caged: Book 2—Trapped* will be released on August 4, 2015!

# EXCERPT FROM CAGED: BOOK 2 - TRAPPED

Tria laid her head against my shoulder and relaxed against me as I exhaled smoke off to the side so it would stay out of her face. I snaked my free arm around her stomach, and she gripped my forearm with her slender fingers.

"Are you going to tell me something about yourself tonight?" she asked.

"No," I told her with a firm shake of my head. "I was kind of thinking it was your turn."

"My turn?"

"Yeah," I said as I took a long pull from the cigarette. "It occurred to me that you haven't really told me a whole lot about growing up here, but you keep trying to drag shit up about my past. I think a little turn-taking is in order."

"So if I tell you something, you then have to tell me something else?"

It wasn't exactly what I had it mind. In fact, the whole thing had been as much of a diversion tactic as actually wanting to know more about her childhood. I wasn't completely sure I wanted to know more about this place while I was still here. I didn't think I'd get out without cracking skulls.

"Actually, maybe that's not such a good idea," I said. "At least, not now."

Tria must have been thinking the same thing.

"Yeah, maybe we should talk about that when we have a little more...distance."

"Yeah."

"But, we could maybe do some of that when we get home?" she suggested.

I sighed.

"You aren't going to give up, are you?"

"Probably not," she said. She turned her head toward me and smiled before leaning back against me again.

I felt her shiver in the night's chilly air and pushed against her back a little so she would sit up again. Gripping my cigarette between my lips, I pulled my jacket off and wrapped it around her shoulders. Tria stuck her arms through the sleeves and wrapped the front part so it overlapped around her torso.

The jacket was insanely huge on her, and I should have found it comical, but I didn't. Instead, my cock took very specific notice of how she looked and decided to attempt escape from the crotch of my jeans, which made me groan.

"What is it?" Tria asked as her eyes narrowed a bit to focus on me.

For a moment, I couldn't answer. I just looked at her and tried to figure out what the hell was going on inside my head. I flicked my cigarette out onto the gravel road and wrapped another arm around her.

"It's just you," I finally answered. "The jacket doesn't fit you at all, and it kind of looks like you're wearing one of those giant bean-bag chairs. I ought to be laughing, but I'm not because it's so fucking hot at the same time—seeing you wearing something of mine."

She widened her eyes a little.

"Like everything else about you," I heard myself say. "It's how beautiful you are when you're pissed off at me. It's how you smile when you're making me breakfast. It's your eyes, your voice, the smell of your hair. It's how your skin feels against mine."

I hugged her against me a bit more.

"Just like this," I clarified, not wanting her to think—despite the moody little bastard's lack of self-control—that this was just about wanting in her panties. It was that, too, but it wasn't *just* that. "Everything about you makes me want you more."

# MORE BOOKS BY SHAY SAVAGE

**Surviving the Storm Series:**

Surviving Raine

Bastian's Storm

**Evan Arden Series:**

Otherwise Alone

Otherwise Occupied

Uncockblockable (a Nick Wolfe story)

Otherwise Unharmed

Isolated

Irrevocable

**Stand Alone Novels:**

Transcendence

Offside

Worth

Alarm

**Novella Collection**

Savaged

# ABOUT THE AUTHOR

Shay Savage lives in Cincinnati, Ohio with her family and a variety of household pets. She is an accomplished public speaker, and holds the rank of Distinguished Toastmaster from Toastmasters International. When not writing, she enjoys science fiction movies, masquerading as a zombie, is a HUGE Star Wars fan, and member of the 501st Legion of Stormtroopers. When the geek fun runs out, she also and loves soccer in any and all forms - especially the Columbus Crew, Arsenal and Bayern Munich. Savage holds a degree in psychology, and she brings a lot of that knowledge into the characters within her stories.

Made in the USA
Middletown, DE
06 October 2022

12028746R00176